P9-ASG-782

THE FLY ON THE WALL

Tony Hillerman's second novel, and the only one not featuring Lt. Joe Leaphorn or Sgt. Jim Chee of the Navajo tribal police, *The Fly on the Wall* was originally published by Harper & Row in 1971 and has been unavailable in hardcover for nearly two decades.

Set in the capital of a midwestern state, this down–home thriller explores the dilemma faced by a veteran newspaper journalist investigating a political scandal. On the eve of the gubernatorial election, his report can make or break the leading candidate, whom he favors, and he must decide what role journalism should play in politics as he finds himself the target for murder.

THE FLY ON THE WALL

TONY HILLERMAN

Published by arrangement with Harper & Row Publishers, Inc.

Originally published by Harper & Row in 1971.

First Armchair Detective Library edition: October 1990

1 3 5 4 2

The Armchair Detective Library
129 West 56th Street
New York, New York 10019–3881

Library of Congress Cataloging–in–Publication Data

Hillerman, Tony.
The fly on the wall / Tony Hillerman.
—1st Armchair Detective Library ed.
p. cm.
Reprint. Originally published: New York: Harper & Row, 1971.
—ISBN 0–922890–32–3 (trade):$19.95
0–922890–30–7 (collector): $25
0–922890–31–5 (limited): $75
I. Title
PS3558. I45F5 1990
813'.54—dc20 90–39567

Printed in the United States of America

INTRODUCTION

The Fly on the Wall was to be my BIG BOOK.

The idea for it had rattled around inside my head for years while I worked as a newspaper reporter. It had become so important in my mind's eye that I was afraid to start it. Instead, as my first book I wrote *The Blessing Way*—a training exercise. Could I make the transition from the short form of newspaper and magazine articles to long and convoluted book length fiction? Could I move from the hard flinty facts of journalism to the plastic of fiction? I would find out by writing a mystery set on the Navajo Reservation. If I could handle that, I'd try to move onward to the Big Book about the moral/ethical dilemma faced by those who report the news.

The title, of course, is from the metaphor the late Walter Lippmann gave us for the perfect objectivity of the perfect reporter—observing society with the insect's thousand eyes, and communicating what is seen with no more involvement or emotion than a housefly. Give the citizens of our democracy all the facts and let the citizen interpret them for himself. The goal, as usual with ideals, is as impossible to reach as infinity. You cannot give the citizen all the facts about everything and he could not absorb them if you did. The merit lies in striving for this objective perfection. At least, that's the theory. Or is there a line that should be drawn between the citizen's right to know about public affairs and the public official's right to privacy? Is there a time when the reporter should temper "the facts" with his knowledge of "the truth." Should professional newspeople follow the example of the showbiz Dan Rather types of television "news" and let our opinions show in our stories? I am among those who believe that, thank God, the average American is better able to judge from the facts than the average TV anchorman. But the debate goes on.

The state capital which models for the story is the one at Oklahoma City. Funds were exhausted there before the dome was built but otherwise all states seem to have used the same architect. The "paper trail" John Cotton follows to run down his story is also typical. Or was. Now those rows of filing cabinets filled with contract specifications, bids, work orders, change orders, payment vouchers, etc., have been replaced by computers. Cotton today would have to learn computer code and access procedures. The fictional method used to swindle the taxpayers is very much like one Loyd Hackler and I exposed years ago in the New Mexico State Highway Department. However the idea isn't unique. It is probably used in varying forms in the other 49 states. And conspiring to rig bids with advance information has been used by our military–industrial complex for years to milk taxpayers. It explains why so many military academy graduates and their buddies in the weapons industry can fly around in private jets.

Fly on the Wall didn't turn out to be the Big Book I had hoped to make it. It dwindled as it took shape and became an adventure yarn with the plot turning on an ethical question. Even before I had finished it, I was itching to get back to the Navajos of *The Blessing Way* in what was to become my continuing effort to do that right.But Big Book or not, *Fly* has always been a favorite of mine. To my joy, it became popular among the newspaper people and particularly among those who are, like Cotton, investigative reporters. One reviewer described it as the best reporter novel ever published. The editors of Garland Publishers included it in their *Fifty Classics Of Crime Fiction*.

Rereading it for me is a nostalgia trip. Reminds me of my days sniffing along the "paper trail" in search of corruption. And it also reminds me of fishing the little high meadow streams of northern New Mexico for those little cutthroat trout back when the mountains could still offer that rare dividend of lonely isolation.

Tony Hillerman

Author's Note

Both the state capitol used in this book and the politicians who inhabit it are products of the author's imagination. However, I acknowledge my debt to Larry Grove, Don Peterson, Loyd Hackler, Mary Goddard, Paul McClung, Hugh Hall, Howard Wilson, Pete Peterman, Bob Brown, Phil Dessauer, Peter Mygatt, Frankie McCarthy, Carter Bradley, Jim Bradshaw, John Curtis, Jesse Price, and the others who have been my friends, competitors and allies in the news profession—and to all those statehouse newsmen who know how it feels to be the fly on the wall.

THE FLY ON THE WALL

>1<

John Cotton had been in the pressroom almost an hour when Merrill McDaniels came in. He had written a five-hundred-word overnighter wrapping up the abortion-bill hearings in the House Public Affairs Committee. He had teletyped that—and a shorter item on a gubernatorial appointment—to the state desk of the *Tribune.* Then Cotton had stood at the window—a tall, wiry man with a longish, freckled, somber face. He had thought first about what he would write for his political column, about how badly he wanted a smoke, and then had drifted into other thoughts. He had considered the dust on the old-fashioned window panes, and the lights—the phosphorescent glow of the city surrounding the semidarkness of the state capitol grounds. In the clear, dry air of Santa Fe there wouldn't be this glow. Each light would be an individual glitter without this defraction of cold, misty humidity. Twenty blocks away, by the river below Statehouse Hill, the glow was faintly pink with the neon of the downtown business district. It outlined vaguely the blunt, irregular skyline: the square tower of Federal Citybank, the black glass monolith of the Hefron Building, the dingy granite of the Commodity Exchange—the seats of money and power rising out of a moderately dirty middle-aged Midwestern city, clustered beside a polluted Midwestern river. Not very large and not very small. About 480,000 people, the Chamber of Commerce said. Exactly 412,318 by the last federal census, not counting the satellite towns and not counting those who farmed the infinity of cornfields and the hilltops of wheat that surrounded it all.

Farm-belt landscape. Rich. Nine-hundred-dollar-an-acre country. Beautiful if you liked it and Cotton had thought again that he didn't like it. The humid low-level sky oppressed him. He missed the immense skyscapes of the mountains and the deserts. And he thought, as he had thought many times before, that one day he would write Ernie Danilov a letter and tell the managing editor he was quitting. He would enjoy writing that letter.

And then, just a few minutes before McDaniels walked in, he sat down again at his desk. He typed "At the Capitol" and his byline on a sheet of copy paper and wrote rapidly.

Governor Paul Roark remains coy about the U.S. Senate race upcoming next year. But if you make political bets, consider these facts:

1. The tax-reform package the Governor and his supporters are now trying to ram through the legislature would make an excellent plank for a campaign in the Democratic senatorial primary.

2. Friends of incumbent U.S. Senator Eugene Clark say privately that they're dead certain Roark will fight Clark for the nomination. They see Roark's campaign as a last-gasp effort of the once-dominant liberal-labor-populist-small-farmer coalition to retain its slipping control over the Democratic party machinery.

3. Roger Boyden, Senator Clark's press secretary and hatchet man, has

moved back from Washington. Boyden isn't talking, but those he has been contacting say he's mobilizing Clark's supporters for a primary battle against Roark.

4. An "Effective Senate Committee" has been registered with the Secretary of State as a repository for senatorial campaign funds. The listed directors include an aide of Congressman William Jennings Gavin and two long-time allies of National Committeeman Joseph Korolenko. The veteran Congressman and Korolenko—himself a former Governor and ex-Congressman—are close friends of Roark and supported his race for Governor four years ago.

It was exactly at this point that McDaniels came through the pressroom doorway. Cotton was leaning back in his chair, looking at his note pad. Halfway up the empty room, the Associated Press teletype said, "Ding, ding, ding," and typed out a message in a brief flurry of clicking sounds. And there was McDaniels wobbling into the room, fat, rumpled and obviously drunk.

"Johnny," McDaniels said, "you're working

late." McDaniels's smile was a joyous, drunken smile.

"Yeah," Cotton said. His voice was curt. Cotton didn't like drunkenness. It made him nervous. When he drank seriously himself, he drank in the safety of solitude. He didn't know exactly why he didn't like drunks, any more than he knew why he didn't like people putting their hands on him, why he always shrugged the hand off his shoulder even when it was a friendly hand. He recognized it as a weakness and he had tried once or twice—without success—to understand this quirk.

McDaniels tossed a stenographer's notebook onto his desk, sending an avalanche of papers cascading to the floor. He sat down heavily and fumbled with copy paper. Cotton felt himself relaxing, relieved that McDaniels was not in the mood for alcoholic soul baring. The Western Union clock above the pressroom door showed 9:29, which meant Cotton had thirty-one minutes to write four or five more brief items to complete his column, punch it into perforated tape and teletype it three hundred miles across the state to the *Tribune* newsroom before the overnight desk shut down. Plenty of time. Cotton wasted a few moments of it wondering where the *Capitol-Press* reporter had been doing his drinking. Probably down the hall in the suite of the Speaker of the House. Bruce Ulrich always had a bottle open.

Across the room, the UPI telephone rang. It rang four times, loud in the stillness. Two page boys, working late for some committee, walked past the open door, arguing about something. Their voices diminished down the corridor, trailing angry echoes. McDaniels started typing, an erratic clacking. Cotton inspected him, regretting his curtness. It hadn't been necessary. Mac's drunkenness was past the stage at which it would threaten the arm-around-the-shoulder, the maudlin, all-guards-down indecent exposure of the private spirit. And since the snub hadn't been necessary it had been simply rude. Cotton looked at the humped figure of McDaniels and felt penitent.

McDaniels mumbled something.

"What?"

"Said can't find my notebook."

"You threw it on the desk," Cotton said.

Mac groped among the papers, found a notebook, peered at it, put it down. "That's an old one," he said. "Full. Need to find the one I'm using now."

"Maybe it fell off," Cotton said. He got up

and looked over McDaniels's shoulder. In the lead paragraph, Mac had misspelled the name of the committee chairman and left out the verb.

"You know what you ought to do, Mac? You need to go home and sleep it off. I'll call your desk and tell 'em you got sick and had to go home."

"Maybe so," McDaniels said.

"If you send in a story like you're going to write with all that booze in you, you're in real trouble. I'll tell 'em you got food poisoning."

McDaniels thought, his forehead wrinkled with concentration.

"Yes," he said. "Good idea." He got up carefully.

"I can tell them you said to use AP on the committee hearing," Cotton said. He said it hurriedly. Mac was peering at him, his eyes watery.

"Y'know what I'm celebrating?" McDaniels asked. He spoke slowly, forming each word gingerly, beaming at Cotton now. "I've got me a hell of a story. A real, screaming, eight-column ninety-six-point, earth-shaking bastard." He put his glasses on, slightly askew, and then took them off again and put them carefully back in the case. "Going to make the heads roll, and thrones topple, and rock this old statehouse right down. I got it solid now and in a day or two I'll have all the loose ends, and when I break it, Johnny, you know what I'm going to do?" He waited for an answer, peering at Cotton.

"What?" Cotton said reluctantly.

"You son-of-a-bitch, I'm going to give you part of it."

"That's fine," Cotton said. "But how're you going to do that? You print in the morning and the *Tribune* is an afternoon paper."

"Got more than I can use," McDaniels said, careful with the shape of each word. "I'll give you the background the night before I bust it and you can get it out in advance for your column the next day. Make it look like you were right on top of it."

"What the hell is it?" Cotton asked. "Something about somebody big?"

"Something about stealing the taxpayers' money. Something about a big screwing for the good old taxpayer."

"That's not news," Cotton said. "Who's doing the screwing this time?"

But McDaniels wasn't listening to the question. McDaniels was looking at him, his eyes watery. And then McDaniels was saying: "Johnny, you're a good son-of-a-bitch. You know that? You know, all my life I never broke a really big one like this. Never did. Mostly worked on little *pissant* stuff. All my life I wanted to win the Pulitzer Prize. Wanted one of the big prizes." He put his hand on Cotton's arm. Cotton flinched, his biceps rigid. "Wanted somebody to pay attention to me. Always wanted . . ."

Cotton pulled away from the hand. "Go home," he said. "Take a cab."

"Yes," McDaniels said. "O.K." He paused at the door. "You're a good son-of-a-bitch, Cotton."

From McDaniels's retreating figure Cotton glanced upward at the white face of the clock. It was an act of professional habit, and now of nervous release. It was twenty-two minutes before ten, still plenty of time. He dialed the *Capitol-Press* city-desk number on McDaniels's phone, gave Mac's excuse to a harassed-sounding copy editor, and went back to his own typewriter. He spent perhaps a minute wondering about Mac's story—about whom he had caught stealing. Then he put the question aside and typed rapidly.

A primary-election showdown
between the young Governor and Gene
Clark would split the state's
Democratic party machinery

approximately down the middle. If Roark runs and loses, the losing effort would almost certainly cost the Korolenko-Gavin bloc its balance of power in party decision making.

Backers of Senator Clark have made obvious inroads into that balance in the past three years. The election last year of George Bryce as district attorney of the Third Judicial District illustrated how Clark's forces have extended their grip.

Bryce is a former partner in Clark's law firm. He won the Democratic nomination despite the bitter animosity of the Gavin-Korolenko people. The election put a Clark man in control of law enforcement in the state's most politically sensitive area—the district which includes the state capital.

Whether or not . . .

Cotton stopped typing, aware of movement to his left.

A tall, dark-haired man in a blue topcoat was poking through the litter of papers on McDaniels's desk.

"Looking for something?"

The man didn't look up. "McDaniels forgot his notebook," he said. "He asked me to get it for him."

"I think he threw it on top of all that stuff," Cotton said. He went back to his typing, finishing a summary paragraph and adding four much briefer items. A lot of it wasn't new but it made a fairly good column, Cotton thought. It would be read by maybe 40 percent of the *Tribune*'s 380,000 subscribers, of whom—if the *Tribune*'s latest readership survey was accurate—less than half would plow their way to the final sentence.

Cotton noticed the man in the topcoat was gone. The pressroom was empty. He thought again about McDaniels's story. Mac had been excited, which was surprising. No one in the pressroom was ever excited. He glanced at the clock. Nine forty-four. Sixteen minutes left. He pulled the copy paper from the typewriter, pushed the lever on the teletype to "send," tapped on the "bell" key, and then punched out:

HV COLUM REDY. YOU THERE? JC944P

The machine was silent. Cotton pushed the key to "tape" and began retyping the column into tape, his fingers moving fast on the electric keyboard.

The teletype thumped twice, then typed out:

OK, JOHNNY. GO HED. TL

It was then Cotton heard the sound. He jerked his head toward the pressroom door and listened. The sound lasted maybe three seconds, or four. It started abruptly, loud, and then diminished. Then there was only silence. Above the pressroom door the clock clicked, inhaled electricity and purred briefly. It became officially 9:45 P.M.

Cotton punched "MIN PLEASE" on the keyboard and stood up—still looking toward the door. By day, this echoing fourth-floor Senate wing of the capitol was a buzzing, rattling medley of sounds. Laughter, angry conversation, shouts, tapping high heels, slamming doors and the whine of elevator motors were bounced by the grimy marble of the corridors and mixed in a discordant symphony always present just outside the pressroom door. But at night the immense old building was virtually empty and its silence imposed a hush on the few who still occupied it.

Thus the sudden sound violated custom and protocol. But it wasn't that which took Cotton through the pressroom door into the semidarkness of the corridor. There was something animal in the sound, something ugly and primeval which prickled the skin and demanded investigation.

The sound had come from the left, from the direction of the central rotunda. Cotton walked slowly from the corridor into the broad foyer directly under the capitol dome. The lights here were off but there was a dim illumination from below—lights from the lobby three floors below reflecting upward.

Cotton stood, listening. Footsteps. A figure emerged from a corridor in the House wing and then stopped at the edge of the foyer.

"Was that you?"

"I heard it, but it wasn't me," Cotton said.

The man walked toward him, skirting the marble railing which circled the open center of the rotunda. Cotton recognized him, a clerk in the office of the House Sergeant at Arms. But he couldn't remember his name.

"What the hell was it?" the man asked. He looked around the foyer carefully, at the four broad corridors which led into it from the House and Senate wings and then upward at the fourth-floor mezzanine railing above. "Nobody here," he said, looking at Cotton again.

"It damned sure wasn't me," Cotton snapped. "I heard it down in the pressroom."

From a floor somewhere below came a stutter of voices—an excited sound. Cotton suddenly understood the noise, what had made it. He and the clerk walked to the railing, looking down.

"Good God," the clerk said. "God."

At the edge of the Great Seal of the Commonwealth embossed in the marble tile of the lobby floor a body was sprawled. It looked from this height, Cotton thought, like a broken doll. By the body, a man in the khaki of a capitol custodian was kneeling. Another man stood beside him, only the top of his hat and his shoulders visible.

"That's what we heard," the clerk said. "He fell from here."

"Here or over the third-floor railing," Cotton said. "Let's hope it was that. That would give him some chance of being alive."

There was no use calling the *Tribune* on it now. The next edition wasn't until 11 A.M. tomorrow. He thought about it. The later the A.M. reporters knew about it, the better. They would get the story soon but every minute that passed before they did would mean more missed editions and more details that would be fresh for the afternoon cycle. Still, he had sent McDaniels home. He should protect him at the *Capitol-Press.*

Cotton leaned over the balustrade and cupped his hands. "Is he dead?"

The man in the hat looked upward, his face a small white oval. Cotton didn't hear his answer.

"What?" he shouted.

"He's dead," the man yelled.

Cotton trotted back to the pressroom and switched the teletype key from tape to manual.

> BE MIN WITH THE COLUM. JUST HAD
> FATAL. UNIDENTIFIED DROPPED DOWN
> CENTRAL ROTUNDA. WILL ADVISE. JC

And then he called the *Capitol-Press* desk and asked for the city editor. The switch button clicked. In the receiver Cotton heard the background sound of teletypes. A voice near the phone was saying, "all right, then, damn it, get it written." And then it was talking into Cotton's ear.

"Yeah?"

"This is John Cotton. McDaniels went home sick and I'm backstopping for him. Your mail edition out?"

"Running now," the voice said. "What ya got?"

"Just had a fatal out here. Somebody did a dry dive in the rotunda. Just a minute ago. I'll go down and get an identification and call you back."

"We're locking up the two star at ten-fifteen," the voice said. "We can save a hole for it."

"It may not amount to much," Cotton said. "But if it's a biggie, I work for the *Tribune,* and if anybody asks you, it's McDaniels covering for you."

"O.K.," the voice said. "If it's a good one—somebody big—call me back quick, before you wrap it up. I'm playing a second-cycle story on the President's press conference and if your fatal is some hotshot I could move the President inside and lead with your jumper."

On the way down in the elevator Cotton thought that it might be somebody fairly big. At least it would most likely be somebody in state government. A tourist wouldn't be in the capitol at night and there must be more convenient places for an intended suicide to do his jumping. It would be somebody in government, probably not a run-of-the-mill clerk. Probably somebody with enough responsibilities to keep him working in his office at night. Or maybe some legislator. Suicide of anyone on the public payroll raised interesting possibilities. Might be worth a two-column head, or one column above the fold.

Cotton pulled the door of the antique elevator open on the first floor and trotted toward the lobby floor of the rotunda. The feeling was familiar, a knotting in his stomach, a tightness in his chest. When he had been a police reporter, he had felt it often—this approach to violent death—without getting used to it. They always looked surprised. No matter the circumstances. The suicide gassed in his garage, the motel night clerk with a robber's bullet through his neck, the middle-aged woman pinned beneath her car. The details were different but the eyes were the same. The intellect believed in death but the animal in man thought it was immortal. The eyes were always glossy with outraged surprise.

Four men stood by the body now, talking quietly. Cotton recognized the clerk from the fifth floor, and the custodian, and the man in the hat. The fourth man was fat, a Game and Fish Department employee, but Cotton didn't know his name.

And then he looked downward. He saw it would not be a big one for the night city editor of the *Capitol-Press.* Not a play story.

Probably a one-column head below the fold at best. Maybe no better than page two. The surprised eyes staring sightlessly up at the capitol dome six floors above were those of Merrill McDaniels.

2

House speaker Bruce Ulrich pounded twice with his gavel. "Chair recognizes Sergeant at Arms."

"Mr. Speaker, a message from the Governor."

"The house will receive a message from the Governor."

Alan Wingerd, the Governor's press secretary, came down the aisle from the double doors, paused briefly to say something to the Majority Leader at the front-row aisle desk, laughed, and then handed the Clerk of the House a folded paper.

"The Clerk will read the message from the Governor," Ulrich said. Ulrich put down the gavel and returned his attention to the newspaper on his desk. Cotton had noticed earlier, with some satisfaction, that Ulrich was reading the first edition of the *Tribune.* The banner said ROARK ASKING $150 MILLION ROAD FUND.

The Clerk of the House was reading in his clear, prissy voice.

"Honorable Members of the House of Representatives of the 77th General Assembly,

"I am hereby asking the Majority Floor Leader to submit for your consideration three bills, the passage of which I feel is essential to the safety and convenience of the people of this commonwealth.

"The first of these bills would adjust the road-users' tax in certain categories to increase revenues an estimated seventeen million dollars per annum. The second of these bills would authorize issuance of bonds against this revenue. . . ."

Cotton yawned and glanced down the press table. At his right, Leroy Hall was reading his way through the stack of bills introduced in the morning session. The AP and UPI chairs were vacant. The wire-service men were in the pressroom filing new leads. In the next chair Volney Bowles of the *Journal* was working a Double-Crostic in a *Saturday Review*. Beyond him, in the last chair, sat Junior Garcia. Garcia seemed to be asleep.

Hall jabbed Cotton with his elbow. He was a skinny man, in his fifties, his gray hair cut in a bristling burr. "Cousin John," he said, "you see that *Capitol-Press* story on McDaniels's inquest. You think it was an accident?"

"What else?" Cotton said. "You knew Merrill. He didn't jump."

"You said he was drinking," Hall said. "You'd have to be pretty drunk to fall over that balustrade."

"He was stiff."

Hall was looking at him questioningly. "Mac didn't hardly ever drink much?" It came out as another question, irritating Cotton.

"You think somebody pushed him? Like who? You're sounding like a beginning police reporter."

"I guess I just feel bad about it," Hall said. He was looking down, drawing doodles on his note pad—elaborate daggers with jeweled hilts. "Did you know we used to work together on the Portland *Oregonian* before it folded? He was general assignment and I was covering the county building."

Cotton was only half listening. The clerk's voice was droning on: ". . . recognize the reluctance of this distinguished body to increase the burden of taxation on the motor-carrier industry. However, this industry will benefit disproportionately from the expeditious construction of a safe network of highways and . . ." This call by the Governor for a road-users tax increase, a bond issue and a crash program in highway construction had come as a surprise—a rarity in a gossipy statehouse where almost everything leaked. That meant little time for reaction to develop. Cotton was watching the floor. The Minority Floor Leader was leaning over the desk of the Majority Whip. The conversation might be casual, since the two men were long-time friends. Or, since the Majority Whip was a Gene Clark Democrat, it might be negotiations for a Republican—Clark Democrat coalition to kill Roark's road plan. Cotton signaled for a page boy and started jotting a note to the Minority Leader. Hall was still talking.

"He'd always wanted to be a political writer," Hall was saying, "and he would have been good at it. D'you know he had a leak in the Governor's office?"

"How do you know?" The note asked the Republican Floor Leader if he would try to stall Roark's road bills by asking to have them referred to two committees, if he had any substantial Democratic support and if he had enough votes for the double referral.

"He knew about this Roark road-fund

bond-issue scheme before we did," Hall said. "He made some crack about it last week—joking about it."

"Why didn't he write it?" Cotton handed the note to the page.

"I've been wondering," Hall said. "I didn't think anything about it. Thought it was just some crap he'd picked up from the motor carriers' lobbyist. But, when Wingerd gave us the advance press release this morning, I knew Mac must have had some early word, and it must have come from one of Roark's people." He laughed. "It damned sure didn't come from Jason Flowers." The Highway Commission chairman's animosity toward the *Capitol-Press* and all associated with it was widely known.

"Other people in the Highway Department had to know about it, too," Cotton said. He started to tell Hall what McDaniels had said about the big story he was going to break, but checked the impulse. Suddenly he wanted to do some careful thinking about those drunken confidences and about McDaniels.

"I didn't know him all that well," Cotton said. "I thought maybe he was still green on political reporting. You know—hearing some tip and getting excited before he checked it." McDaniels had to be green. Why else tell Cotton about his hot story? Why risk it? Because the booze made him friendly? Because in his drunkenness he was reaching out to touch someone—reaching with the only thing he had to offer? Cotton found the thought uncomfortable.

"No," Hall said. "Merrill was a pro. A good digger."

Cotton noticed that Hall, without seeming to do so, was also watching comings and goings on the House floor. "You think they're going to pull something?"

Hall looked surprised. "What do you mean?"

Cotton laughed. "You bastard. You know what I mean. You're just hoping it won't happen on my time."

"It's already an A.M.'s story. But relax. Nothing's going to happen."

The clerk's singsong voice worked its way through the final page of Roark's message. ". . . highways which are a disgrace to this great state and an increasing danger to the motoring public." The page boy handed Cotton a folded slip of paper. It read:

Not for quote:
1. We'll move for a double referral.

2. The Clark people aren't playing.
3. Probably not.

Cotton looked at his watch. Nineteen minutes before his three-star-edition deadline. He got up.

"Just out of curiosity," Hall said, still drawing daggers, "are you screwing me out of my lead for tomorrow?"

"Those are my intentions," Cotton said. "To do unto Leroy Hall what Leroy Hall has so often done to me."

In the pressroom, Cotton didn't take time for the typewriter and editing. He punched the information directly into teletype tape and filed it.

INSERT IN ROARK ROAD-FUND STORY, SUBS FOR SECOND PARAGRAPH. WHEN THE MAJORITY LEADER INTRODUCED THE GOVERNOR'S THREE-BILL PACKAGE, REPUBLICAN MEMBERS TRIED TO DELAY THE PLAN WITH A MOTION TO REFER THE BILLS TO WAYS AND MEANS COMMITTEE AS WELL AS THE TRANSPORTATION COMMITTEE.

LACKING SUPPORT OF THE ANTI-ROARK DEMOCRATS IN THE HOUSE, THE MOTION SEEMED CERTAIN OF DEFEAT.

Cotton signed the insert with the time and his initials and hurried back to the House chamber. He had put his neck out a mile. If things went as the Minority Leader said, the *Tribune* would have this development a cycle ahead of the *Morning Journal*—a fact which Managing Editor Ernie Danilov would remember about twenty-four hours. If something went awry, if for some reason the Republicans switched signals at the last moment, nobody would ever forget he had been wrong. The nervousness Cotton felt as he hurried down the corridor was a totally familiar feeling. Cotton and most of the other newsmen for the afternoon papers lived with it—took such calculated risks routinely, two or three times a week, during the high-pressure days of the legislative session. They wrote in the past tense at 1 P.M. of things that would happen at 3 P.M. The game demanded cool nerves, a savvy of the situation and an accurate judgment of news sources. But, if you didn't play it, the morning papers broke all the stories.

The red light was shining on the KLAB-TV television camera in the balcony now and the Minority Leader had the floor mike. A young man with a thin face and long sideburns was in McDaniels's chair. Cotton didn't know him. ". . . an act of extreme discourtesy," the Minority Leader was saying. "This request is a reasonable request. If the Ways and Means Committee is to make sensible decisions on the financing of state programs it must have full information about all such programs. I do not say the refusal of Mr. Speaker to submit these bills to Ways and Means was made in bad faith. But I do commend to the honorable members of this house the thought that Mr. Speaker has acted without mature consideration." The rich sound of the Minority Leader's voice faltered and there were shouts of "Call the question" from a half-dozen scattered desks. The Minority Leader, Cotton noticed, was very much aware that the television camera was on and was reluctant to surrender the mike. Ulrich pounded once with his gavel.

"I urge this honorable House to vote no on the motion," the Minority Leader said. He sat down.

"Question to close debate been moved and seconded," Ulrich said. "All in favor. Opposed. Carried." He banged once with the gavel. "Motion's now to table the motion. All in . . ."

"Explain the vote," the Majority Leader said.

"Yes vote means we leave the bill only in the Highways Committee. No means we double-refer it," Ulrich said. "In favor say Aye."

There was a roar of Ayes.

"All opposed Nay."

There was a roar of No's from the Republican side of the aisle. Cotton noticed the Clark Democrats didn't join the chorus. He wondered why not.

"Ayes have it," Ulrich said. "Motion's tabled."

Cotton looked at the Minority Leader, wondering if he would risk a roll call. The Minority Leader appeared engrossed in something he was reading. There would be no test of strength today. Again Cotton wondered why the Clark people had missed this opportunity.

"Did you do it to me, Cousin John?" Hall asked.

"Cousin Roy, I didn't leave you a crumb. You'll have to rewrite me."

Ulrich was settling the House down to a long, routine afternoon of working its way through inconsequential bills waiting their fate on the calendar. Cotton moved down the table and sat in the AP chair next to the man with sideburns.

"My name's Cotton. I guess you're replacing Merrill."

"George Cherry," the man with sideburns said. "They pulled me off of general assignment until they can get a political man out here."

"It was too bad about Merrill."

"I hardly knew him," Cherry said. "Just saw him in the office now and then."

Cotton stared out across the House floor. A representative was trying to explain a floor amendment he was proposing to some sort of insurance bill—a fat man with a fat, rusty voice. Across the immense, rococo shabbiness of the room, a swarm of grade-school children were being herded into the spectators' gallery by two teachers. Cotton was surprised at himself, and shocked. He was considering whether he should lie. If he did, it would be a professional lie, told to a fellow member of the brotherhood for professional reasons. It would therefore be a violation of taboo. Nothing was written about it in the pressroom rules, and nothing was said about it, ever. But it wasn't done. Reporters screwed one another when they could. The P.M.'s warred among themselves, and collectively against the morning-paper reporters; the AP-UPI vendetta resumed each day; and the name of the game was cutthroat. But the game had its rules. One evaded. One was secretive. One covered his tracks. But one didn't *lie* to another newsman. In a profession which risked a hundred mistakes in a working day, and published them on rotary presses, and saw years of being right destroyed by being wrong in one edition, the lie was too dangerous for tolerance.

But now Cotton found himself considering it. It would be a small lie. Harmless and impossible to detect. Its purpose was not even entirely serious—a simple yen to satisfy curiosity. Cotton made no decision. A lie might not be necessary, or it might be fruitless.

He would see.

"Did you find Merrill's notebook?"

"There were three or four in all that junk on his desk," Cherry said. "Which one?"

"He would have had it with him when he fell. That night when he left, he forgot it and he sent some guy to get it for him."

"I don't know anything about it," Cherry said. He looked at Cotton, his eyes neither friendly nor hostile. "Why?"

The lie didn't form. Instead there was the acceptable mild evasion.

"Merrill said he had some information he was going to give me for my column. Something he didn't want for a story. I figured it would be in his notebook."

"What about?"

"He didn't say," Cotton said. Either McDaniels had been working with his desk on the story or he had kept it to himself until he had a string around it. In the first case, Cherry would know all about it and would be interested in knowing if Cotton knew anything. In the second case, Cherry would know nothing at all and Cotton had no intention of alerting him.

"Maybe our police reporter has it," Cherry said. "He picked up all of Merrill's stuff at the morgue. Billfold and all that. Gave it to Merrill's widow, I guess."

"It's probably old stuff now, whatever it was," Cotton said. And then he changed the subject.

3

The *Capitol-Press* police reporter was a very young man named Addington with a sandy mustache and sandy eyebrows and pale blue eyes. "I don't think so," he said. "Let's see." He ticked the items off on his fingers.

"A billfold, a bunch of keys in a key case, some coins, eighty-seven cents I think it was, glasses and a case for them, a handkerchief, two ballpoint pens, a comb." Addington's voice stopped. He thought. "A cigarette lighter, part of a pack of cigarettes, a pair of dice and a couple of those discs you get in one of those gas-station contests. There wasn't any notebook."

"No notebook," Cotton said.

"They didn't give me one."

Cotton had found Addington sitting at a table in the central station interrogation room, working his way through the day's log of complaint calls. "I'll go ask the records sergeant," Addington said.

Cotton stared at the half-finished pack of cigarettes Addington had left on the table. Eighteen days now since he had smoked, going on nineteen. Two of the cigarettes were half out of the pack. Cotton felt saliva forming in his mouth. He had matches in his pocket. When Addington returned he would say, "I bummed one of your cigarettes," and Addington would think nothing of it. But then Cotton would be back on two and a half packs a day by tomorrow. And eighteen days of misery would be wasted. He looked away from the cigarettes. In a few minutes Addington would be back almost certainly with confirmation that there had been no notebook on McDaniels' body. Cotton would think about that when the time came. Now he thought about police-station interrogation rooms, which came in various shapes, colors and furnishings but which all managed, somehow, to look depressingly like this one.

The light through the barred windows on the back wall changed suddenly from the gray of twilight to garish yellow as the lights over the POLICE ONLY parking lot went on. From somewhere down a corridor came the sudden clanging of a steel door closing. And then the faint animal smell, the universal odor of all jails. And with the smell the old, sore memory was with him again. The juvenile division officer saying: "Were you trying to kill him, John? Were you?" And his own voice repeating, "No, no. No. He was my friend." The interrogation room at Santa Fe had been about like this one—like all of them, everywhere. Grimly impersonal, devoid of comfort. Wooden chairs and the heavy table covered with vinyl cold under the forearms, and Charley Graff in St. Vincent's with a concussion and a broken jaw and his own knuckles cut and aching and his mind trying to find an answer to satisfy the officer.

Why had he done it? He honestly hadn't known. It had taken him months to understand that brutal rage. Understanding had come slowly, by bits and pieces. First came the knowledge that the girl had not been really important to him. (When had he started thinking of Alice Beck—blonde, slender, sexy and silly Alice Beck—as "the girl"?) If it had been someone other than Charley he had found with her in the back seat of their car, his reaction would have been nothing more than disappointment and disgust. He had been halfway through boot training at Camp Pendleton before he had fully understood that his sick, homicidal fury had been based in self-contempt for his own weakness. He had thought at first the car had something to do with it. They had worked almost three years to buy it—he and Charley—pooling their funds, savoring their high-school poverty, and looking ahead to the trip through Canada which would celebrate their graduation to manhood. Charley had defiled all this. Charles Albright Graff (frail, witty, happy, ineffable friend) had known that Cotton intended to marry Alice, just as he had known all Cotton's thoughts, all his hopes, the peaks of his happiness and the pits of his despair. This was what Charley had betrayed. And it had taken Cotton months to know that even this was not enough to explain his savagery.

The memory of it still ached in his mind. His fists striking the bloody mouth that had so often laughed with him, feeling Charley's pain as much as Charley must have, but striking again and again as if to kill something within himself by killing it in Charley. And he might, indeed, have killed had Alice's screaming not attracted the man who had pulled him away and taken all of them to the hospital emergency room. Killed Charley, but not this new knowledge that Charley's betrayal had planted within him. He had only gradually—over the months—realized that Charley had simply completed a lesson he had been too slow to learn. That each human spirit must travel alone, safe only in isolation. He had forgiven Charley then, and started a letter to him. But he hadn't finished it. Innocence was ended. There had been nothing, now, to say.

A young policeman in a motorcycle helmet walked in, looked at him curiously and walked out again. Cotton wrenched his thoughts away from Charley Graff and found himself wondering about Janey Janoski. He wondered specifically if Miss Janoski (or was it Mrs. Janoski?) had ever learned this elemental lesson in interpersonal relations. He doubted it. There was something reckless and vulnerable about Janey Janoski—the shield lowered too easily. Or was this woman's apparent openness itself a façade behind which the genuine woman lived? He was thinking about that, doubting it for a reason he couldn't identify, when Addington reappeared through the doorway. He had a sheet of pink paper in his hand.

"No notebook," he said. "Here's the invoice. Everything I remembered, except I forgot two books of paper matches and one of those slips you get when you buy gasoline on your credit card."

He handed the invoice to Cotton. It told him nothing that Addington hadn't except that the billfold contained currency, a twenty and seven ones.

"O.K.," Cotton said, "and thanks a lot for the trouble."

McDaniels had carried no notebook with him on his five-story drop down the rotunda well. It was time now to think about what, if anything, that might mean.

Cotton drove slowly through the light dinner-hour traffic toward Capitol Heights and his apartment. The problem seemed uncomplicated. McDaniels had come into the pressroom drunk. McDaniels had tossed his notebook on his desk. Cotton recalled that clearly. Mac had tried to write his night lead on the tax hearing. Mac had announced he was celebrating cracking a really big story. Mac had left, saying he was going home to bed. A little later the man in the blue topcoat had come in looking for the notebook. How much later? Cotton couldn't be sure. But he did remember the man had picked up the notebook. It was in his hand when he left. Something was in his hand. Maybe the notebook. And then some time had passed and

Cotton had heard the sound McDaniels made screaming his way down the well of the rotunda. But Mac hadn't had the notebook when he hit bottom. Why not? The obvious simple answer was that Blue Topcoat hadn't given it to him. Another why not? The man had said Merrill had sent him back to pick it up. Had Mac fallen before the man reached him with it? Too much time for that.

The traffic signal at Capitol Avenue turned amber ahead of him. Cotton braked to a stop—thinking hard. Plenty of time—as he remembered it. A new thought struck him. If there had been as much time as there seemed, why was Mac still on the fourth floor? It was no more than thirty steps to the nearest elevator from the pressroom door. Mac had been going straight home. What the devil had kept him in the foyer all that time? Or had it been as long as it seemed?

Cotton flicked down the turn indicator, signaling a left on Capitol. He would detour past the statehouse and check the signoff times on the teletype copy he had filed that night. That would tell him exactly.

A raw autumn wind was blowing out of the north as Cotton trotted up the sidewalk past the now-leafless capitol rose garden. Lights were burning on the seventh floor of the

Health and Welfare Building. Health and Welfare, in trouble with the Senate Social Services Committee, would be working late. But the statehouse itself was almost totally dark. Cotton let himself in through the press entrance, under the west-wing stairway at the Sub 1 floor level. He hurried past the Game and Fish Department offices, past the doors of the State Veterinary Board, the Funeral Directors and Embalmers Commission, the Contractors' Licensing Office, and the Cosmetology Inspection Bureau. He reminded himself, as he did almost every day when he used this route, that there might be good hunting among these obscure agencies forgotten in the capitol catacombs. In fact, he had a tip jotted in his notebook about the Veterinary Board. An anonymous caller had told him the director was letting his wife use agency gasoline credit cards. When he could find time he would check it out.

Cotton thought about time while the elevator whined its way slowly toward the fourth floor. Addington hadn't asked him why he wanted Mac's notebook. Had he asked, he would have told him just about what he had told Cherry. But he would have been honest about it; he would admit it was just a matter of curiosity. He had notebooks of his own crowded with story ideas dying on the vine and no time to work them. It was simply that Mac had been excited. And that excitement, if Mac was as case-hardened a pro as Hall claimed, was worth some curiosity.

The pressroom was empty. Cotton sorted quickly through his spiked teletype copy and pulled off the file for Monday. When McDaniels had left the room it had been twenty-two minutes before his deadline. The message from the *Tribune* city room giving him the go-ahead to transmit his column was signed off at 9:45 P.M. That meant seven minutes had passed before Mac fell.

The swivel chair squeaked as Cotton leaned back. He stared at the ceiling. What had delayed Mac seven minutes? A trip to the john? That might account for it. That or meeting a politician willing to talk to a reporter even if he was drunk. Cotton walked slowly to McDaniels's desk. No matter what had delayed Mac, the man in the blue topcoat had had plenty of time to give Mac his notebook. So what the devil had happened to it? Maybe, it occurred to Cotton suddenly, the man hadn't found it. He thought backward, recreating the scene, seeing Mac in the doorway, Mac tossing the notebook on the desk, remembering that a little later Mac couldn't find it. He had found a notebook, but he had said it was an old one—filled and set aside for filing.

Cherry had made no effort to sort out McDaniels's desk-top accumulation. There was still a deep stack of carbons of bills introduced, a pile of outdated Bill-Finders, old House and Senate working calendars for the past several weeks, and a litter of press releases. But no notebook. Not even the old filled one. In the second drawer of the desk, Cotton found four spiral notebooks—all pages filled with Mac's scrawl. Notes on the last page of the newest one concerned a press conference the Governor had held in September, just before the Legislature had convened. Cotton looked at the first page. There were Mac's notes on an appointment to the Public Employees Retirement Board made late in July. Mac had filled the book in a little more than five weeks. Cotton arranged the other notebooks in chronological order and went through them, looking for datable material. The arithmetic was simple enough. At the average rate Mac filled notebooks, there must be at least two missing. Probably the most useless deduction of the year, Cotton thought, but it probably meant Blue Topcoat had picked up the filled notebook that had been on Mac's desktop. And maybe that meant the notebook Mac had still been using was still around somewhere. Cotton sorted through the desk-top jumble again and then reached his hand down between the back of the desk and the wall. A pile of old papers, months of desk-top slippage, had accumulated there, caught atop a hot-air vent. On top of this pile, Cotton's fingers encountered the cardboard cover of a spiral notebook.

He flipped through it hurriedly. About two-thirds of the pages were filled with McDaniels's jottings. On the last such page were his notes on Tuesday night's Taxation Committee hearings. Cotton remembered that McDaniels had thrown his notebook onto the desk that evening and then, when he was trying to write his story, couldn't find it. He had apparently thrown it a little too hard.

The complaining whine of a police siren somewhere down Capitol Avenue filtered through the dusty windows. It made Cotton conscious that he was sitting at a dead man's desk, sorting through the privacy of a dead man's papers. He felt slightly furtive.

"Elliot—sez need only bout 18 milyn adnl to balance genl fund next fiscal. Sez estimates of the State Ed Assn sheer nonsense. If the approp com keeps its head, we won't need any new taxes." Those were the last words scrawled on the page. The last note taken by Merrill McDaniels, political reporter. A quote from a half-senile country banker-politician. A lie told for political purposes. How did McDaniels intend to use the quote? He had worked next to the man for more than eight months and he didn't know him well enough to answer. It was a sad, lonely thought and he turned away from it. The words could be used, as Representative Howard Elliot intended, to mislead the public. Or they could be used, with the hard facts of general-fund revenues and impending budget appropriations, to prove Elliot ignorant, or a liar.

The sound of the siren died away. Except for the faint, changing murmur of traffic on Capitol Avenue the pressroom was still. A long, narrow room, a row of tables in the middle and its dingy walls lined with desks. It had occurred to Cotton long ago that these work stations were arranged more or less in the informal pecking order of their owners, or their owners' publications. To the left of the high, unwashed windows was the old roll-top of Leroy Hall, the unchallenged if unproclaimed Numero Uno of the pressroom, winner of the Pulitzer Prize for bagging two county commissioners and a district judge in a land-zoning–bribery affair, chief of the *Journal*'s capitol bureau, whose "Politics" column reached 450,000 subscribers daily. Across the window, the desk of T. J. Tobias, the room's senior citizen, who had written politics for the *Evening News* since the early Roosevelt administrations, who had scores of political scalps to his credit, and who remembered too much, and drank too much, and coasted now into retirement, relying more on nostalgia than on facts. And next to Tobias, Eddie Adcock, ex–Associated Press and now syndicated, writing for twenty-five or thirty small dailies and specializing, so it seemed to Cotton, in embarrassing county chairmen whose patronage efforts showed. Across from Adcock, Cotton's desk, and above it one of the more exotic examples of the graffiti which had been accumulating on the pressroom walls for generations.

It was an ink drawing, about two feet square, of a housefly. The drafting was careful, with each of the thousand facets of the bulging fly eyes carefully suggested by the pen. The fly had been there, already stained and yellow, when Cotton had taken over the desk seven years ago. Old Man Tobias had told him that he thought it had been glued into its position back in the 1930's by a reporter who had subsequently fallen from grace and gone into public relations.

After wondering about the drawing for months, the thought had dawned on Cotton that it must represent Walter Lippmann's famous concept of the newsman as "the fly on the wall," seeing all, feeling nothing, utterly detached, utterly objective. By then, Cotton had become comfortable with this grotesque ugliness staring down at him. And the drawing remained, reminding him, and all who glanced at it and knew its meaning, that the reporter was supposed to be a little more than human. Or a little less.

For some reason the stare of this symbolic insect now oppressed Cotton with a sense of loneliness and isolation. He glanced away from it, past the collection of erroneous headlines tacked above Pete Kendall's desk (ROARK WON'T RUN FOR GOVERNOR. DEWEY ELECTED. GOVERNOR PREDICTS CALM ON CAMPUSES,) past the cluster of teletypes at the AP-UPI working stations, past the desks of the *Capitol-Press*, the *Daily Independent*, the *World*, the *Morning Bulletin*, the *Beacon*, the *Times*, the *Gazette*, the *Evening Sun*, and, finally, over to the desk of Jake Mills of Broadcast Information Network and, segregated near the doorway, the four television stations. The performing apes, Hall called them, using the pressroom without being part of its hard-bitten, cutthroat camaraderie. Tolerated but not accepted—like birdwatchers in a club of foxhunters.

Cotton turned his thoughts back to the notebook. Tomorrow he would tell Cherry he had found it and offer it to him. The ethics of the situation didn't require him to tell Cherry what Mac had said about his big story. And the traditions of the game argued against it. Cherry probably wouldn't want the notebook. Cotton was fairly sure *he* wouldn't want it once his curiosity was satisfied. Unless the fox Mac was chasing looked unusually fat, he couldn't imagine how he could find time for it.

He read his way idly into the notes, working from the back of the book. McDaniels had operated abut the way Cotton did—recording the spelling of names, occasional figures, key phrases from interviews, and a rare complete sentence for direct quotation. Like most newsmen, Mac used his notes only for the specifics his memory wouldn't retain. Cotton worked through six pages, matching details with his recollection of capitol news developments—looking for anything which didn't fit.

The seventh page stopped him. It was filled with columns of figures.

S-007-211-2778	Rebar cnt	121,000	usd	97,000
S-007-272-2112		109,000		91,100
S-007-411-2772		92,300		85,900
S-007-437-2442		142,000		130,600
S-007-255-2616		186,200		171,000
	halg sb	390,000	actl.	412,720(in tms)
		412,000	actl.	438,000
		290,500		311,300
		187,000		201,000
		313,000		363,000

An entire page of such tabulations, penned in neat rows, identified with code letters like "pcem pp," and "alm pp," and "gding," and "wting." Idle curiosity turned to absorbed interest. Cotton studied the numbers, looking for a pattern. He could see only that they were arranged in groups of five. That suggested nothing except—by the sheer size of some of them—that McDaniels's fox might indeed be fat. The ten-digit numbers might be account numbers coded for computer bookkeeping, or purchase order numbers, or almost anything. The abbreviations (if that's what they were) were gibberish. Cotton, who wrote "that" with a "tt" in his notebook, used "gv."

for "governor," and "xgr." for "legislature," thought about "The Goldbug," the Poe short story that turned on breaking a cryptogram to find pirate treasure. That could be done, he guessed, by working through the notebooks to determine what letters Mac tended to drop out of words.

Deeper in the notebook he found four other pages of similar numbers, interposed with other notes. Some seemed to represent the day-to-day routine of capitol coverage. Others he couldn't identify with published stories. There seemed to be, he finally decided, three or four unwritten stories represented in the jottings. One seemed to concern the State Insurance Commission, one involved loose accounting for cigarette tax stamps—a story Cotton had already been tipped on himself—and the third seemed to turn on the State Park Commission. The pages of figures might be part of any of them—or a story of their own.

He snapped the notebook shut and leaned back, looking at the fly on the wall without seeing it. Given time and McDaniels's clippings for the past few weeks he could sort it out. But where would he find the time?

4

The clock on the walnut-paneled wall was old and ornate. Its small hand stood almost exactly on 10. The large hand clicked two marks past 12. Governor Paul Roark was two minutes late for his Thursday-morning press conference. In approximately 180 seconds, John Cotton—senior man among the P.M. reporters—would get down from the windowsill where he was slouching and walk out of the Executive Conference Room, and the six other reporters waiting there would follow him. Tradition gave the Governor five minutes of grace. The rule had been proclaimed a dozen administrations back by a United Press reporter long since transferred and forgotten. He had argued that the Governor was—after all—still a public servant. To wait for him longer than five minutes would be to undermine the relationship between newsmen as watchdog-auditor-guardian-of-the-public-trust and the Chief Executive as politician and feeder-at-the-public-trough. And while the rule had been born in philosophy, it had lived in practicality. P.M. reporters, with edition deadlines looming, could ill afford to waste more than five of the crucial sixty minutes between 10 and 11 A.M.

Cotton looked at Alan Wingerd, the Governor's press secretary, who had handed out ditto copies of a Roark statement announcing the appointment of Tommy Gianini, identified as a prominent Tahash County civic leader and businessman, to the State Pardon and Parole Board, and was leaning against the wall, looking bored.

"He's late, Alan," Cotton said. "If he's not going to show we've got work to do."

"Got tied up on the telephone," Wingerd said. "He'll be here."

Governor Roark walked in. "Here he is now," the Governor said. "Sorry I'm late."

"You have anything besides the handout?"

"No," Roark said. "I'm available for questions."

"This guy you're putting on the parole board," Volney Bowles said. "Isn't he the Tahash County Democratic Chairman? How does that fit with your campaign statement about not giving jobs to party officials?"

Roark's smile lost nothing. "Delmar is the chairman, Tommy is his brother."

"O.K.," Bowles said. "See any conflict there?"

"None," Roark said. "If you rule out everybody related to party officials you don't have much left to appoint."

"Has Gianini got any kinfolk in stir?" Bowles asked. "Why did he want the job?"

Roark's smile frayed. "Mr. Gianini has no relatives in prison to my knowledge."

"To my knowledge," Bowles said. "Are we supposed to quote you as saying you know Gianini doesn't have any felons in the family, or that you don't know whether or not your new Parole Board member has kinfolk in prison?"

Roark laughed. "Come on, Vol," he said. "I said I was sorry I was late."

"Vol's on a diet," Cotton said. "A hard-boiled egg for breakfast, a hard-boiled egg for lunch and a broiled steak for dinner. It makes him mean as hell."

"I've got a couple for you," Junior Garcia said. "Will you sign or will you veto House Bill 178? And what are you going to do about that situation down in LeFlore County?"

"What's House Bill 178?" Roark asked.

Everybody laughed except Wingerd, who looked glum. House Bill 178, if signed, would legalize parimutuel racetrack betting. The Democratic National Committeewoman, a woman of grandiose temper and considerable clout, raised racehorses. The word in the pressroom was that Roark had made a secret primary campaign commitment to the Committeewoman that he would sign a race betting bill on the unlikely chance she could get one passed. The word was, further, that the secret had leaked, as political secrets tend to do, and that Republican leadership had conspired with the tourist and gambling blocs. The press table subsequently had witnessed the spectacle of the Senate Minority Leader, a Baptist layman of notorious piety, voting for legalized gambling. The Governor had thus been handed the choice of outraging the Committeewoman and Motel Association with his veto, or the do-gooders with his signature.

"I've forgotten about House Bill 178," Roark said. "Why don't you guys join me? If you concentrate hard on more pleasant things, like suicide, you can forget all about House Bill 178."

"We're making book on it," Garcia said.

"Eight to three you'd rather piss off eighty thousand Baptists than tangle with the old lady."

"The Constitution gives me fifteen days to make the choice," Roark said. "For the record, the Governor said he has not yet studied the bill and is not fully cognizant of its contents."

"How about LeFlore County then?"

Cotton wasn't interested in LeFlore County. The affair involved an employee in the circulation area of Garcia's paper who had got himself involved in some sort of conflict-of-interest controversy of no particular importance. He pulled out the McDaniels notebook and looked again at the pages of figures, looking for enlightenment.

Borrow 28 34

P M Asp. 1.09 1.50

A1 C.C. Half Sec. 24 in. D 16 ga. L.F. 8.50 15.00

16 ga. 16 gauge was the bore of a light shotgun, or it might be the thickness of metal. The numbers which followed seemed to be in dollars, but might be simply decimals representing something else. And what did "borrow" mean? It meant borrow, to go into debt. Cotton snapped the notebook shut and

slipped it back into his pocket. It might as well be Sanskrit.

Roark had managed to dispose of Garcia's question without saying anything damaging and was responding to the UPI man's question about a bill to make the directors of conservancy districts elected instead of appointed.

There were patterns in McDaniels's numbers, that was clear. Many of them ran in sets of two's or three's, as if they were comparisons in weight, or price, or size. And they weren't code. Cotton was sure of that. The abbreviations were from some technical jargon, further complicated by the reporter's personal shorthand. But the sense of the pattern continued to elude him. And he could not find any clues in the calls Merrill had been making in the days before his death. In the Supreme Court library Mac had checked out the briefs in an unimportant four-year-old civil suit and spent—if the court librarian's memory was accurate—more than an hour reading them. But his notes reflected only the case numbers and the date of trial. Whatever information Mac had gleaned from his reading must have been general, trusted to memory. The following day he had gone to the Utilities Commission. There he had chatted with the commission clerk about a pending telephone rate hearing, as reflected in his notes. But he had also pulled the incorporation file on Wit's End Inc. In his notebook, he had written the names of the incorporators, and the date of filing, and the word "crossed" followed by a question mark. A call to Marty Knoll in the Park Board information office established that McDaniels had called on Knoll the next day, asking about Wit's End state-park resort concessions. ("I got him the hearing files and he read them," Knoll had said. "What's going on?" And Cotton had lamely replied that he was just curious, which—unlikely as it must have sounded to Knoll—was true.) And the curiosity remained. On the surface it seemed likely that Mac was checking out a tip that the politicians were moving in on the state-park concession profits, and that the tip—like 80 percent of such tips—had proved sour. The trouble with that guess was the names of the five incorporators of Wit's End rang no political bells in Cotton's memory—and his memory stored the name of every county chairman of both parties, every legislator for the past five sessions, and most of the motley clan of aides, assistants, well-connected payrollers, henchmen and hangers-on. The only name he remembered seeing before was A. J. Linington. A. J. Linington had been one of the attorneys in the civil case McDaniels had checked—the attorney of a labor union which had been sued by a construction company in some sort of labor disagreement. This opened a second alternative—that Mac was interested in Linington. But the connection was tenuous.

Whitey Robbins had just asked the usual question about Roark's political plans and Roark was giving his usual noncommittal answer. "In sum," the Governor was saying, "this is the season for worrying about our tax-reform program and our project to bring this state's highway system into the twentieth century. Later, after the Legislature adjourns, I may find time to worry about politics."

"Governor," Cotton said, "were you surprised by the move in the House to double-refer your highway bonding authorization bill?"

"I was surprised." His smile denied the statement.

"Did you notice that most of the Democrats who often vote against you voted with you this time?"

Roark grinned. "I didn't notice." His grin broadened. "Which ones do you mean?"

"Let's call them friends of Senator Clark," Cotton said. "Do you see any significance in their voting with you this time?"

"On the record, no, I don't. Can I talk off the record?"

Cotton glanced around the conference room. Robbins was shaking his head.

"No," Cotton said. "No off the record. But I'd buy attribution to an informed source on the Governor's staff. How about you, Whitey?"

"That's okay."

"Not with me it isn't," Roark said. "Leave the answer as 'No,' or 'No comment.' "

"That's all I have," Cotton said. "Anybody else? Thanks, Governor."

The conference had lasted only fifteen minutes, far shorter than usual.

Cotton obeyed a sudden impulse, caught the Governor in the doorway. "Paul," he said. "How about a few minutes in private?"

The view from the high windows in the Governor's office was to the west, across the wooded hills where the capital city's most expensive residential district was built. Cotton noticed that the trees were leafless, the morning continued to be bleak, and the Governor—standing by the window—was in a good mood, which might mean he would be talkative. He was talking now. Yes, he had said, there was something to be said for giving Cotton a frank, off-the-record, for-background-use-only analysis of the Senate race. And now he was philosophizing about the anatomy of politics.

"This tax-reform plan, for example," Roark was saying. "If we can punch it through the Legislature about a half-million taxpayers will like it and ten thousand will hate my guts. The half-million taxpayers don't care much, and don't understand it very well, and have short memories. But the utility companies, and the bankers, and the big real-estate operators, and all the fat cats who have been getting a free ride—those birds don't forget who gored their ox."

"They don't," Cotton said. "But that's not important to you unless you're running for the Senate nomination. Have you decided?"

"I'd rather talk completely off the record."

"Make it not for attribution, for my background only."

"None of this sources-close-to-the-Governor crap?"

"If I use anything you tell me, it'll sound like it came right off the wall."

"Well," Roark said, "I've decided in a sense. I've decided I want to run. I think you reporters know that. If it was now, I'd run. I think it looks fairly good for me. A fair chance. But it may not look good by April. Something could sour it. A hundred things could screw it up."

Roark walked slowly from the window to his desk and sat down, a trim, handsome man who moved with a natural grace that Cotton admired and envied. He looked at Cotton for a long, silent moment. Then he said: "Korolenko thinks I could beat him, and so does Bill Gavin. They're both old pros and they know a lot of people, but maybe they hear what they want to hear. Both of 'em hate Clark. What do you think, Johnny? Can Clark be beaten?"

"I don't know," Cotton said. "He'd kill you on the East Side and he runs strong in the suburbs. You'd need a heavy turnout unless you get more party help than I can see now, and you'd need a good batting average on your legislative program, and you'd need a break or two between now and election. And you'd need maybe five hundred thousand dollars."

"Exactly," Roark said. "Exactly. Today it looks pretty good. Next month we could have my highway program killed, and my tax reforms gutted, and somebody caught stealing in one of my agencies, and two or three bad headlines about something else, and it could look hopeless. A hundred things could screw it up."

"But as of now you're getting ready," Cotton said. "Have you found the money? Or are you going to spend your own?"

"I don't have that much. And nobody ever won in this state spending his own money," Roark said.

"That's right. So who's going to finance the campaign?"

"Some of it's committed, more or less. At least Korolenko tells me we can count on enough."

"How much does Joe think is enough?"

Roark evaded the question, as Cotton knew he would. He talked generally of campaign costs. With television spots costing $2,000 a minute money wouldn't stretch far. Gene Clark would be superbly financed by banking and defense industries, as always, but Clark's enemies would spend something to get him out of the Senate. After fifteen minutes, Cotton had a fair picture of the Governor's tactical thinking and a few specific odds and ends of facts. The shakeup in the Randolph

County Democratic Central Committee had been Roark-inspired, to eliminate a diehard Clark booster. An appointment last month to the State Fair Board had cemented Roark's command of support from the Dales City municipal organization. A current League of Women Voters project to investigate tax-collection procedures had been indirectly and secretly inspired by the Clark organization in hopes it would air inefficiencies in Roark's State Revenue Bureau. And so forth. Some of it would have to be checked, but most of it would be useful.

"What I think I'll do is wait until the Legislature adjourns, and then get a little polling done by some reliable outfit and take a look at the results. Then I'll make the decision. I may not announce until just before the filing deadline. And now I've got to get some work done."

"One more question," Cotton said. He watched Roark's face. "Merrill McDaniels had an appointment with you last week. What was he asking about?"

Roark leaned back in the swivel chair. He looked at Cotton, surprised.

"I wouldn't ask a question like that normally," Cotton said. "And I wouldn't expect you to answer it. But it can't matter now. He's dead."

"And what do you think about that?" Roark asked. "Did he jump?"

"I don't think so. He was drunk, but he was happy drunk. He didn't do it on purpose. Merrill was feeling good that night. He was going to give me some dope for my column. I don't know what it was. So I'm asking around."

"Let's see," Roark said. He made a tent out of his fingers. "He wanted to know about pay scales for state capitol personnel in the new budget . . . how much raise and that sort of thing. And he asked me . . . Wait a minute." Roark leaned his elbows on his desk and grinned at Cotton. "Now I've got a question for you. McDaniels asked me a bunch of questions about that highway-bond-issue plan of ours. You bastards weren't supposed to know about that until I sent the message to the House. How'd he find out?"

"Simple," Cotton said. "Somebody told him. He found himself a leak."

"Like who?" Roark asked. "Nobody knew about it. Just Alan Wingerd and *he* wouldn't leak anything out of this office."

"Somebody had to know about it. Where'd

you come up with that $136 million cost estimate? Somebody did that work for you."

"That came out of a study the Highway Commission made last year."

"But somebody in highways had to know about it. You didn't just spring that out of the blue on your Highway Commission."

"I discussed it with the chairman," Roark said thoughtfully. "But I think you'll agree that Jason Flowers isn't likely to get chatty with the press—and especially not with a reporter from the *Capitol-Press*."

"No," Cotton said. Flowers was a prominent capital lawyer, big in the social set, who had feuded with the local paper for years over a dozen civic issues and once sued the editor for libel. "But you know how it works. Flowers tells some guy on the golf course, and the guy tells his wife, and before long somebody knows, and somebody talks to McDaniels."

"But he didn't put anything in the paper about it," Roark said. "How come? He knew about it at least two days before I sent the message to the House."

Cotton had been asking himself the same question. He didn't want to discuss the possible answers until he had thought it through.

"Who knows?" he said and shrugged. "What else did he ask you about?"

"I'm not sure I remember all of it. He wanted to know whether I would push for adoption of the higher-education budget without any cuts, and how active I thought the Motor Carriers Association would be in fighting the highway bonding plan, and he asked me whether the Highway Commission cleared it with me when they appointed Chick Armstrong as Executive Engineer, and . . ."

"Did they?"

"I'm not sure I remember. I think Flowers mentioned they had picked Armstrong. But it might have been that he discussed it with me after the appointment was announced."

"And what else did Mac ask about?"

"Something about concession policies at the state parks. And he asked about that goddamn House Bill 178. That's about it."

An idea was taking vague shape for Cotton—a nebulous idea of the sort of story McDaniels must have been shaping.

"Governor," he said, "did Merrill ask you whether you were a stockholder in any companies doing business in the state? Did he ask you what stocks you owned?"

Roark's face showed brief surprise and then anger.

"He did. I told him that was none of his business. And I'll tell you the same thing. I resent the casual way you reporters presume that nobody's honest except yourselves. My personal property is my private affair."

"It would be my business if there's a conflict of interest," Cotton said.

"Well, there isn't," Roark said.

"One more question. How much did you tell Mac about your highway bond plan?"

"Not much. He already knew all about it. I told him I hoped to hell he'd wait two or three days until it was official. I asked him to hold off on it but it didn't occur to me he would." Roark looked at Cotton. "Imagine," he said. "Finding a nice guy in the pressroom. It boggles the mind."

It was eleven minutes until 11 A.M. when Cotton left the Governor's office. Enough time—if he ran up two flights of stairs instead of waiting for the elevator—to tell the desk that the press conference had produced nothing of value so the hole saved for him could be filled with another story. As he trotted up the steps he decided he would tell the slotman to rely on AP and UPI for capitol coverage today. He felt an urgency, a stirring of excitement. He hadn't learned much from Roark. But he had learned that the story McDaniels had been chasing must have been very big indeed. From what Roark had said, Mac had somehow nailed down a clean exclusive on the highway bonding plan, and he had tricked the Governor into confirming it for him. But he had chosen to sit on the story. Why? Certainly not because the Governor had asked him to. Such requests were routinely rejected. No reporter would have suppressed such a story simply to accommodate a politician. To do so violated ethics, common sense and competitive instincts. Mac must have sat on the bonding story to protect his source. And yet he hadn't hesitated to let the Governor know he had a leak somewhere. That didn't seem to matter. For some reason, Mac wanted the information confirmed even though he didn't plan to use it. He had confirmed it by using a hoary old reporter's trick. He had presented the Governor his rumor as if it were fact and Roark had walked right into the trap.

The confirmation would have proved to McDaniels that he could trust his source. Maybe it proved other things. The way Mac had handled it told Cotton two things. McDaniels had been a highly competent reporter. And he had passed up a clean beat on the highway bonding story to avoid any risk of endangering the other story he was developing. That story must, therefore, be about as Mac had described it—an "earth-shaking bastard!"

⪢ 5 ⪡

Cotton sat in a stenographer's chair, his heels supported on the rim of Janey Janoski's wastebasket. He watched the rain streaking the windows of the Legislative Finance Committee office. He thought: Damn the rain.

"Just a minute," Janey Janoski said. "Just a minute. It's here somewhere."

"It's on the jump page," Cotton said. "About halfway down the column."

"I don't care where it is," Janey said. She folded back the front page of the *Morning Journal,* looking for it. "Leroy didn't have any reason to put it in."

A man stood at the bus stop by the east entrance of the capitol, absolutely motionless, enduring. Cotton put him on the bus, took him downtown, switched him to the airport limousine, bought him a ticket at the TWA desk, boarded him on the 11:05 flight to Albuquerque Sunport—mentally rescuing a human being from the dreary day.

"I should get back to work," Cotton said.

"Listen," Janey said. "Listen to this. 'The invoice for the shipment bore the signature of Arthur L. Peters. Personnel records show Peters resigned his job as accounting clerk in the Bureau's Tobacco Tax Division less than a month after the stamps were delivered. He is now employed by Bradbury-Legg, a capital accounting firm. Peters said he had "no idea" what happened to the stamps.' "

Janey handed the *Journal* to Cotton. "He didn't have any reason to put that in," she said.

"It's the rain," Cotton said. "You're in a hell of a mood this morning."

"You know Art Peters. He's that tall, skinny man who was always there with all the records when the committee was hearing those cigarette-tax bills. He's not a crook."

"Leroy didn't say he was a crook." Cotton's voice was noticeably patient. "He said Peters's signature was on the shipment invoice and that Peters said he didn't know what had happened to the stamps."

"But you know how people think," Janey said. "There's the implication. People read that and they say, Well, well. Peters got the stamps, and he quit his job and now five hundred thousand cigarette-tax stamps are missing. And they say the newspaper wouldn't have put it in like that if he wasn't mixed up in it."

"You know what we should do, Janey," Cotton said. "We should pick up your telephone there and call the airport and fly out to Albuquerque or Tucson or someplace decent and let the sun shine down upon us."

"I'll bet Peters loses his job."

"I didn't write the goddamn story," Cotton said. He looked at the headline, wishing he had.

500,000 CIG TAX
STAMPS MISSING

The headline was three columns wide in 42-point type. On another, duller day it would have won play position. But this morning the streamer read: PLANE HITS SCHOOL; 32 DIE. The stamp story was typical Leroy Hall, written in crisp sentences.

A half-million cigarette tax stamps with a face value of $50,000 are missing from Revenue Bureau stocks.

The stamps disappeared after the shipment from Decal, Inc., of Chicago,

> was delivered to the bureau last July 9. State law requires tobacco dealers to affix the stamps—for which they pay the state $100 per 1,000—to each pack of cigarettes before it is sold.
>
> A Revenue Commission spokesman conceded that the stamps are missing and that they might have reached the hands of cigarette bootleggers. Since discovery of untaxed cigarettes in vending machines last fall, the bureau has been making routine inspections to assure that all smokes sold have the stamp affixed.

He knew what each paragraph said, and he knew how Hall had come across the story. Cotton had received the same anonymous tip (and so had Merrill McDaniels), and had dutifully added it to his list of things to be checked when time allowed. It had been a spite call. He had known that there was a good chance it would check out probably and usably true. But he had put it off and Hall had beaten him to it.

Cotton let his eye follow a bead of water tracing its way down the window pane, thinking of how Hall would have worked his way through the invoice records—checking stamp orders against sales to wholesalers and then against inventory supplies; looking for a small squirrel of a story proving that the bureau was buying more than it needed from a company which kept a State Senator's law firm on a retainer; finding instead a bobcat of a story—a receipted shipment which didn't reach the supply room. The water bead merged into the general wetness on the pane. Janey, who had been talking steadily, was still talking.

". . . and that all sounds very nice, and proper, and worthy. But why do you have to hurt someone when it doesn't do any good?"

"I don't know. It's one of the details that make a story sound credible. Leave out the specific stuff and it sounds like you made it all up."

"I don't buy that," Janey said. "You guys just don't think about whom it hurts."

"Boy," Cotton said, "you're grouchy today." He pulled McDaniels's notebook out of his coat pocket. "I've got something here that will take your mind off your troubles. A mental exercise."

"What is it?" Janey put on her glasses, which were square with horn rims. They reminded Cotton that Jane Janoski was a pretty woman and of the pressroom gossip about her. He put the opened notebook on the desk in front of her.

"The problem is figuring out where those figures came from, or what they mean."

Janey picked up the notebook.

According to the gossip she was a lesbian. Or she was a secret swinger, conducting an affair with none other than Governor Paul Roark. Or she was the devoted mistress of the vice chairman of her standing committee. Or she was a Vietnam war widow mourning her husband. For the first time Cotton found himself speculating on which, if any, version was true.

"Where'd you get them?"

"That's not the question," Cotton said. "The question is what they mean."

"Those initials don't mean a thing to me," Janey said. "Rebar. I've heard that somewhere. It's something technical, I think."

"It must be," Cotton said.

"Part of it is some sort of tabulation," she said—still studying the figures—"and part of it might be computer account coding." She looked at Cotton over her glasses. "What does 'borrow' mean?"

"Neither a lender nor a borrower be," Cotton said. "It's what you do when the rent comes due."

"Maybe it has some technical second meaning," Janey said. "Is it fair to use the dictionary?"

"I looked up rebar," Cotton said. "It wasn't there."

"But I've got the world's biggest dictionary," Janey said.

Cotton followed her to the *Webster's Unabridged International* on its stand in the bill-drafting office. She turned pages.

"Rebar. Here it is. 'Music. To change the position of the bar lines in a composition.' That help?"

"I don't see how."

Janey turned more pages.

"Borrow. 'The opposite of lend.' We knew that one. 'Term used in arithmetical subtraction.' That doesn't help. 'How about the stops on an organ'?"

"No."

"How about 'a nautical term, relating to sailing close to the wind'?" Cotton laughed.

"How about 'the material removed from a borrow pit and used as a base in road and highway construction'?"

Cotton felt immensely silly. "That's it," he said. "Borrow. Of course. I should have thought of it."

Janey looked at him curiously. "Is it important?"

"It means you won," Cotton said. And it meant he knew now the source of Mac's story.

"The figures came out of some highway construction project?"

Cotton recovered his notebook. "Right. You're good at puzzles."

"No I'm not," Janey said. "Now I'm puzzled about what this was all about."

It occurred to Cotton that he had developed this habit of wasting time in the Legislative Finance Committee office because he enjoyed Janey Janoski. It occurred to him that it would, indeed, be pleasant to take this skinny, emotional, unpredictable brunette to the airport and continue this conversation somewhere where the sun was shining. He felt a sudden impulse to know her—to say: Janey Janoski, which one are you: the lesbian, the mourner or the lover? With that thought came another, surprising and shocking—Janey would tell him. If he asked her in the right way, Jane Janoski would show him her soul with all its scars. Cotton felt a surge of uneasy dismay. Or was it pity? The same concern one felt for a fingertip with the nail removed?

"You're looking at me funny," Janey said. "Does that mean you're actually going to let me know what you're working on?"

"I don't know for sure myself," Cotton said. "I think that when you add those figures together just right they tell you somebody's had his fingers in the public till."

"Are you going to catch another Art Peters?" She smiled and he could read nothing in the smile. But it stung. And, unreasonably, it angered him.

"I'll make a deal," Cotton said. "I'm going over to the Highway Building now and see if I can find the end of the string. You can come along and help. And, if we catch someone like Arthur L. Peters, I'll give you a chance to talk me out of it. You can decide whether we bag him."

"Like going rabbit hunting," Janey said. "But I have a chance to save the rabbit."

≫ 6 ≪

Janey had been too busy to go to the Highway Building, remembering a list of committee bills which still needed researching and mail to be answered. But she had gone, first protesting that she shouldn't and then joining him in rationalizing why she should.

"Maybe you'll find that all those seven thousand tons of highway construction records are written out longhand," Cotton had suggested, "by three thousand clerks on Republican patronage. And you suggest a bill making typewriters mandatory and you're the hero of every Democrat on your committee."

"Written out by quill pens," Janey said. "Or maybe when we read those construction specifications we'll notice that what they're mixing into the roadbed is really peanut butter, and I'll tell Gene Oslander about it, and I'll really be a hero."

Cotton thought about it, and laughed. Representative Oslander was a wholesale grocery broker. "If they're using peanut butter, you can bet Oslander's already subcontracting it," he said.

And Janey had laughed at that, although maybe it wasn't really funny. But the rain had stopped now, and the mist was rising, and there was a scent of leftover summer coming from somewhere, and it was fun walking like this—skirting the puddles on the wet sidewalk. *Fun,* Cotton thought. That's a good, old-fashioned word. He hadn't used it much. He tried to remember the last time.

And then he was signing into the highway records room—and Willie Horst was leading them down the central corridor, past endless rows of blue steel filing cabinets, under a sky of fluorescent tubes. Past tables where file clerks worked, past a pretty sweatered girl in a miniskirt. Cotton looked at the girl and noticed that Janey had been aware of the look.

"The completed jobs start down here," Horst was saying. "They're filed chronologically by the project acceptance date. And the file's also chronological. Starts with the bidding specs, and the invitation to bids, and the bids, on down through all the work-in-progress reports." Horst was a tall, stooped man with large ears and a habit of allowing long pauses between sentences while he sorted out exactly what he wanted to say. Cotton had time to think that the next sentence would be a third reminder of how important it was for them not to get his paperwork out of order.

"When you go through that stuff, put each page face down on the table and then the next page face down on top of that," Horst said. "Then when you put it back in the folder it's the way it was when you took it out."

"We won't mix it up," Cotton said.

Horst stopped and pulled out a drawer. "Here's where last year's starts. Down the aisle and back toward the end of the room is earlier. And after three years old it goes into the microfilm files."

"We'll start here," Cotton said.

Horst stood, looking at him doubtfully.

"We just want to do a little spot checking," Cotton said. "If we have any problems, we'll come up and ask you."

"Put it back like it was," Horst said.

The file Cotton pulled and carried to one of the work tables at the side of the room was labeled "FAS—27(2) 5 1322." It included at least twenty folders and more than enough paper to fill a bushel basket. "The FAS means it was a Federal Aid construction job on the secondary highway system, and the two in parentheses means it's a two-lane job," Cotton said. "I think the five means it's in the Fifth Highway Maintenance District."

Janey looked from the pile of file folders down the rows of cabinets. "Good lord," she said. "We found the haystack. But how can you expect to find the needle?"

"I'm showing you how a smart, well-trained, highly skilled, dedicated newspaper reporter goes about his duties," Cotton said. "He brings somebody along to help with the work. You didn't think I brought you along for the companionship?"

"Seriously," Janey said, "it's impossible."

"I don't think so. It just takes time."

It took approximately thirty minutes to complete the first step and it might have taken less—Cotton told himself—had his thinking been clearer. They found the specification sheets attached to the invitations to bid and combed them carefully—looking fruitlessly for the same pattern of figures which appeared in McDaniels's notes. There was no such pattern.

Janey glanced at her watch. "Altogether I'll

take an hour," she said. "Then I have to get back to work."

Next they looked at the itemized bid sheet, listing the asking prices for all contractors trying for the job.

And there it was. Cotton felt a stirring of excitement, a remembered feeling. In boyhood he had felt it. An animal track, fresh in melting snow.

"See it?" Cotton said. He put the tip of his ballpoint under the line.

"Rebar," he read. "1.20, 1.11, 1.32, 1.09, 1.14. Mac got his figures off a bid tabulation sheet."

"And there's that Al C.C. Half Sec. 24 in. D. 16 ga. L.F.," Janey said. "What's that?"

"That must be corrugated aluminum culvert," Cotton said. "Twenty-four inches in diameter and sixteen-gauge metal. And the L.F. means the prices quoted are for linear feet." He shook his head. It should have been obvious from the first. "And rebar is reinforcing bar—the steel bars they use to reinforce bridges and pavement."

Janey smiled at the sourness of the statement. "So why didn't a highly skilled, dedicated reporter think of that?"

It was well past her self-imposed one-hour deadline before they found the contract which had been the source of some of the notebook figures. They had worked their way methodically back through the files, taking alternate cabinets, looking only at the bidding tabulation sheet and checking only the prices in the columns McDaniels had noted.

"Hey," Janey said. "I think this is it."

Cotton closed the drawer in which he was working and squatted beside her.

"See. The numbers match."

Cotton checked the tabulation: Rebar 1.19 1.07; and down the page: Borrow .82 .89.

"Yeah," Cotton said. "He didn't write them all down. Just the second and fourth columns." He glanced at the bottom of the page, where the figures on each line were multiplied against the number of unit amounts involved and then added for the total money bids on the project. McDaniels had made note only of the prices offered by the lowest bidder and his nearest competitor. He looked at the top of the columns for the names of the bidding companies. The low bidder was Reevis-Smith, Constructors, Inc. The name rang a bell. The company sued by the labor union in the Supreme Court case McDaniels had checked.

"Well, now," Cotton murmured. "That's interesting."

"What?"

"This must be it," Cotton said. "Let's take the whole file over to the table."

There he carefully checked off the figures in McDaniels's notebook against the bid tabulation. Of the 108 items on which the contractors had bid, Mac had noted the prices by the two lower bidders on only seventeen. In each case, the Reevis-Smith offer was either noticeably higher than the others or noticeably lower. He pointed this out to Janey.

"But what does it mean?"

"Beats the hell out of me," Cotton said. "Let's think about it."

"I don't know enough about it to know what to think."

"Let *me* think, then. You listen."

Janey smiled at him. "That's a nice way to say shut up," she said. "I like tactful people."

Cotton thought. He stared at the wall behind the table. The wall was off-white and clean. Reevis-Smith was high on some items, low on others. It didn't seem to mean anything. All of the other bidders were also high on some items and low on others. What mattered was the total when it was multiplied out and the line totals added together. That represented the total price of the project, the amount paid to the contractor, the cost to the taxpayers. And Reevis-Smith had offered the lowest total price. But no! It didn't work that way. The bids were on *estimated* amounts. The contractor was paid for the amount of materials actually put into the road, the actual amount of work done.

Cotton began flipping hurriedly through the file folders, looking for the final acceptance sheet. There these actual amounts would be totaled, showing the final, total cost of the project after its completion. He knew now what Mac had found, and what he would find. There would be a big overrun in the total amount paid. He would find that Reevis-Smith, which had (he glanced at the bid sheet, checking the figure) bid in the job at $2,837,350, had finally been paid several hundred thousand dollars more than that.

"I'm listening and all I'm hearing are the wheels going round in your head," Janey said. "But what are you looking for now?"

"In just a minute I'm going to show you what we highly skilled, dedicated reporters call an overrun," Cotton said. "Reevis-Smith bid the job at two million eight and we're going to find it collected a lot more than that."

He found the final acceptance sheet.

"It should be on this." Janey, he noticed with satisfaction, looked impressed.

The total project summary figure was near the bottom of the page. It was $2,839,027.

"Right?" Janey asked.

"Wrong," Cotton said. He leaned back in the chair again, feeling deflated. What the devil had McDaniels been after?

"Not much difference?"

"Less than two thousand dollars," Cotton said. "Two thousand on a project of almost three million. Nothing. Anyway, they never hit it right on the nose."

Cotton stared at the wall in front of him, thinking. The miniskirted blonde became visible in the corner of his eye—restoring something in a file cabinet to his left. Cotton held his focus on a mark on the plaster, aware that Janey had glanced at him.

"What could it be?" He asked the question to himself and Janey ignored it.

"Well," she said. "Enough of this hunting rabbits. Back to researching bills and answering mail."

"I'll walk back with you."

"That's not necessary." Cotton sensed something in her voice. Coolness? She got up. "You think," she said.

Cotton looked after her.

"Wish me luck."

She looked over her shoulder at him, half smiling. "I don't know. I think I'm wishing the luck to all the Art Peterses in the Highway Department."

After that Cotton tried thinking for a while. Nothing offered itself. And then he began working his way through the file, reading memos from the project engineer to the construction engineers, memos from the Bureau of Public Roads to the Administrative Engineer; reading landfill compaction reports, reading change orders, reading analyses of the solubility of roadbed material, reading gravel hauling slips, finding nothing and finally finding himself forgetting what he was looking for.

He got up, stretched stiff muscles. Miniskirt was out of sight. Far down the room two file clerks, man and woman, worked heads down at a table. There was the faint sound of a radio playing somewhere. Advertising insurance.

Cotton walked to one of the narrow basement windows and looked out, eye level with the wet grass of the lawn. The rain had started again. A gray drizzle.

What had McDaniels found in that file? He

leaned his forehead against the glass. Cold. Where had it gone—that mood he had felt walking around the rain puddles with Janey Janoski? What had it been? Fun? Was that the word for it? He thought about fun. It lost its shape and its meaning as words did when he thought of them and became a visual shape. Three letters representing a sound. On the misted window, he marked the symbols FUN, examined the shape, wiped it away with a finger, and looked again out across the dripping grass.

McDaniels wrote down only the high numbers and the low numbers. Why? High on reinforcing bar. Low on roadbed material removed from borrow pits. High on aluminum culvert. Low on . . .

He turned abruptly away from the window, hurried back to the table and sifted through the files. One of the change orders he had noticed involved aluminum culvert, and one involved roadbed materials. He found the subbase order first. It noted a reduction in borrow material between Station 217 and Station 218 by 470 cubic yards. Under "Explanation" someone had typed: "Change in grade due to on-site drainage requirements." Immediately under it in the file was the order changing the amount of aluminum culvert used. It noted that 316 additional linear feet of culvert was added to the project between the same stations and "Drainage requirements" was typed in as the explanation. Both were signed "H. L. Singer, Project Engineer."

Cotton reinserted the pink carbons into the file at an angle so they would keep their place in the chronology but be easy to find. He flipped quickly through the work-in-progress papers. There were dozens of the change-order sheets, week by week—scores of them. And the pattern was quickly apparent. The changes on materials on which Reevis-Smith had bid high were almost always increases—thus increasing the contracting firm's high-profit items. But changes in items like road-bed materials, excavation and compaction—items on which Reevis-Smith had bid low—were almost uniformly reductions. And, without exception, they bore the signature of H. L. Singer.

Cotton rocked backward in the chair, smiling.

Mr. Singer, Mr. Singer. You have run out of string. Mr. Singer, you hapless bastard, you didn't cover your tracks at all.

He looked at his watch. Almost four. An hour before the records room would close.

He worked steadily, rapidly, efficiently, knowing almost exactly now where to look—transferring figures from the records to his notebook. He finished with the file labeled "FAS—27(2)5 1322" and began checking other project files for contracts won by Reevis-Smith on which H. L. Singer had served as project engineer. There wouldn't be time today to finish the job. That would take hours. He would simply try to scout its dimensions—determine how extensive this corruption had been. There would be time for pinning it all down, and wrapping it all up another day. H. L. Singer would keep. There was no possible way for Singer to escape.

Outside, the cold rain was turning to snow. Cotton was too engrossed in his hunt to notice.

7

The card was the deuce of clubs. It fell across the queen of diamonds and the jack of diamonds.

"I have just busted the diamond flush of Cousin John with the double blank," Hall said. "I hope all you guys appreciate how carefully I'm dealing."

"I believe that made me three deuces," Cotton said. He turned up the corner of the hole cards and looked at a spade queen. "Yeah," he said. "I'm working on the world's smallest full house."

Hall dropped the five of hearts in front of Pete Kendall, who had the nine of clubs and the ten of spades showing. "No help," Hall said.

"Pay attention when you're dealing," Kendall said. "I don't need that goddamn five."

The next card gave Junior Garcia a pair of

fours and a jack showing, and the next one was the ace of hearts, which gave House Speaker Bruce Ulrich an ace, trey and king up.

"Fours bet," Hall said.

Garcia put his cigar in the ashtray and tossed four white chips into the pot. "Four dollars," he said.

Ulrich folded. Hall had already dropped. Cotton considered the odds. If Garcia had another pair it was probably jacks, and he had one of Garcia's jacks. There was about eleven dollars in the pot. "Call," he said.

Ulrich relit his cigar butt and blew a heavy blue cloud across the table. "You know," he said, "if Roark really has got some running money lined up he might beat Gene Clark. He's been the best Governor this state's had."

"You've just damned the man with faint praise," Hall said. "That's like saying he's the world's tallest runt."

Kendall was studying his hole cards, his expression foreboding. "Or the world's most moral grandma raper," he said. "Like saying as lively as a three-toed sloth. Lovely as a bucket of guts. Honest as . . ."

"Kendall's on a simile kick again," Hall said. "You see his story on the abortion bill yesterday? He said Senator Wheelwright opened debate like a lioness opening an antelope."

"I wish I'd said that," Garcia said.

"You will," Kendall said. "Lacking the quota of spades required for a flush, I fold."

"Kendall learned that fancy stuff on the Corpus Christi *Caller,*" Hall said. "They even write sports like that in Texas. 'The forward wall of the Longhorn defense was in hideous disarray.' Stuff like that."

"I once wrote that the Southern Methodist passing attack, like sweet corn, traveled poorly, losing flavor with each mile from the Cotton Bowl corn patch. And got it past the desk." Kendall's expression changed from morose to merely grim with the remembered triumph. "Stole that one from A. J. Liebling," he said. "Deal the cards. It's like playing with a bunch of Brownies."

"Pot's right," Hall said. He dealt Cotton the jack of spades and Garcia the seven of clubs. "Pair of jacks," Hall said. "Jacks are tall."

"Let's not change the bet," Cotton said. He pushed four white chips into the center.

"What the hell happened to Whitey?" Kendall said. "He's been gone an hour." Garcia was studying Cotton's cards.

"What'd he say he was going to do?" Kendall said. "Wasn't he just going to call something in to his desk?"

"He said the *Gazette* wanted some information about the Health Department funding," Ulrich said. "But he had to drive back out to the newsroom to get it."

"It's just six or eight blocks," Kendall said. "If he wants to play poker he ought not screw us around like this. I don't like a five-handed game."

"You don't like losing," Hall said. "You know that quotation from Shakespeare: 'When the city desk calleth one, one goeth.' "

"Come on, Junior," Ulrich said. "Call or fold."

Garcia put the cigar between his teeth. "My mother told me not to call unless I could raise. I'm going to raise the son-of-a-bitch a little." He added three blue five-dollar chips to the pot.

"Just to get the shoe clerks out," Hall said.

Three fours, Cotton thought. Or maybe a club flush. He felt a sudden hunch that his seventh card would be a queen, giving him a winning full house. Cotton had learned years ago to resist hunches in poker.

"You bought a pot," he said, folding the hand. "What did you have?"

"Knock off all the talking and deal the cards," Kendall said.

Cotton won his own deal, a five-card stud hand, with a pair of tens, and then folded the next two hands of draw. While Ulrich shuffled he got up and made himself a bourbon and water. As he dropped in the ice cubes the telephone on the kitchen wall rang.

"Get the phone," Hall said. "If it's for my wife, tell 'em she's out playing bridge."

"Hall residence," Cotton said.

"This is the *Gazette.* Is Whitey still there?"

"He went back to the capitol to get some sort of information for you," Cotton said.

"That was damn near two hours ago. He hasn't called in and we're on deadline. I think the son-of-a-bitch skipped the country."

"He better not have," Cotton said. "He borrowed my car."

"If he comes back tell him to call the desk," the voice said.

Back in the den, Cotton found Ulrich had dealt him four diamonds in a draw hand. He called the opening bet, drew a small spade and folded. He considered briefly why Whitey hadn't called his office and hadn't returned. Maybe car trouble. Cotton's car was a battered Plymouth sedan. The left rear fender was rumpled and rusty and it needed a change in spark plugs, but it was usually reliable.

Cotton sipped his drink. A little too much bourbon. He watched Hall call Garcia's bet and thought, with pleasure, about Janey Janoski. Monday he would drop by her office and tell her what he had found. But what had he found?

He hadn't, he was fairly sure now, found the story that had excited McDaniels. Not if McDaniels was a seasoned pro in the reporting game. The story wasn't *that* good. His calculations indicated that the juggling of overruns on the project he had multiplied out might have increased the Reevis-Smith profits something like $28,000. He had found four other contracts in which Reevis-Smith worked with Singer as project engineer. In each of them the pattern seemed to be similar. But, if they were no worse, the total would amount to less than $100,000 on construction valued at more than $13 million. Not enough to excite a pro.

Garcia dealt him a seven of diamonds. Cotton looked at his hole card. Four of spades. He folded, and began shaping in his mind the story as it would probably appear. It would be a tough one to write—and a hard one for the reader to understand.

"Highway Department records indicate that last-minute changes in at least five road-building projects have served to increase the profits of Reevis-Smith Constructors, Inc."

He considered the sentence—whether the facts he had would support the statement. They would. Would they support adding the qualifier "substantially" after the verb "increase"? Probably not.

"In all five projects, changes ordered after the contract was awarded tended to decrease the amount of items—such as roadbed materials—on which Reevis-Smith had offered low prices and to increase the amount of items on which Reevis-Smith had bid higher than other contractors.

"In total, the changes appeared to have increased the contracting company's profits about"—Cotton guessed at what the figure might be—"$90,000."

Ulrich pushed the deck in front of him.

"They're cut. Deal."

Cotton anted a quarter and dealt draw. He dealt himself a pair of threes, and a queen, nine, five.

Ulrich opened. Garcia folded. Hall raised the bet to seventy-five cents. "This isn't a hand. It's a foot," Kendall said. He dumped the cards on the table. Cotton folded and dealt to the callers.

And the next paragraphs would be what the Highway Department said about it, and the comment from whatever Reevis-Smith official was stuck with commenting. They would be what Hall called the "lying-out-of-it paragraphs."

"Chief Highway Engineer C. J. Armstrong said that such change orders are common. He pointed out that original working plans for highways often have to change considerably during construction because 'as the road is being built we learn more about the demands of the terrain and the condition of the rock and soil on which we are building.'

" 'We give the engineers in charge of the project a lot of flexibility to adjust the work to meet conditions as they develop,' Armstrong said.

"H. L. Singer, who was project engineer on all five jobs, agreed. 'It just happened that when we got those jobs started we found we had more rock underground than had been estimated, so we cut down on the roadbed requirements,' Singer said. 'And it also happened that the drainage situation looked worse than the survey indicated, so we added more culverts.' "

That wouldn't be exactly what they would say, but it would be close. And then there would be a dozen more paragraphs pointing out that this odd sort of profitable coincidence didn't happen with other contractors, and that if the specifications had been written accurately in the first place, Reevis-Smith would not have been low bidder on any of the five jobs, and adding details of what the change orders involved and how they were made. It would run maybe eight hundred words, and it would be worth maybe a two-column off-play head on the front page on an average day. And, when enough time had passed for it to be fairly well forgotten, Singer would be eased out of his Highway Department job and there would be some quiet, never-admitted tightening-up of specification writing and change orders, and then everybody would be very good, or very careful, for a year or two.

"Come on, Cotton," Kendall said, "queens bet. You've got a pair of goddamned ladies."

"Dollar," Cotton said. A good enough story. But not a prize winner. And far from good enough to explain McDaniels's excitement. Maybe he had found a way to prove a link between Reevis-Smith and Singer. Maybe the bribing had been careless. But bribery was never careless. More likely this wasn't the story at all. Even if you could prove bribery this one wouldn't win the Pulitzer. More likely—much more likely—one of the other leads Mac's notes seemed to contain was the source of the hot one.

On the seventh card, he still had queens and sevens. They cost him fourteen dollars in total to Ulrich's small straight.

A little after eleven Cotton's luck improved. He bumped into a high straight with a well-concealed full house and took a forty-seven-dollar pot from Hall and then won two small draw pots. But the deck was generally cold and he had trouble keeping his mind on the action. The conversation drifted from ribald speculation about what Whitey might be doing in his long absence, to Roark's senatorial ambitions, to Ulrich's strategy for squeezing Roark's tax-reform bill through the house, to the extramarital affair apparently being conducted by the State Treasurer with one of his secretaries.

"I don't like to think ill of the dead," Garcia said. "But I wondered for a while there if old Merrill didn't have something like that going for him."

"I don't think Mac did any screwing

around," Ulrich said. "Not like Cotton here, anyway. Not wholesale."

"Cotton doesn't enjoy it," Kendall said. "He's laying all the statehouse secretaries out of a sense of duty. He thinks it improves their efficiency."

"It's not that," Ulrich said. "He's doing it for his friends. Doesn't want us to worry that he might be impotent."

"I used to see Mac's car parked over at the Highway Maintenance Division office quite a bit," Garcia said. "The only story you get out of there is the once-a-year alibi about how come it took so long to get the snow off the highways."

"When was this?" Cotton asked.

"Week or ten days ago. I drive by the district office on my way to work, and there was old Mac's car. Three or four times. Figured maybe he had a girl out there."

"It's your bet, Cousin Garcia," Hall said. "Notice how chatty the son-of-a-bitch gets when he starts winning? Mac didn't cheat on his wife."

"Two white ones," Garcia said.

The phone rang.

"That'll be Whitey with some improbable excuse," Hall said. He folded his stud hand and went into the kitchen.

Ulrich raised the bet to four dollars, which surprised Cotton. The Speaker of the House had a queen, ten, three showing. And Garcia was betting an exposed pair of sevens. Cotton had a nine down, and had paired it on his fourth card.

"Either you're lying or you've been laying in the weeds," he said. "Which one?"

"I don't remember," Ulrich said. "I forget what I have in the hole. It was some sort of face card."

Cotton studied Ulrich's cards and then Ulrich's face. Neither told him anything.

"You've got three alternatives," Ulrich said. "You can call, or you can raise, or you can fold."

"Or I can cut my throat," Cotton said.

"John," Hall said, "you better take this call. My night city editor has a story about you being dead."

Cotton spun in the chair. Hall wasn't smiling.

"They're pulling your car out of the river," Hall said. "The driver wasn't in it but they got your name by checking back on the license tags."

"Whitey," Cotton thought. The phone felt cold on his ear.

"This is John Cotton."

"John, this is Glen Danley. We're about ready to kill you off in our final home edition. Was your car stolen or what?"

"Whitey Robbins borrowed it," Cotton said. "He's the capitol man for the *Gazette.* What happened?"

"All we have is a story that moved a little while back on the AP state wire. Just a minute. I'll read it to you."

Danley read in the steady, paced voice of a man practiced in dictating over the telephone.

"The car of John Cotton, widely read political columnist for the Twin Cities *Tribune,* plunged off a bridge into Rush River near the state capitol late Tuesday. Police were dragging the rain-swollen stream for the body of the driver.

"Witnesses said the driver was the only occupant. Police said the accident happened when a semi-trailer truck swerved in front of the car on the narrow, antiquated bridge and forced it through the railing. The truck did not stop and was sought by police.

"The identity of the driver was not immediately established. However, Cotton could not be located at his apartment or at his desk at the capitol and Police Captain James Archibald said, 'We presume he was the victim.'

"Cotton, forty-one, had covered the state politics for the *Tribune* for nine years and his 'At the Capitol' column had statewide readership.

"A native of Santa Fe, New Mexico, Cotton joined the *Tribune* staff after serving as police and general-assignment reporter on the Denver *Post.*

"That's it," Danley said. "I didn't know you used to be on the *Post.*"

"I was," Cotton said. He felt numb.

"Who do you say had your car?"

"It was Whitey Robbins. He's the capitol man for the *Gazette.*"

"Robbins," Danley said. "Like the bird?"

"Two *b*'s and an *s* on the end," Cotton said.

"How about the first name?"

"William," Cotton said.

"Age and address?"

Cotton's numbness was changing gradually to anger. Whitey Robbins was somewhere in the mud at the bottom of Rush River.

"I don't know," he said, and hung up.

He dialed the AP number. From the next room, from the poker table, low voices. Hall had told them. The mourning for Whitey Robbins had begun.

"Associated Press."

"This is John Cotton. You better get a kill out on the story about my car in the river. Whitey Robbins was using it."

"He was? Oh. Damn, John. I'm sorry about that. I mean I'm sorry we did that to you. You know how . . ."

Cotton cut him off. "Have they found the body yet? And when did it happen?"

"We got out carbon on the fatal from the *Capitol-Press* about nine-thirty," the voice said. "And then Addington called us from the police station about ten thirty and updated it about the car being registered in your name and more details."

"Have they recovered his body?"

"Not when we checked." The voice paused. "It's R-o-b-b-i-n-s, isn't it?—the guy with the *Gazette*. What's his first name?"

"William," Cotton said, and hung up.

He stared at the phone. The story would have made the 11 P.M. newscasts. There must be somebody he should call to assure that he was not at this moment drowned under a polluted river. But there was no one. There was literally no one—he realized bleakly—who would have heard of his death with shock and grief and sorrow. Once, Charley Graff would have mourned him—feeling the same stunning agony of loss that he had felt when the nurse emerged from the intensive-care room and told him and his mother that his father was dead. Twenty-seven years ago, but Cotton remembered the feeling exactly. Remembered how he had felt, and how his mother had looked—bloodless and withdrawn, her sight turned inward, her eyes not seeing him. His mother had mourned, she and her bottle. But who, now, would mourn for him? He thought about it, his hand still on the telephone receiver. Leroy Hall would feel a certain sadness, he knew. Hall would miss the competition and the endless banter and the careful, guarded friendship. And Ulrich would be genuinely sorrowful for a while, and Junior Garcia, and perhaps Kendall, who was, under the cynicism, a sentimental man. The others in the newsroom would simply be shocked, sorry it happened, reminded unpleasantly of their own fragile mortality. And some of the women might miss him—a little—for a while.

And who would mourn Whitey? Cotton picked up the telephone book and began sorting grimly through it for the William Robbins number. Sometime tonight that telephone would be ringing and Whitey's wife would answer and a police desk sergeant would invite her down to the morgue to identify what had been her husband. He couldn't save her the pain, but at least he could soften the shock.

He took a deep breath and began dialing the number, asking himself as he did whether he should also call Jane Janoski. But what would he say? "Miss (or is it Mrs.?) Janoski. I thought you might like to know that John Cotton is still alive. I presume, as this call clearly tells you, that you give a damn one way or the other." And what would Jane Janoski say? He was curious about that. Less about the words he would hear—which would be polite—than about the way they would be spoken. But not curious enough to be tempted. The burned hand doesn't test the fire.

The telephone was ringing now. In a moment he would be—as gently as possible—making Mrs. William Robbins aware that her husband had been in an accident. He took another deep breath.

> 8 <

The policeman rang the doorbell at John Cotton's apartment Saturday morning at almost exactly 8 A.M. Cotton had slept until seven—an hour later than his workday rising time—and was sitting at his breakfast table over a third cup of coffee, reading the editorial page of the Twin Cities *Journal.* He had finished the *Capitol-Press,* working his way through it methodically in search of information useful to him. When he finished the *Journal,* he would find out about recovering his car, or what was left of it, and learn what the police knew about the accident. The 7 A.M. newscast had reported that Whitey's body had been recovered from the river and a semi-trailer truck believed involved in the accident had been impounded by police.

The officer at the door was very young,

very neat, and very officious. "Are you John Cotton?"

"That's right," Cotton said.

"Get dressed," the officer said. "They want to talk to you downtown."

On another morning, in another mood, Cotton might have been amused. This morning he wasn't. The name on the officer's badge was Endicott.

"Come in, Mr. Endicott, and pour yourself a cup of coffee and have a seat while I get some clothes. Do you have the warrant?"

"There's no warrant," Endicott said. He looked uncomfortable. "They just want to talk to you down at headquarters."

"Who wants to talk to me?" Cotton asked.

Endicott obviously didn't want to say.

"To hell with it then," Cotton said. "Go back and tell them I'm busy and whoever it is can call me at the pressroom Monday and make an appointment."

"It's Captain Whan," Endicott said. He looked even younger now. "He just told me to come and get you."

Cotton's irritation shifted from Endicott to Captain Whan. He handed the officer a cup of coffee and dialed the police number. Whan was in.

"I understand somebody down there wants

to talk to me," Cotton said. "What about?" Cotton enjoyed the long pause that followed the question.

"We'll talk about it when you get here," Whan said.

"I've got things to do today," Cotton said. "I guess I'll just skip it then."

There was another pause.

"We want to talk to you about your car and about William Robbins," Whan said.

"I want to talk to you about that, too," Cotton said. "I'll be right down."

Cotton regretted his display of toughness all the way to the station with Endicott. He'd had no real reason to push the captain. It had been petty. If he needed information from Whan, as he might, he would pay for the pettiness.

Whan, now, was being pointedly polite. He told Cotton that Cotton's car was in the police garage, that the right side had struck a pier and was caved in. Whan was a young man, perhaps five years younger than Cotton, with his hair cropped short, and dark, intelligent eyes set deep in a dark, intelligent face. He quickly established details of Cotton's identity, the circumstances under which Robbins was driving his car, when Robbins had left the Hall home, and where he was going. The questions then became personal, centering on how well Cotton had known Robbins, what he knew of his life.

Cotton answered fully and freely, making restitution for his rudeness. Whan's interrogation technique was efficient, Cotton noticed, wasting no time and allowing for no vagueness in answers. He wondered how well the captain would fare with a politician—someone like Ulrich when Ulrich had reasons not to be frank and candid.

The question now took a turn which puzzled Cotton, centering on Robbins's family and social life.

"I'll be blunt, Mr. Cotton," Whan said. "Did Robbins, to your knowledge, have any girl friends?"

"As far as I know, he didn't. I don't think he did. He was an honorable man. I don't think he would have cheated on his wife." Cotton interrupted Whan's next question. "Let's save some more time, captain. You've got to have a reason to be asking questions like that one and there wouldn't be a reason if you were sure it was an accident. Wasn't it an accident? Do you have any reason to think it wasn't?"

Whan's intelligent eyes studied Cotton.

"It looks like an accident."

"So why are you fishing around for someone with a motive?" Cotton said.

"We try not to overlook anything," Whan said.

"I don't think there's anything to overlook," Cotton said. "The statehouse is a gossipy place. A guy horses around, everybody chats about it. They chat about me, for example. But there was never any gossip about Whitey. I don't think you're going to find a vengeful husband. And I don't think you'll find any professional enemies. Whitey wasn't as mean as some of us in the way he reported. And besides, all of us work with politicians. They're pros. They know the rules. They know they're going to get caught now and then and they know it's part of the game—nothing personal. Nobody had any reason to kill Whitey Robbins. But I'd like to know why you think they might have."

"I told you," Whan said. "We're just being careful."

"You've got the truck now," Cotton said. "Who was driving it?"

"We don't have the driver."

"A semi-trailer truck driver shouldn't be hard to trace. Who'd he work for?"

Whan's eyes were alert for reaction.

"The truck was stolen," he said. He allowed

himself a slight smile at Cotton's expression. "Now let's save some more time. You're going to ask me why anyone would steal a semi-trailer truck because you've been a police reporter and you know there's no way to fence it, or even to fence what you strip off of it, and because the thieves go for the late-model, sporty hardtops."

"The thought occurred to me," Cotton said.

"Or maybe it was teen-agers—some kids doing it on a dare," Whan said. "Things like that happen. But it wasn't." Whan looked down at a note pad on his desk. "The makes we get on the driver from the witnesses put him from about twenty-five up to forty years old. He was wearing large sunglasses, had blond hair and a bushy mustache. A big man, bulky looking."

"I'd like to see the investigation report," Cotton said. "And the stolen-property report."

"I'll get copies made," Whan said. "Couple of other small things. Maybe they mean nothing at all. The truck was abandoned down near the railroad yards in the industrial district—the sort of place nobody notices a parked truck very fast. I guess all that does is prove our driver was smart, or that he didn't panic."

"But it makes you think of advance planning," Cotton said.

"Usually—almost routinely—when you pick up a stolen vehicle it's been wiped. But some of the pros wear gloves and don't have to bother. This guy wore gloves. So he didn't need to wipe it, except where the ignition wiring was jumped. I guess he took the gloves off for that."

"So you're looking for a reason somebody would knock Robbins off a bridge on purpose," Cotton said. "I'm sorry but I don't know of any reason. I don't think there was one. I think you've run into a coincidence."

"You're probably right," Whan said. He fished out a cigarette and snapped his lighter.

Cotton examined Whan's face, concentrating on not thinking of how he hungered for a smoke. He felt a respect for this policeman and a sharp, puzzled curiosity. Whan had told him a good deal more than he needed to tell him. He was sure the captain had a reason for this unorthodox exposure of police speculations.

Whan exhaled a cloud of smoke.

"Probably it was a coincidence," Whan said. "That's alternative one—an accident pure and simple. A stolen semi-trailer, a man who doesn't know how to handle it, a mishap on a bridge. Alternative two is a premeditated homicide by someone who wanted to kill William Robbins." Whan leaned forward and placed the cigarette carefully in the ashtray slot, his eyes on Cotton's eyes.

"Have you thought about the third alternative?"

"What?" Cotton asked. He was genuinely puzzled.

"It was your car," Whan said.

Cotton said nothing. He was thinking that Robbins and he were both tall and lanky, both blond.

"If nobody had a reason to kill Robbins, does someone have a reason to kill you?"

"Yeah," Cotton said slowly. "I see what you mean. It's an interesting idea."

"Think about it," Whan suggested.

Cotton thought about it. He thought about three National Guard officers indicted after his stories exposing falsification of travel expenses, about a state health director fired after his series on nepotism in the department, about a State Senator defeated for re-election in the wake of the *Tribune* series on conflicts of interest, about others injured, outraged or offended down through the years.

"I've got some enemies," Cotton said. "I've

hurt some people. But they're politicians. They're smart. They run risks and if they get caught they tend to be philosophic." He stopped, thinking about it again, and feeling vaguely deprived that even the animosity he inspired was casual, impersonal. Or was there some sort of ironic justice that a man with no one to grieve for him had no one to hate him?

"No," Cotton said. "You have to rule out your third alternative."

"Why don't you keep thinking about it?" Whan said. "And if you have any interesting thoughts, give me a call."

It was almost noon when Cotton got back to his apartment. He had stopped at the police garage and inspected the soggy remains of the old Plymouth. It had been worth maybe $600, but he had driven it six years and he would miss it. He had called his insurance agent from the garage to arrange to file a claim. Finally he had taken a taxi home, riding glumly through the gray day. The coffee was strong but drinkable. He poured a cup, made a salami and lettuce sandwich, considering Whan's line of questioning. The captain, he thought with wry amusement, considered him a possible murder victim on the hoof. The captain was taking advantage of a unique opportunity—interviewing the victim before the homicide. Except it made no sense.

At the table, he unfolded his copy of the accident report and read through it carefully. There had been two witnesses, a teenager crossing the bridge walkway and a woman who had pulled onto the bridge just as the accident happened. Their reports were about the same. The truck, identified by the boy, was a green cab-over diesel pulling an empty flatbed trailer. Cotton turned to the stolen property report:

ITEM: 1970-model Mack diesel tractor, cab-over flatbed trailer attached. Dark green. Transportation Commission Tax No. 92772 in white on both doors. License LA3-8302.

TIME: Noticed missing about 5 P.M., Friday, October 15. Last noticed on lot about 8 A.M., same date.

PLACE: Equipment lot at 1100 Third Street.

OWNER: Reevis-Smith, Constructors, Inc.

Cotton pursed his lips. Small world, he thought. Damned small. How many coincidences did that make? Two accidental deaths within a week. Both statehouse reporters. That was one. And the second reporter crowded off a bridge by a truck stolen from a company being investigated by the first reporter. That was two. Or maybe two and a half by the time you sorted it out.

He read the remarks. The equipment manager had missed the truck at closing time Friday when equipment check-in was verified. He had presumed a company driver was making some unauthorized use of it, or had taken it to the shop for a tune-up without filing a required report. He hadn't realized it was stolen until Saturday morning.

Cotton checked the time. The theft hadn't been reported until shortly before police had found the vehicle.

Outside, the dirty sky dragged down at the rooftop—a steady, cheerless drizzle. Cotton closed his eyes. Santa Fe would be a pattern of sun and shadow—clear blue sky over the La Bajada plateau and early snow clouds fighting with the wind to control the mountaintops. The air would be chilly, and the sun hot, and the forest of aspens above the Horse's Head an ocean of gold. The ravens in the cottonwoods by St. Catherine's Indian School would be raucous with autumn.

He opened his eyes and examined the grayness outside his window. He felt cold. Too much coincidence.

9

Congressman William Jennings Gavin died sometime in the small hours of Sunday morning. He managed the event as he usually did—to the maximum inconvenience of the working press. City editors, not warned by the customary ritual of preliminary illnesses, found the obituaries in their files hadn't been updated for years. And the fraternity of political writers—not alerted to impending death by reassuring statements from press aides—were caught unprepared for morbid speculations required of them by any sudden vacuum in the political command.

It occurred to John Cotton, when the Sunday-morning call came from his state editor, that he had never given the slightest thought to the political effects if Congressman Gavin died. Bill Gavin didn't seem to be the sort who would.

"You know what we want," the state editor said. "Who Roark will appoint to replace him, and crap like that. We'll hold your Monday column over until Tuesday."

"Roark's not going to talk about the appointment while the body's still warm," Cotton protested. "They never do that until after the funeral. All I can do is guess."

"O.K., guess then," the state editor growled. "The first time in twenty years the son-of-a-bitch broke any news on the P.M. cycle and then he does it on Sunday when we don't have an edition."

Cotton made three telephone calls: to Alan Wingerd to confirm that Roark would have nothing to say; to Joe Korolenko, to discuss the question of impact with this astute student of working politics; and to Ulrich, who often knew what Roark was thinking as soon as Roark did. Ulrich could tell him nothing—except that the Legislature would recess Monday and Gavin's body would lie in state in the House chamber. Korolenko wasn't much more helpful. He sounded depressed. Gavin had been his friend for forty years.

"I don't know who we'll ask Paul to appoint," Korolenko said. "You can't really replace Bill Gavin. You damn sure can't fill the gap he leaves in the party."

"Will Gene Clark be able to pick up part of Gavin's people?"

"No comment." Korolenko snapped out the words.

"O.K., Joe," Cotton said. "Let's just chat about it then. It will be not for attribution. I just want to get a feeling for it."

"If we're just talking as friends, sure, Clark will pick up some of the wreckage. The hyena always gets his bite."

"How about the State Executive Committee?"

There was a long pause. Seven committee members were Gavin people, part of the controlling Korolenko-Gavin-Roark coalition. The pause lengthened, telling Cotton that Senator Clark's encroachment on the committee must be more serious than he had thought.

"Clark will pick up one," Korolenko said. "That's all we'll lose. I think."

"You think?"

"Who knows anything for sure these days," Korolenko said. He sounded tired.

"No ideas about the replacement then. How about the names of some people from the third district who might be considered?"

"I owe you a favor, John. I've owed it to you for four years now, and I pay my debts. You know that. But I just haven't had time to think about it yet. When I do, I'll call you."

Cotton wrote the column then, throwing away three false starts before he finished it. He spent four paragraphs reporting why Gavin's death would be a blow to Paul Roark's senatorial ambitions and then shifted into background.

> Since he completed his term as Governor 25 years ago and won the first of his 13 consecutive terms in Congress, Gavin had been one of the pins keeping the Democrats in this state from splintering along lines of factional interest.
>
> Gavin and Senator Eugene Clark have disagreed on policy matters for years.

He reread the sentence, thinking it was a notable understatement. Clark was a sophisticated, urbane political creature, with a sort of country-club, Hamiltonian distaste for mass man. Gavin had been a sort of latter-day populist, who never lost his rapport with, and popularity among, the blue-collar workers. The Clark-Gavin relationship was a genuine animal dislike bordering on hatred.

Cotton considered working in a paragraph

on Korolenko's health. The old man looked bad and was in his seventies and there were rumors he had something incurable. But today such speculation seemed too ghoulish.

The rest of the column was sheer guesswork, carefully qualified, concerning the sort of horse trading which might be involved in the appointment of a man to fill the Gavin vacancy until the next election. Cotton read it without pleasure, folded the three typed pages into his coat pocket, and took a taxi to the capitol.

He signed off the column on the teletype at 10:43 and flicked off the switch, conscious of the total silence. In an hour and seventeen minutes it would be appropriate to eat lunch. He could go home, play one or two games of solitaire, and then it would be time to open a can of . . . He considered the alternatives. Creamed chicken soup. Or he could walk around for an hour and drop into a café and buy something. Neither alternative had any appeal. He stared down the newsroom, his eyes stopping at the desk of Whitey Robbins. There was a paper in the typewriter—a story which would never be finished. A flutter of motion at the window, a house wren on the sill. Cotton had intended not to look out the window at the grayness of the day. Now he felt a bleak, overpowering loneliness. Somewhere from far away there was a muffled sound. Perhaps a janitor slamming something, if janitors worked on Sunday. Perhaps a door closing. The silence returned, buzzing in his ears. If it had worked out differently and he had married someone he would rush back to the apartment and he'd say, "Wife, I'm low today," and his wife would say . . . He frowned, trying to think what a wife would say. He couldn't make it work. The wife needed a personality. She became Janey Janoski. Janey would say something wise. Janey would say, "It's this goddamn weather. Let's fly away to one of those sunny places you always talk about." And he would say, "What about Ernie Danilov?" And she would say, "He got along without you before he met you. He can get along without you now."

Cotton walked out of the pressroom, down the dark hallway—hearing the echoes of his footsteps. He pushed the elevator button and waited. A clanking sound came up the shaft, and the creaking of the cables. Then he turned abruptly, walked back to his desk and riffled through his Directory of Public Employees. He ran his finger down the J's. It was listed simply as Janoski, Jane, Executive Secretary, Legislative Finance Committee.

He dialed her home number.

"Hello."

"This is John Cotton. I thought you might like to hear what I found out about that highway contract."

"What did you find out?"

Cotton paused. The feeling was familiar but he hadn't suffered it since high school. "Ah. Well. Could I tell you over lunch? Have you had lunch yet?"

It was more than a mile to the Copper Pot but Cotton walked. A tall, slightly stooped man who had forgotten to get a haircut last week and whose suit needed pressing, walking rapidly across the damp parking lot, whistling. Walking past the few parked cars, glancing at the man sitting in the dark blue Cadillac and smiling because the man looked vaguely familiar, not noticing the blue topcoat tossed over the back of the seat beside the man, not noticing (because he was thinking of Janey Janoski) that the man did not return the smile; that the eyes of the man were studying him in cool appraisal.

10

At ten minutes before nine Monday morning, Cotton stood in the senate gallery, looking down at the lying-in-state of William Jennings Gavin. He was thinking of the luncheon meeting, and of Janey Janoski, and deciding once again that he had talked too much and listened too little. It had been fun, but the memory was disappointing, and slightly puzzling. Janey's enthusiasm for his success in the Highway Department files had been brief—quickly changing to questions about the identity of H. L. Singer. And, when Cotton could identify Singer only as a project engineer, she'd returned to questions about the impact of the story on reputations in general. Then somehow they'd wound up talking about novels, and Cotton had talked (endlessly, as he recalled it) of the novel half finished in his desk drawer, and of how he should finish it. Most of the lunch had been pleasant, and then they had walked through the cold, almost deserted downtown streets, peering into the windows of closed shops. But now his mind returned, like a tongue to a sore tooth, to the moments of friction. Janey's distaste for his story could be the normal reaction of a Roark Democrat—conscious that even a small dent in the administration's image did its small damage. But he thought about the gossip. That Roark's marriage was on the rocks, that Roark had a mistress. And of Janey's name among the dozen possibilities the gossips listed. He was aware that the television lights had gone on again and that Leroy Hall, standing beside him at the gallery railing, was leaning over for a better view.

"He's saying, 'I'm glad you're dead, you rascal you,' " Hall said.

"Who?"

"Our good Senior Senator," Hall said. "If the boobs watching TV tonight can read lips, that's what they'll see Cousin Gene Clark is saying."

Senator Clark, his white head bowed and reflecting the portable lights, stood before the open casket while two cameramen recorded his display of sorrow.

"Gavin would have enjoyed watching that," Hall said. "He really would have enjoyed it."

A fat woman under a large hat replaced Clark at the casket. Behind her the line led back through the east aisle of the Senate chamber, past two National Guardsmen standing at parade rest at the door, and out into the hall. Most of them were older people. Cotton recognized an assistant state treasurer, a secretary from the Corporation Commission, a retired legislator, and two county Democratic chairmen in the slowly moving line. Others looked familiar—faces he had seen at political conventions and campaign rallies. Most of them he had never seen before. They looked like what Hall called the "real people."

"A lot of poor people," Hall said. "The kind of people old Bill never forgot, and they're not forgetting him. When Clark dies, it will look like a combined convention of the Rotary Club and the Chamber and the Bankers Association."

"That was a hell of a column you wrote this morning," Cotton said. The column had been superb. Hall had ignored the obvious political speculation. He had put together a series of remembered incidents in Gavin's career—a promise kept, a betrayal punished, an old favor repaid, a skirmish lost, a battle won. Tales told with affectionate nostalgia. And the effect had been almost poetry.

"I worked on it," Hall said. "I liked the man." He turned abruptly and looked at Cotton. "And I like Joe Korolenko. And I respect Paul Roark for what he's trying to do. And I can't stomach Gene Clark. But I think you feel about the same about all of them. Nothing at all. Like you were a psychologist watching rats in the maze. I never could understand that about you."

Hall's intensity surprised Cotton, and embarrassed him a little. He looked out across the chamber, at the profusion of funeral flowers around the bier, thinking about what Hall meant.

"I like some of them better than others."

"But not on company time," Hall said. "When you're writing, it's 'a plague on both your houses.' You say, 'Folks, here we have two gray rats: Eugene Clark and Paul Roark. Both politicians. Same goal. Power. Get the power and you get the money.' "

"It's not that simple," Cotton said. What the hell was the matter with Hall today?"

Leroy was looking down at the slow-moving line. The only sound was the shuffling of feet, an occasional muffled cough.

"The great electorate," Hall said. "The citizenry of the state. You think, Give 'em the facts and they'll make the right decisions. But they're not reading past the headlines. They're watching *I Love Lucy* and getting their instant political wisdom from some former disc jockey with a sincere smile on the ten-o'clock news. The bastard couldn't name the National Committeeman for you, but he's got credibility because they like his teeth."

Cotton said nothing.

"Cousin John, we've sold ourselves a bill of goods, you and Junior and I, and Volney and all of us. We buy this business of give them the facts and man decides in his enlightened self-interest. How about changing it—being realistic? Deciding that sometimes they're not going to digest the facts and come to the enlightened conclusion. You know it's true. You've seen it, time after time." Hall looked up, his eyes on Cotton's eyes. "How about making a selection sometimes of what facts they can handle—giving them what's good for them?"

"You feel like playing God?" Cotton laughed. "I'm not ready for it."

"O.K.," Hall said. "Forget it." He turned

from the railing, from Cotton, and walked away.

Cotton looked after him, puzzled at the anger, and wondering what Leroy Hall had been trying to say to him.

≫ 11 ≪

It was a quarter to five when Cotton returned to the newsroom and found the message in his typewriter.

He was tired. He had spent most of the morning going through records in the State Park Commissioner's office. He had found nothing—or virtually nothing. Wit's End, Inc., held—as McDaniels's notes indicated—a contract for developing new state parks. But he could find nothing irregular. Bidding for the developing had been competitive. Wit's End had been low. Cotton had left at lunch—guessing that McDaniels had either followed a bum lead or had found a way to prove something that Cotton couldn't even suspect. He lunched with the thought that he had accomplished nothing beyond making the Park Commission staff nervous, and curious about why Cotton was interested in Wit's End, Inc.

He spent the afternoon at the Corporations Commission. His luck started good. In the Insurance Department office, Tom McGaffin remembered McDaniels's visit and even remembered the files Mac had asked to see. They involved Midcentral Surety, and after almost two hours of tedious cross-checking, Cotton found that some of McDaniels's notes had been taken from records covering bonds the firm had provided to guarantee performance on public construction projects. Such bonds were required by law to protect the state in the event a contractor failed to complete a job properly. Cotton found nothing peculiar except the volume of the company's business. Midcentral seemed to be writing the performance bonds for six of the state's larger highway builders (including—he noticed—Reevis-Smith) and for a good many of the public-school building jobs around the state. That had seemed promising until he discussed it with McGaffin.

"I don't know anything special about it," Tom had said. "But I'd guess you're going to find they found themselves a good, cheap source of back-up money. That would mean they could beat the competition for a while."

McGaffin explained that the bonding surety companies generally lack the capital to guarantee a dozen or so multi-million-dollar jobs simultaneously and thus they reinsure their risks with a major national insurance company.

"I'd guess Midcentral found an insurance company hungry for business and got a special deal on reinsurance."

"How do I check it out?"

"You could get it from the contract file of any state agency they're dealing with. If they're bonding a public school, the school-board contract file would show who's bonding the project and whether the bond is reinsured. Same with those highway projects. You'll find a record on the way the bond is handled."

On his way back to the newsroom, Cotton decided none of what he had found looked very promising. McDaniels's park contract notes seemed to dead-end unless some new information could be found in some source outside the official records. And the insurance files were simply confusing. Mac must have had a reason to check them. He must have seen some significance in the odds and ends of figures, dates and names he had jotted into his notebook. Again, there must be some outside key to which McDaniels had had access. Either that or the notes were nothing more than relics of a reporter's wasted time—notes taken for stories that simply had not checked out. But that seemed to mean that McDaniels's big story lay in the peculiarities of Reevis-Smith contract overruns and underruns. And the Reevis-Smith story wasn't really very exciting.

Cotton walked into the newsroom intending to go directly home. But the message aroused his curiosity. It bore Junior Garcia's initials.

"Wingerd wants to see you. Says he'll be working late in his office and will wait for you."

Wingerd was obviously doing nothing but waiting when Cotton walked into his office. He was sitting behind his oversized desk—a desk which made him look even smaller than he was.

He peered at Cotton through thick-lensed glasses, his narrow head bent slightly on its skinny neck.

"John," he said, "sit down. I've got two things to ask you about and the first one is hardest so let's take it first." He moved around the desk and stood by the window, looking out into the early darkness. "Harder for me, anyway," he said.

"What is it?"

"You're working on something," Wingerd said. "McDaniels was working on something and now you are. Maybe different things. I don't know what it is." He turned and faced Cotton again. I hadn't noticed, Cotton thought, how frail he is.

"That's the point, I guess. I don't know what it is. Roark's just about at the Rubicon. He's getting everything done that he can to make the race and it's at the point pretty soon where he won't be able to turn back without hurting himself." Wingerd shrugged. "I don't have to tell you how it is. It's close. Maybe he shouldn't run. He needs to know everything he can know."

Cotton found Wingerd's discomfort painful. He wanted to hurry it. "Like what, for example?" he said.

"Like what you're working on." Wingerd paused, peering at Cotton.

Cotton thought about it, surprised.

"Or, if you can't be too specific, maybe you could let us know if it will hurt the Governor. You know, embarrass the administration. Have a political impact."

"To tell the truth, Alan, I don't know myself."

He stopped, liking Wingerd but wondering how much he should tell him.

"You don't *know*?" Wingerd said. He obviously didn't believe it.

Cotton made his decision.

"I'll tell you as much as I can, and you tell me as much as you can."

Wingerd looked at him a moment. "Good enough."

"I can't tell you much. I've been doing some checking in three areas. The Highway Department, and the Insurance Department of the Corporations Commission, and the State Park Commission. I've got a story out of the Highway Department worth maybe off-play on page one on a dullish day. When I get it wrapped up and ready to go, that is. It won't help Roark a bit, because it makes his Highway Department look bad. But on the other hand it doesn't seem to involve him, or even any of his highway commissioners, in any direct way. He won't enjoy it, but it won't hurt him much."

Cotton paused for comment and received none. "It's too early to tell about the others. I honestly don't know what I have. It looks like nothing. And as far as I know they won't gut Roark if they do work out. Frankly, I doubt if I get anything I can write."

"Somebody cheating a little?"

"That would be about it," Cotton said. "If it's anything at all."

"Thanks," Wingerd said.

"Now. My questions. How did you know I was working on something? And what do you know about what McDaniels was working on?"

"This has to be between us, only." He looked at Cotton, acknowledged Cotton's nod.

"You boys already know this. At least we knew it happened when I was writing for UPI. We sort of keep track of what you're doing when it's outside the routine."

"Oh?"

"Like today I get a call this afternoon from somebody in the Insurance Department, and I learn you've pulled the files on Midcentral Surety. And like I already knew you were working the highway construction records." Wingerd looked embarrassed. "I used to work for United Press International," he said, "but now I work for the Governor's office. It's the job."

"Why not?" Cotton said. "It's part of the business. Now, how about McDaniels?"

"That's how I made the connection. Mac had been looking into the same records. The Midcentral outfit and into highway construction files and over at the Highway Maintenance Office."

"And the Park Commission?"

"Yeah. That too."

"What was he after?"

"Same as you, I guess."

"I'm not so sure," Cotton said. "Do you have any hints?"

Wingerd took off his glasses and rubbed his eyes. "Let me think about this a little," he said. "I have a habit of thinking like a reporter and forgetting I'm a Governor's flac. I'm not going to say anything to help you embarrass him. Not while I'm taking his money."

"I don't want something for nothing," Cotton said. "Maybe you can't help. But if you do help me, I'll remember I got help from the Governor's office. You know what I mean. I won't forget it. Maybe a sentence in the third paragraph says, 'Governor Roark's office cooperated in the investigation.' Or maybe I can't do anything but give you time to get braced for it."

"The next couple of weeks are the most important," Wingerd said. "After that we're past the point of no return."

"I understand that."

"And I can't tell you much, partly because I don't know much. But I know Mac was checking into who was behind Midcentral." He peered at Cotton, guessing Cotton had been doing the same.

"You mean like who was handling reinsurance of performance bonds?"

Wingerd said, "Yes," but he looked surprised. That wasn't what he meant, Cotton thought. What did he mean? Did he mean McDaniels was checking on who owned the company?

"What else?"

"Well." Wingerd peered at Cotton again. "He was trying to get hold of the freight-company hauling slips on some highway jobs."

"Hauling slips on what?"

"Materials. You know. Gravel. Steel. Stuff like that."

"What was he doing at the Maintenance Division?"

"I don't know. All I know is that he had about three-four visits with the District Engineer."

"How about the Park Commission?"

"He was nosing around the development contracts on those new lake resorts."

"What else do you know?"

"That's it. That's all I know. I wonder how you two happen to be working on the same stuff."

"Maybe I can tell you later," Cotton said. "But what was the second thing you wanted to see me about?"

"I don't think there's any way to do this without giving you the wrong idea," Wingerd said. "I want to offer you a job."

"A job?"

"Roark needs somebody to handle his campaign. And then he'll need an executive secretary for his Senate office. And it won't be me. At the end of his term as Governor, I'm quitting."

Cotton said nothing. This was totally unexpected.

"What are you making? Maybe twelve, fifteen thousand? You'd have to negotiate some for the campaign job. Maybe twenty thousand. Maybe he can go more. The job on the Senate staff would be about twenty-five thousand or so."

"If he wins," Cotton said.

"I think there'd be a contract. If he loses

and can't provide the staff job, there'd be a settlement in it."

"I don't know," Cotton said. "I don't think I'm interested."

"Think about it. Roark wants to talk to you tomorrow after you've thought."

"No. Really," Cotton said. "I'm not interested. It's not my line of work. Why don't you get Junior Garcia . . . or maybe Volney Bowles. Junior would be good at it."

"You'd be better," Wingerd said. "And Roark wants you for it."

"I appreciate it," Cotton said. "Really. It's an honor. But no. I don't like the idea."

"Well," Wingerd said, "I wish you'd think about it." He looked exhausted.

12

Cotton switched on the light with his elbow, deposited his two sacks of groceries on the kitchen table and walked back into the living room. A box sat almost exactly in the center of his coffee table. It was a cigar box with the word SURPRISE printed large on its top. Cotton stood, frowning at it. The box hadn't been there when he left for the capitol. After his coffee he had started a game of Spider. The box now sat atop the array of cards in the unfinished game. He glanced at the front door. The lock had clicked behind him when he left, he was sure of that. And it had been locked when he returned. He picked up the box and opened it.

There were a sudden sharp pop and a puff of blue smoke. Cotton jumped, dropping the cigar box.

"Son-of-a-bitch," he said. The box was on

the carpet, its lid open. In it—fastened with adhesive tape—was a small green plastic container, its lid partly open, the remnants of blue smoke drifting out. He stared at it, shaken at first, and then angry. He squatted, examining the container. Molded into the plastic on its top lid were the words: SECRET BOMB. CIGARETTE CASE.

"Very funny," Cotton said. A toy. He pushed the lid fully open. Inside was a spring, which—when the lid was released—slammed a tiny clapper down on a cap. The exploded cap, the sort used in toy pistols, was still in place. Also in the box, Cotton noticed then, was a small photograph taped face up.

Cotton unfastened the tape and looked at it. It was a Polaroid photograph of the back of a man walking across the statehouse lot. His own back, Cotton realized.

He sat on the sofa and examined the print. Nothing was written on it. He picked up the box and turned it over. Nothing written there. And then the telephone rang.

"John Cotton."

"Cotton, listen." The voice sounded muffled, barely audible. "You opened the box. You'd be dead now if we wanted you dead. Maybe you . . ."

"What?" Cotton said. "What about the box? Who is this?"

"Listen." The voice was low but insistent. "Don't talk. Listen." It was a muffled whisper. "You saw the photograph. That could have been a bullet in the back of your head. But we took your picture. We want to show you how easy it would be. Maybe you don't have to die. It's up to you."

"What?" Cotton said again. He couldn't comprehend it.

"It's up to you, Cotton. If you stay in the capital, you can't stay alive. If you want to stay alive, you have to leave. You have to leave tomorrow. And you can't come back. If you come back, we will kill you."

"Look," Cotton said. "What the hell is this? Is this some sort of joke?" He was shouting.

"Where's your car?" the voice asked. "Is that a joke? Now listen. Here's how it was. Just a moment." Cotton heard a rustling of paper. " 'Subject left the residence of Mr. Leroy Hall at about five minutes before ten P.M. He walked down the sidewalk and approached the white Plymouth. Then he turned back and reentered the Hall residence. He came out again within a minute, got into the car and drove up Spruce to A Avenue. He turned left on A to the intersection of Eleventh and right on Eleventh toward the Eleventh Street bridge. Action was taken as planned on the bridge. There may have been a witness in a green Rambler station wagon. Truck abandoned without witnesses.'" The voice had been reading. Now the pace became conversational. "Exactly as planned except someone named William Robbins borrowed your car and he happened to look something like you."

"But what is it?" Cotton asked. "What's going on?"

"We think you may interfere with us," the voice said. "Here's what you must do. Listen carefully." The whisper slowed now, spacing the words. "Do not go to the capitol tomorrow. Stay in your apartment tonight. Do not use your telephone tonight. If you do, we will know it immediately. Tomorrow morning call a taxi to pick you up at eight. Go to the airport. Buy a ticket. Get out of town. If you come back, there won't be another warning. You will simply be killed."

"But how about . . ."

"Your job? You will be watched, here and at the airport. When your plane leaves, a telegram will be sent to the editor of the *Tribune*. It'll tell him you are resigning, that you are sick and that you are leaving the state."

"Boy," Cotton said. "Danilov will love that."

"One more thing. After you hang up, your first thought will be to call the police, report this call, and ask for protection. Maybe you'll get an officer assigned to watch you a day or two. Maybe not. But, even if you do, think how easy it will be to kill you. Think of the ways we can do it." The voice paused. "You'll think of eight or ten, but there are dozens you won't think of. And we will be ingenious, because there is a lot at stake."

The voice paused again. "Goodbye."

"Wait a minute," Cotton said. "Don't you want to know . . . what I decide?"

"It doesn't really matter much what you decide."

Cotton listened to the dial tone. And then he slowly replaced the phone. The John Cotton reflected by the night on the inside of his glass patio door looked back at him, a slouchy nondescript man with a lined, long-jawed face. Its expression stunned at first, then grimacing, and then glancing away from the door to the telephone as if for assurance that the telephone was really there. It was a joke, of course. Was it a joke? Something planned by Junior, perhaps, and Vol Bowles?

It doesn't really matter much what you decide.

It wasn't a joke. Or was it?

Cotton got up and walked toward the kitchen; then turned abruptly, moved to the glass doors, checked the lock and pulled the drapes closed. He picked up the cigar box, turned it in his hands, placed it carefully on the coffee table and sat again, thinking.

He walked down the sidewalk and approached the white Plymouth. Then he turned back and reentered the Hall residence. He came out again within a minute, got into the car . . .

Cotton remembered now, clearly. Hall's front door opening and Whitey Robbins in the entry hall. "Forgot my hat," Whitey had said. "It's still raining."

No one could have known that. Not unless they had been waiting outside, watching.

Cotton went into the kitchen and mixed himself a bourbon and water. Then he started packing.

13

The cloud cover began breaking over what must have been western Kansas and ended over eastern New Mexico. Cotton could look down now, under the wing of the 707, and see the late-morning shadows cast by the mesas across the grassland of Guadalupe County thirty thousand feet below. To the north, the Sangre de Cristo range showed the white of early snow on its eastern slopes. He made out the shape of Grass Mountain, and Pecos Baldy, and the ragged line of the Truchas Peaks—jutting to thirteen thousand feet above the Espanola Valley.

"It's pretty country," Mr. Adams said. "I envy you your vacation. I wish I was going fishing tomorrow."

"It's been years," Cotton said. "I hope I haven't forgotten how."

The man had boarded at O'Hare field in

Chicago, where Cotton changed planes. Cotton had guessed he was a seasoned traveler—basing the guess on two shreds of evidence: Mr. Adams had picked an aisle chair on the seating chart—a choice Cotton thought he would make himself when he had flown enough to tire of looking out plane windows at the tops of clouds. And he had an easy, friendly facility for starting idle conversation, which Cotton suspected one who traveled endlessly among total strangers might develop to pass away the time. At the capital airport, Cotton had picked out among those waiting three men who might be watching him. One had hurried off to board a United flight to New York, one had disappeared, and his last, and most likely, prospect, had disillusioned him by meeting a young woman with two small children amid much hugging and kissing. Thus it restored some of Cotton's faith in his judgment to learn that the man whom the stewardess placed next to him was indeed a seasoned traveler—a salesman for National Cash Register who worked out of Denver, and who was now heading for home, and who liked to talk about hunting.

"I always start mine the first week in November, when deer season opens in the San Juans up above Durango. But once in a while

I've hunted down in New Mexico—mostly back there on the west slope of the Jemez. Is that where you fish?"

"Usually up on the Brazos," Cotton said. "Way up high above the falls but below the meadows. Do you know that country?"

"I guess not," Adams said. "How do you get in there?"

"There's an old Forest Service logging road that leads west from the highway between Tres Piedras and Antonito. It winds past San Antonito Mountain, and up San Antonio Creek, and then past the Lagunitas Lakes and over the ridge, down into the gorge of the West Fork of the Brazos. Maybe thirty miles of dirt, but the fishing is good. Not many people know about it."

"How about deer up there? Is that where you're going tomorrow?"

Cotton hadn't actually seriously decided to go fishing. It had been nothing more than a conversational ploy. But, as he thought about it, he felt the pull of the silence, and the sun, and the cool high-country breeze, and the remembered thrill of a trout fighting on his line.

"That's where I'll go," he said. "I can hardly wait."

The NO-SMOKING—FASTEN SEAT BELTS sign

flashed on. Cotton watched the crest of Sandia Mountain move under the plane's wing, its thick dark green fir forests broken with bright yellow splashes of aspen. And then the rumble of wheels going down and Albuquerque was sprawled below them.

The Frontier Airlines 707 landed at Santa Fe airport just at noon. Cotton took a cab to La Fonda, and ate a late and leisurely lunch at a table by the massive fireplace. He sat, legs stretched, finishing the pewter pot of coffee, watching the piñon logs consuming themselves in the flames, and marveling at his mood. He should, he thought, feel self-disgust, shame at running. But he felt none of this. Instead he felt more relaxed than he could remember. Loose and easy. Relieved. Free.

For the first time since he had hung up the telephone (How long had it been? Only about eighteen hours. That seemed incredible.), Cotton felt he could think about all that had happened Monday without lapsing into mind-buzzing confusion. He sipped his coffee, reviewing Monday as if it involved some other person—some stranger. It seemed to have nothing at all to do with the real John Cotton, who sat here with the warmth of the piñon fire against the side of his face and a meal of La Fonda's chile con queso equally warm inside him. Considered through this odd, comfortable lens of detachment, the events of yesterday seemed fantastic. He had once, briefly, during an illness of the regular man, written movie reviews. What could he call Monday's series of events? Bum plotting? Too much for the audience to swallow? Something like that. Why would whoever-it-was first force his car off a bridge in a well-conceived plan to kill him and then politely call him on the telephone and warn him away? Why all the trouble, the box and the photograph, when it would have been simpler to shoot him—and certainly surer? Cotton grinned at that, thinking he had run, sure enough, and that an audience would hardly buy a hero with such rabbity habits, who ran without shame or the slightest twinge of conscience.

He refilled the cup with the last coffee from the pot and added sugar and cream.

To hell with it, Cotton thought . . . Screw 'em all. Screw Danilov. Screw the entire, total, bleeding zoo. He would write a letter to Hall one of these days and tell him a little—but probably not much. And he would write Janey Janoski. No, he would call Janey.

And tell her what? The whole business, probably.

You know that rabbit I was hunting, Janey? Well, he turned out to be a tiger and he chased me out of town.

The irony might appeal to her. He wished that Janey were here—sitting across this table from him—and the wish was suddenly intensely strong. He turned his thoughts to Wingerd, remembering Wingerd's tired, lined face, Wingerd's eyes watery behind the lenses. The offer from Roark might have been tempting for the money in it if he had needed money. But he didn't. Not particularly. A single man whose vices are inexpensive could hardly avoid stacking up some savings over the years. And the idea of being a politician's handler was unappealing. It was working the wrong side of the street, and years of considering office holders as the natural adversary had conditioned him against a switch. Even for Paul Roark. He pursed his lips.

Even Roark? He had turned down Roark's offer at about five. The phone call had come at about seven. Would it have come if he had accepted Roark's offer? What happened in Wingerd's office after he left? Had Wingerd picked up the phone and reported to someone the failure of a job offer that was really a bribe? The speculation rankled. It meant accepting that he had totally misjudged Paul Roark. That the man was either ruthlessly ambitious or utterly corrupt. And it meant accepting that Wingerd would involve himself in murder. Wingerd, who was basically still a member of the fraternity, a lifelong newsman, a wearer of the badge.

He paid the check and walked out through the lobby, exchanging "Good afternoons" with a youngish man hurrying toward the bar. "A politician," Cotton thought, and quickly felt ashamed of the guess. He had somehow forgotten this about Santa Fe, this casual friendliness. On the plaza he sat on a bench and submitted to a shoeshine. For his quarter, he learned that the boy's name was Arsenio Rodriguez, that St. Michael's had moved to a new site on the west side of the city, had become coeducational, and no longer accepted boarding students; and his shoes, when the conversation was over, were no worse than before.

He walked up San Francisco Street past the Cathedral, along the long brick wall which once guaranteed the privacy of the girls at Loretto Academy. (It was now, he noticed, closed and empty. Where had all the girls gone?) The sun was warm, the air cool. The ravens were still operating in their noisy fashion out of the cottonwoods along the Santa Fe River. Cotton felt an impulse to whistle, and did so—some tune he had heard somewhere.

He turned up the river, using the unpaved pathway on the river side of Alameda Street, and crossed on the Delgado Street bridge. It was here, he remembered, that the secrets of the atomic bomb had been handed to the Russians. Doctor Klaus Fuchs, wasn't it? British physicist on the staff at Los Alamos, who had picked this little concrete span as the meeting place with the courier from the Soviet embassy. Cotton wasted a moment looking at a plaque commemorating this dark but historic deed. Under the bridge a small, clear stream of water was running—telling Cotton that the Public Service Company had not turned off the river as it usually did in the autumn. That meant that the summer had been wet, that the reservoirs up Santa Fe Canyon were full, and that autumn fishing would be good. He would walk back downtown and buy himself his fishing gear. He would arrange to rent a car—or better a pickup truck—from Hertz. And tomorrow he would go fishing. But first he had a mission to complete.

In five minutes he was walking east on Acequia Madre, along the mother ditch which fed Santa Fe's network of minuscule irrigation canals, walking slowly past familiar adobe walls. Behind the walls were the houses which—when he was a boy—were the homes of friends. Here was where Eloy Sisneros had lived. (The sign on the mailbox now said Thomas Sanchez.) And there was the house of the Saiz family, whose youngest daughter (what was her name?) had once been the object of his amatory ambitions.

At the corner of Camino Sin Nombre he was hurrying. And there it was—three houses down the narrow unpaved street. Smaller than he remembered, and a little grubbier with increasing age, with the block wall he remembered walking along now missing some of its blocks. A small girl doing something with a rope on the front porch, the cottonwood in which he and Charley had built their treehouse missing from the side yard, a fat woman emerging from the side door and looking curiously at the stranger who stood there by the street looking at her house.

Cotton turned and walked away. He was puzzled at himself—and half angry. What had he expected to find? This was exactly what he had consciously expected—certainly no worse. Then why this intense disappointment? Had his subconscious anticipated the cottonwood and Charley Graff in it? Some journey backward to warmth, to someone to be alive with? Tomorrow, perhaps, while he fished it would sort itself out.

> 14 <

John Cotton sat against the fire-killed fir snag and considered his problem. The pool was behind an outcropping stratum of granite. It was maybe four feet deep and it would be home for several cutthroat trout. Since the pool was deep and protected, one of them would almost certainly be large. But Cotton could see no way to get a hook into the deep water without spooking the fish. A growth of willow overhung it. He had tried fifteen or twenty casts from downstream. Each time he had either hooked a willow twig or the line, caught by the vagrant breeze, had fallen short into the current. Drifting the salmon egg in from upstream hadn't worked either. The current whipping past the outcrop slid the fly line past the backwater pool. It might be possible to crawl close enough to the pool from the opposite side. In a little while, he would wade across and try it. But now he was hungry. He opened his creel, still stiff with newness. Among the seven small trout, cold, limber and slippery in the wet grass, he had pulled to protect them, he found a can of Vienna sausages.

He ate absently, trying to think of the pool, of the tense expectancy when his hook finally hit its surface, of the sudden excitement when the trout struck. Instead he found himself thinking of numbers in McDaniels's notebook, of the thin smoke seeping from a plastic toy in a cigar box, and of the anger of Roy Hall's outburst in the House gallery. Hall's cynicism justified his presence here, justified the sensuous comfort of the warm, high-altitude sun on the back of his jacket and his pleasure in this day. But Hall's cynicism was Hall's, and not his own. Hall's was deeper, eroded by more years into a different personality. Cotton turned it over in his mind. Perhaps Hall, basically, was a pessimist while he was an optimist—still believing that man was more than a biped shorn of feathers, that the public, given some information, could govern itself. Or perhaps it was the opposite—that Hall cared more than he did and felt more deeply. For the first time since he had packed his bags in his apartment, he felt guilt.

He had no business being here. He should be back at the capitol completing whatever job it was that McDaniels had started. But there was the catch. What job? He had no doubt at all that the threat against him was intended to protect something from public exposure. But what? He tried to re-create the chronology. His car had been bumped off the bridge after he had spent the afternoon in the Highway Department records. But it must have been planned before that. So he might have inspired this murderous fear in the Park Commission office, or by the questions he asked in the Insurance Department, or even by the files he had checked out at the Supreme Court library. By Monday—before the cigar box and the telephone call—he had poked just about everywhere he knew McDaniels had poked.

Cotton dug a hole in the peat moss and buried the empty sausage can. He simply didn't know where to start looking. If he could find the story and break it he would destroy any reason for killing him. But could he stay alive long enough to find it?

The breeze had died now. Cotton could hear it faintly in the spruce which topped the ridge behind him. But here, and through the marshy meadow across the stream, nothing stirred. From far to the east, across the timbered ridge which climbed toward the truncated peak of Broke Off Mountain, a file of puffy white clouds were being pushed slowly across the deep blue sky by a wind which didn't reach this valley. Cotton listened, straining his ears for the dim, echoing clap of sound which would mean a hunter's rifle shot far away across the timbered hills. He had heard nothing all morning and he heard only silence now. Most of the mule deer which browsed this high country in the summer must have moved to warmer levels when the aspens turned. There would be little now to draw the hunters this high into the mountains.

The last sign Cotton had seen that other humans shared this planet with him were the sheepherders who had ridden up when he had stopped to try his luck on San Antonio Creek. An old man and a boy, riding horses still frisky with the morning cold. Cotton grinned.

"Me llamo Cirilio Maestas," the old man had said, *"y este est mi nieto, Antonio Maestas."* Cotton had thought—with instant disapproval—that the boy was about ten years

old and should have been out of the mountains and into the classroom at least a month ago. And then Maestas had shown him the raw bearskin bundled on the pack horse, and told him that the boy had shot it, and looked at the boy with such pride and love that Cotton immediately retracted all considerations of truancy.

"I was after some strays and the boy was there at the camp when Señor Oso came down out of the timber after the sheep. And Tony here got the rifle out of the tent and when *el oso* charged him, the boy here, he shot him."

The rifle was an old, worn, short-barreled .30-30 carbine—not the sort of weapon with which a prudent man would shoot a six-hundred-pound black bear. And certainly not a bear that was uphill from him.

"Antonio no es niño," Cotton had said. *"Es hombre. Muy hombre."*

At that Antonio had blushed, and Cirilio Maestas had unpacked his pot and made coffee while the boy rode back up the ridge to keep the sheep moving. They talked while the coffee brewed, the old man asking what had happened in the world since he had ridden in for groceries a month ago.

Nothing Cotton could think of seemed as

significant as Antonio, thin and small, standing among the scattering sheep with that rusty carbine facing the downhill charge of the bear. But he told Cirilio Maestas of a new federal ruling on mutton and wool imports, and a plan to increase social security payments, and that he had read in the *New Mexican* that the Highway Department would complete paving the road from Tres Piedras to Taos. And then, when they had finished their coffee, the old man had done something that Cotton wished Leroy Hall could have seen. He had taken a can of Prince Albert from his jacket pocket, rolled a cigarette and laid it carefully on a rock beside their fire. Then he had rolled a second cigarette. Cirilio Maestas had then placed the cigarettes side by side on his palm and extended them to Cotton.

"Quiere usted un cigarillo?" he had asked. It had taken Cotton a second to appreciate the nature of this courtesy—to realize that the old man had paid him the ineffable compliment of presuming Cotton was too polite to accept a cigarette if only one had been rolled. Cotton had accepted the cigarette and smoked it—although he had sworn a month ago never to smoke again and suffered hard

weeks of withdrawal pains to keep the pledge.

Cotton smiled again, thinking of it and of what Hall would say.

There, perhaps, was the difference. Hall wouldn't believe in Cirilio Maestas. "Cousin John," he would say, "romance lives on in your mountains. You sure you didn't meet Don Quixote and Sancho Panza?" Maybe that's the difference. Leroy Hall sees the infinitely corruptible citizen, the Roman mob rejecting Brutus in favor of Mark Antony. John Cotton thinks there's some Señor Maestas in everybody.

He was suddenly aware that something had moved. Upstream a weasel had come out onto a partly burned log which had fallen into the stream. It stared intently into the water, looking for an unwary trout. Cotton noticed its fur was turning white. In a month, when the summer fur was shed, it would be an ermine worth twenty dollars to a trapper. He sat motionless, thinking the animal would vanish if he moved. But then it looked directly at him, curious but not afraid. It occurred to Cotton that the weasel was undisputed lord of the rocky slope behind him and the small wilderness of marsh grass. It had never met anything it couldn't whip. The same had been true of the badger he had seen downstream earlier. It had sat on the cliff above its hole and whistled at him while he fished—a derisive, disrespectful challenge.

Cotton pushed himself stiffly to his feet, and picked up his flyrod. Something had gradually gone out of this day. In two or three more hours long early shadows of autumn would move across this valley. He would take down his flyrod and walk the two or three miles downstream to his rented car and drive the thirty rocky miles back to the highway, and that would be the end of it. The snow was already overdue. Soon this stream would be buried under three feet of it, and the weasel would be pure ermine and he and the badger and snow birds would have these mountains to themselves. And where would he be? He would be where he had to be. This day had been stolen. He could not really enjoy it with an unfinished job heavy on his mind.

He made his cast squatting in the marsh grass well back from the stream. The distance was gauged carefully. About thirty-five feet. Since he couldn't see the pool, see the sudden explosion on the surface that would signal the strike, he would have to feel it. And that meant the line and leader would have to extend straight and tight when the salmon egg hit the water. He aborted the first cast with a quick backward snap of his wrist before it touched the water. It would have been slightly downstream from the point he wanted. But the second cast was exactly right. The line disappeared over the grassy bank and snapped tight instantly. There was a flurry of splashing as the trout fought the hook and Cotton found himself simultaneously trying to rise from his squat, trying to keep the rod tip high, and trying to free the line from the grass. He lost his balance a second and in that second the trout was gone.

Cotton sat back in the high grass and reeled in his line. The trout had been bigger than he had expected—big enough to pull him off his precarious balance when it struck. But trying a second cast would be futile. The fish, stung by the hook, would be wary for an hour or more. And any other trout in that pool would have scuttled to the bottom rocks, thoroughly alarmed by the flurry of action. He might try this pool from this position again on the way back to the car after working further upstream. And as he thought about it he heard a sound.

A man wearing a red cap and a red jacket was walking slowly toward him across the stony slope beyond the meadow. He carried across his chest a long-barreled rifle with a telescopic sight. Cotton watched him through a screen of cattail reeds. Obviously, the man was looking for deer. And since he was looking here, along this stream in the early afternoon, he was probably inexperienced. Deer slept in the afternoon and they did their sleeping far back in the tangled woods on the slopes. Only a greenhorn would be hunting here—the sort of a hunter who might snap off a shot at anything that moved. Before he stood up he would yell at the hunter, Cotton decided. And he would make sure the hunter understood.

The walking man made no sound now. The noise had probably been caused by a dislodged stone. Cotton watched, conscious that there was something familiar about the man. In the next instant, Cotton knew who he was. The hunter was the man he had talked to on the plane to Albuquerque. Who was it? Adams? But Adams had said he was flying to Denver. What was he doing here? Suddenly Cotton found himself asking another question—a question he couldn't answer. Where had this man boarded the plane? Had he followed him all the way from the capital airport? Cotton knew as he asked it, knew with stomach-knotting panic, why Adams was here. Adams probably had boarded late at the capital terminal door, and then had followed Cotton to the TWA gate at O'Hare. His choice of seats would have been no accident. He had picked the seat beside Cotton because he wanted to know Cotton's plans. And with this realization another question answered itself.

He knew now the why of the cigar box which might have been a bomb, the photograph which might have been a bullet, the order to run. At the capital, the death of John Cotton would have been the third in a series of similar deaths—enough to make the authorities wonder if two accidents were really accidents. There John Cotton dead would have been too much coincidence. Here John Cotton dead probably wouldn't be found until next summer. And, if he was found, he would be just another victim of the deer season. A dead stranger—connected to nothing. The telephone call had been a shrewd device to move him where he could be killed without embarrassment, a thousand miles from McDaniels and Whitey Robbins.

Cotton crouched lower in the grass, trying to think. The man was skirting the marsh—keeping his feet dry. On his present path, he would pass within fifty feet of where Cotton hid. He almost certainly couldn't see him. But what would Adams do? Cotton remembered the conversation in the plane—Adams's voice talking of hunting, with knowledgeable, experienced enthusiasm, talking of tracking bear, of flushing elk from heavy cover, of following the trace of javelina in the Big Bend country. He knew what Adams was doing. He was saving time, as he had saved time on the plane by having Cotton describe where he would fish. He had found Cotton's car and followed Cotton's tracks along the stream. Now he was simply skipping a little—taking the easy path. Above the marsh, he would check the stream again. He would find no tracks and he would know almost exactly where he could find his quarry. He would turn back downstream toward the marsh, and the rifle would be cocked.

Adams was passing abreast of him now—making no sound that Cotton could hear over the murmur of the stream. And then he was past, walking slowly, placing his feet carefully. Cotton looked downstream, toward his car. The marsh grass would give him crawling cover for maybe seventy-five yards. After that it was open. Adams would only have to glance back to see him. And, once he was seen, shooting him would require no more than two or three seconds. He might run, but then Adams would hear him instantly. And running in his hip-high waders would be slow and clumsy. He looked across the stream. He could reach it easily through the grass, and cross it behind the outcrop which formed the pool, without being seen. And then he could climb the opposite bank into the clutter of fallen logs left by the old forest burn. No more than fifty yards up the slope regrowth started. Young fir and spruce were already crowding the aspen thickets. If he could reach that cover, he could work his way through the trees without being visible. He had left his car parked in a wide expanse of hillside grass, but, if his memory was accurate, he would have covered most of the way there and to within a quarter of a mile of the automobile.

He waited until Adams had time to be at least two hundred yards upstream before he eased himself over the bank and into the water. The current was surprisingly swift here, sweeping his foot off the rocky bottom, knocking him off balance and sending icy water gushing into his boot. The numbing cold drove the air from his lungs. He leaned against the granite outcrop, cursing, trying to catch his breath, and wondering, frantically, if Adams had heard the splash. Through the willow branches, he could see nothing moving. The hunter must be well above the upper end of the marsh now, checking the banks upstream.

Cotton climbed the bank and ran up the slope. He ran clumsily, dodging the fallen timber where he could, and climbing over the rotting trunks which couldn't be avoided. He ran as if in a nightmare, his eyes now on the obstacles in his path, now on the forest up the slope which promised him life, his mind's eye seeing the face of Adams—Adams's brown cheek pressed against the rifle stock, one eye hidden behind the telescopic sight. The crosshairs centering on his back. Cotton fought a desperate impulse to drop behind a fallen trunk, to burrow under it, to hide as he had seen panicked rabbits try to hide from a hunting dog. He fought the impulse and won, running desperately up the steep slope toward the trees that seemed to get no closer. It was a staggering, uneven run, his left leg burdened by a boot half-filled with numbing, icy water, his lungs gasping for breath. And then he was at the trees and among them.

Cotton fell then, only half voluntarily, behind a cluster of young fir. He lay face down, his forehead across his forearm, trying to control his shuddering breath, trying to think. He crawled around the trees, through the soft bed of fir needles and aspen leaves, and stared down the slope. Nothing moved. If Adams had been near the stream when he made the dash up the slope, the sound of the stream would have covered the sound of his running. If that was true, he had a little time. He sat up, unsnapped the wader from his belt, pulled it off, poured out the water, and wrung out his sock. And then he cut the tops off both waders, sawing with his fish knife through the soft rubber at the knee. That would eliminate most of the weight. As he did, destroying boots he had paid nineteen dollars for the evening before, it occurred to him that perhaps Adams meant him no harm. He had told the man he would be fishing this stream. Adams had been interested in the hunting. Maybe something had delayed his trip home, kept him in New Mexico. And he had taken the day off to hunt. Cotton refastened the straps which fastened the cut-off waders at his knee. But why would Adams take his rifle and his hunting gear on a business trip? There might be an explanation for that.

Instead of pursuing the thought, Cotton remembered the voice on the telephone. ". . . think how easy it will be to kill you. Think of the ways we can do it. You'll think of eight or ten, but there are dozens you won't think of. . . ." Here was one of the ways he hadn't thought of. His impulse to discount Adams as a threat died. He would, he decided, work his way down the ridge, try to reach his car before Adams realized he was running. He stood up. As he did so, Adams appeared from behind a cluster of upstream trees. The man was walking slowly, watching the heavy growth of marsh reeds, his rifle held at the ready. Cotton noticed Adams had snapped the telescopic sight off the rifle. That meant he was no longer counting on an easy long shot at an unsuspecting target. He had guessed Cotton was hiding—that it would be a quicker, close-range shot, that open sights would be better. His hope of reaching his car vanished. There was too much open country to cross.

Cotton watched, fascinated. He felt no panic now. Instead, for the first time in his life, he knew the complete measure of fear. The trick with the cigar box had startled him and the voice on the telephone call had caused him to run. But then he had simply faced a choice between danger and escape—

an intellectual problem logically solved. Now there was no choice. Sometime this afternoon, perhaps within a very few minutes, he would be shot and he would die. He would be shot rather carefully and only once. Adams would want to leave no question that it had been simply a hunting accident. And, if Adams was a competent hunter, there would be no reason for a second shot.

The ground here was deep with aspen leaves, a sunny yellow carpet. Across the valley, between the stark white trunks of the aspens, the first of the clouds was crossing the top of Broke Off Mountain—dragging its bottom across the eleven-thousand-foot crest and leaving behind ragtag fragments of mist in the treetops. Half aloud, Cotton said, "God. Help me. I don't want to die. Not today."

Adams was threading his way carefully through the marsh now—avoiding the half-hidden pothole springs which fed it. Cotton watched Adams stop at the pool where only minutes before he had been fishing, watched as the hunter moved carefully to the bank where Cotton had splashed through the pool. Adams stood there, examining the place where Cotton had climbed the opposite bank. Cotton realized, with first shock and then anger, that Adams was smiling. And then the hunter turned downstream, moving at an unhurried walk. He was looking for a place to cross without getting his feet wet. The casualness of it, the arrogant certainty of the hunter, outraged Cotton.

Cotton moved abruptly, trotting back through the trees, conscious for the first time that he was still carrying his flyrod. His first thought was to drop it there, but why? It weighed almost nothing, didn't slow him down. Instead, he snapped it apart and tied the three pieces with a quick loop of the fly line, thinking what Adams would do. The man must know he would be in this mixed patch of spruce, fir and aspen. Most likely he would move downstream far enough to make certain Cotton couldn't get past him southward toward the car. Then he would ford the stream, walk up into the north edge of the timber. He would work it about the way he would stalk a mule deer hiding in a patch like this. Cotton put himself in Adams's place. He would try to make the animal break cover. But he would try to keep close enough to the open grass which surrounded the woods to make sure that if the animal broke across the open he'd have a clear shot before it reached the ridgeline or the stream. A mule deer, Cotton thought, would have maybe a fifty-fifty chance if it made the break in the right direction when the hunter was in the wrong place. But a mule deer was swift. A running man wasn't. He rated his own chance at zero. Apparently, judging from his deliberateness, so did Adams.

Cotton decided almost instantly what he would do. He would do what he thought Adams would least expect him to do. He wouldn't hide near the south edge of the timber, running toward his car when Adams passed his hiding place. That Adams would expect. Nor would he try to keep away from Adams in the timber. Hide-and-seek in the woods might keep him alive an hour but it wouldn't keep him alive until dark. There were no more than twenty-five or thirty acres of timber—an island bypassed by the old fire. There wasn't enough cover for hiding.

Cotton trotted through the woods, moving northward. At the north end of this timber, the growth of young trees extended to within a hundred yards of the stream. If he could reach the stream without being seen, he might put a substantial distance between himself and the hunter before Adams realized he was gone. At the edge of the timber, where the young spruce were not much higher than his head, he stopped and looked carefully behind him. He could see nothing. If he had guessed correctly, Adams should be in the south end of the timber patch by now. Abruptly, hope returned. And with it fear. He looked toward the tangle of willows which marked the course of the stream. It would take him maybe fifteen seconds to cross it and regain cover. If Adams was where he could see him, Cotton would make a perfect target. He drew a deep breath and ran.

He ran desperately and as silently as he could, trying to avoid loose rocks and the old debris of the forest fire. And then he was at the bank, ducking to the left to avoid dead brush, feeling a surge of wild, joyous exhilaration of escape. At that moment the shot came.

The bullet snapped past him through the brush he had swerved to avoid and then there was a cracking sound of the muzzle blast. Cotton fell, slid against a boulder at the edge of the stream. He lay, gasping for breath, feeling the burning pain in his left forearm. The exhilaration had died with the sound of the shot. Adams had outguessed him, had guessed that he might try doubling back to the stream, and had come within a second of ending this mismatched game. The shot must have been hurried—snapped off just as Cotton reached the bank and, judging from the sound, from at least five hundred yards. But it had barely missed.

A second shot came a moment later, the rifle slug kicking up a spurt of dirt and dead leaves at the crest of the bank and whining over his head. Cotton ducked and then began running up the stream, moving as fast as he could, splashing through the shallows. A limb whipped across his face. He felt little pain. All he could do now was delay it. Postpone the inevitable moment when Adams would run him down and shoot him. What was Adams doing? Racing across the open ground to head him off? Maybe. More likely merely following—closing the gap gradually with a minimum of exertion. There was no place Cotton could go except up the stream. If he left its cover, this chase would be over in the time it took Adams to catch him in the rifle sights and pull the trigger.

Just upstream the ridge bulged down into the valley, forcing the West Fork into a deep, narrow bed pinched between higher banks. Cotton ducked under the trunk of a dead ponderosa which had fallen here. He squatted a moment under this natural bridge—desperate for a plan. The trunk, he noticed, had been used as a path by animals and summer fishermen. But the path would only lead him out for an open shot. No plan formed. Cotton felt panic for a moment and then hard, hot anger. He moved upstream, trying to hurry over water-smooth boulders. He slipped into the current, soaking his legs to the hips. He squatted a moment, trying to control the trembling in his aching leg muscles. As he did, the plan came to him.

The flyrod, still incongruously clutched in his right hand, started the chain of thoughts. He hadn't dropped it because there had been no reason to. It was as natural in his hand as a cane in the hand of a blind man. But now he should abandon it in favor of something that would serve as a weapon. He looked at the fiberglass pole, remembering as he did the sudden tug of the trout pulling him off balance at the pool downstream. And then he had his plan.

He worked his way back downstream toward the tree-trunk bridge and ducked under it. Now he kept in the water, feeling his feet turn numb with the cold but leaving no fresh wet tracks on the rocks. A dozen yards below the fallen tree he pushed his way under the willow brush and squatted behind a streamside boulder—his feet still in the water.

The plan wasn't good. It simply was better

than no plan at all. It depended on Adams's demonstrated aversion to wet feet and on luck, and on Cotton's own skill, and on more luck. He fished his spool of nylon leader out of the creel pocket, spun off ten feet, doubled it and redoubled it, then tied on the heaviest of his spoons—a green metal shape dangling two sets of triple snelled hooks. Then he knotted the leader to the tip of the tapered line.

There was nothing to do but wait. Wait and hope he was guessing right—that Adams had not splashed across the stream somewhere behind him, that Adams would follow the easy going up the west bank and then, when the ridge crowded out the walking space, see the path and know—as any hunter or fisherman would be sure to know—that here it must lead to an easy fording spot. Common sense said Adams would want to cross—to follow the stream along the open ground to east instead of being forced away from the waterway by the ridge. But Cotton felt a sick foreboding. Adams had outguessed him once. He should, he decided, drop this crazy scheme and run again. No. There was no place to run.

A shadow suddenly darkened the boulders. The cloud drifting westward from Broke Off

Mountain was blocking off the sun. With the shadow, the breeze came to life again, breathing faintly through the willow brush and setting up a distant murmuring in the ridgetop spruce. And then it died away. Cotton was conscious of the aching numbness of his ankles, of his beating heart. He could hear absolutely nothing except the stream. And then he heard footsteps.

They came at a fast, steady walk. A soft, regular thudding. Behind Cotton at first and then on the bank above him and to his left. Cotton tensed. He found himself willing, with every fiber of his mind, the hunter to keep walking. Not to stop here to part the brush and look for a hiding man. The footsteps—a barely audible sound—continued past him. And again Cotton heard nothing.

He strained his eyes through the brush, staring at the tree trunk. Adams, too, was probably looking at it now, making his decision. Long seconds dragged past. Red became visible at the west end of the tree trunk. Motionless. Adams was looking, Cotton guessed, upstream and downstream.

"Let him see my wet footprints on the rocks," Cotton prayed. "Let him think I'm upstream."

The hunter walked out on the fallen log

and Cotton moved with him. He had already assured his footing under the current. Now he simply placed his feet and stood, swaying away from the willows, pulling line from the reel as he swung the rod tip back for the cast. Any sound he made was covered by the splashing of the current and Adams was still looking upstream. The hunter walked slowly on the log, balancing himself with the rifle. But, as Cotton flashed the rod forward, Adams glanced around.

The hunter was incredibly fast—even on the narrow, rounded surface of the trunk. He had shifted his feet and spun toward Cotton as the spoon reached him. He was raising the rifle as Cotton snapped back the rod to sink the hooks. The snelled hooks caught on the shoulder of Adams's jacket. Adams jerked back the rifle, fighting to keep his precarious balance, lost the battle against the steady pull of the fly line, and jumped.

In all, it took perhaps three seconds. Time enough for Cotton to know that if Adams landed on his feet John Cotton would die. He hauled back on the flyrod with full strength of his shoulders. It was enough.

Adams, with his upper body pulled forward by the jerk, dropped the rifle, flailed his arms frantically, and crashed chest first into the stream.

Cotton was leaping toward Adams even as the hunter fell. But he checked himself after three clumsy, splashing steps. Adams was pushing himself up from the boulders where he had landed—his right arm apparently useless and blood flooding down from his forehead. He was fumbling with his left hand inside his jacket.

Cotton scrambled back behind the willow brush and over the embankment. And then he ran. Behind him he heard the pop of what was probably a small-caliber pistol—an angry, ineffectual sound.

He covered the two miles to his car in less than thirty minutes, running at first and then—when there was no sign that Adams was following—lapsing into a fast walk. The hunter almost certainly had a broken right arm, as well as other injuries. Whatever the case, there was little chance he would be able to follow fast enough for a rifle shot. Cotton paused at the pickup truck parked under the pines near where he had left his car. He plunged his fishing knife through three of the truck's tires. And then he drove away. And while he drove he made his plans.

15

The seventeenth photograph was of a high, balding forehead, close-set eyes and a long, cleft chin. The eighteenth was of a round-face man glowering at the camera. The nineteenth was Adams—looking younger than he had looked across the aisle on the airliner. But the eyes were the same, and the mouth. And the expression was familiar—open, warm, friendly, even when facing a police identification camera. Cotton found himself wondering how badly Adams had been hurt in his plunge onto the boulders in the Brazos, wondering how much trouble he had had making it out to the highway, thinking that if he had needed help there were deer hunters along the road who would have helped him.

"That one look familiar?"

Captain Whan was straightening the stack

of police identification photographs with his fingertips, his eyes on Cotton's face.

"This is him," Cotton said.

Whan took the photograph and put it back in its file folder.

"Randolph Harge," Whan said. "That tells us something. You sure this is him?"

"I'm sure, but what does it tell us?"

"I'll read it to you. 'Harge, Randolph Allen: Born, Okeene, Oklahoma, March 11, 1930. Sentenced indeterminate term McAlester Penitentiary, May 3, 1946, auto theft. Sentenced, indeterminate term, El Reno Federal Reformatory, July 13, 1949, interstate transportation stolen motor vehicle. Indicted February 9, 1952, armed robbery–assault with intent to kill, acquitted. Sentenced three to ten, Lansing State Prison, May 27, 1954, extortion, assault with intent to kill. . . ." He looked up. "A hard case."

"But it doesn't say why he was coming after me," Cotton said.

"There's more. A charge of murder in Miami. That didn't stick. And held for investigation in a Chicago homicide case, and a kidnapping-extortion charge in Milwaukee in 1969. That one didn't stick either." Whan closed the folder. "The point is these last three felonies were connected to the rackets.

Harge worked for the Organization in Chicago. I imagine he still does."

From down the hallway in the Municipal Police Building there came the sound of someone laughing. Captain Whan was straightening the stack of criminal identification folders with his fingertips. Cotton examined his expression. There seemed to be nothing to read, neither hostility nor warmth. Only blank neutrality. How much could he trust Whan? He had decided on the long drive back to Santa Fe to work with him. He had remembered Whan's suspicions of Robbins's death, remembered Whan's suggestion that he—and not Robbins—might have been the target of the accident which sent his car plunging into the river—the accident which was not an accident. Remembering that, he had placed a long-distance call from Santa Fe, reached the captain at his home and told him what had happened. But on the night flight east from Albuquerque the doubts returned. He remembered then how easily the line between police and criminal can be erased by corruption. Waiting for his flight out of Kansas City, he crossed the bridge again. He thought of the burglary ring which had operated in the Denver Police Department, of the involvement of Florida police in the murder of a judge, of the shooting of a West Texas district attorney by Borger police, of rackets flourishing in Chicago, and in Jersey, and elsewhere, under police protection. And when Whan met him at the capital terminal he had told the captain that he had also called Ernie Danilov from Santa Fe and that the managing editor knew Whan was meeting his flight. He had put it bluntly but Whan had simply laughed. "If you're nervous about me, it's a good sign," Whan had said. "Stay nervous about everybody for a little while and maybe we can get this sorted out."

Now it was almost 2 A.M. and Cotton was no longer nervous. He was merely tired, tired almost to exhaustion. Wednesday had been a long, long day. And now it was Thursday.

"We'll presume that Harge was on an assignment from the people he's been working for," Whan was saying. "The question is what you've been doing that concerns the Organization."

"I told you what I think," Cotton said. "I think Mac was after a story somebody didn't want printed. Whoever it involved killed him. I got his notebook. It looks like there's three unfinished projects he was working on. The State Park concession business. Something or other involving that insurance company, and that collusion on highway contracts. Take your pick."

Cotton became aware again that he desperately wanted a cigarette. Why not? He wasn't likely to live long enough for lung cancer. He thought about asking Whan for one, and rejected the thought. Whan was studying him.

"I nosed around some at all three of them," Cotton said. "I told you that. And I told you there was a fairly good story in the highway situation—but not good enough to kill somebody over. And nothing that I could see in the park concessions or the insurance records looked very promising."

"No use going over that again," Whan said. "Let's talk about a couple of other things. About how McDaniels might have got started on this thing and about what you're going to do next."

"I don't know," Cotton said. "First, I think I'm going to go through that damned notebook again to see if I missed anything. And through my own notes, and then maybe I'll see if I can find out anything more about the highway deal."

"How do you think McDaniels got on to it—whatever it was?"

"All I can do is guess," Cotton said. "Usually

it would be a tip. Somebody gets pissed off at the boss and calls the pressroom and gives some reporter ammunition."

"That would be somebody who knew McDaniels—or at least knew who he was."

"Not necessarily. The reporters have their own telephones but there's also a phone booth in there and that's the number listed in the book for the pressroom. That phone rings, and whoever's not busy answers it. Usually it's somebody wanting information, and once in a while it's a tip on a story."

Whan looked thoughtful. "A tip, you think."

"Hell, I don't know. Maybe he saw something, or heard something, that made him curious. Or maybe he ran across something while he was doing regular routine checking."

"Let's say it was a tip-off from someone," Whan said. "How would he handle it?"

"The first thing, he'd take a look at whatever records would apply. Bidding forms, purchase orders, pay vouchers, payroll, official reports whatever he could find officially on paper. First you want to find out not just whether there's any truth in your leak but whether you can nail it. Whether you can prove it." Cotton paused. He was so tired it was hard to think.

"Let's say somebody tipped me off that you were cheating on your travel expenses," Cotton said. "First I'd check all your expense vouchers for a few months at the city clerk's office. I'd jot down all the dates you were charging the city for using your own car on city business and the places you claimed to have gone. Then I'd look at the city motor-pool records to see if you had a city car checked out on the same days. And I'd go through the billings from the oil companies to see if any of the credit-card slips had your name on them, and the license numbers on the slips, and the dates, and the places they were signed. And then, if this showed you were cheating, I'd go to you and tell you what I had and give you a chance to lie out of it."

"You always ask the guy you're after for an explanation?"

"Always," Cotton said. "That's the way the game's played. You give him a chance to tell his side of the story."

Whan thought about it.

"If I had about twenty good men with nothing else to do I could try to trace down everybody McDaniels talked to for the past month." He rubbed the back of his hand across his eyes. "But it probably wouldn't tell us a thing."

Whan stood up. "You're registered at the Southside Inn as Robert Elwood. One of our people moonlights there as the night clerk. He, and I, and your editor are the only ones who know you're back in town—unless you told somebody else. Let's keep it that way."

"I can't work out this story in a motel room," Cotton said. "I've got to be out talking to people."

"We'll keep an eye on the motel during the day and when you have to leave call here and ask for me, or Lieutenant Bierly if I'm out. Most of the time I can have somebody close."

"Most of the time?"

"Look," Whan said, "I've got four unsolved armed robberies to work, and fourteen or fifteen burglaries, and a homicide case to get ready for the District Attorney by next weekend, and we're short four men in the detective division. I can have a man around you part of the time. When I can't, you sit in your motel room with the door locked and be patient."

"That's what the man who called me said," Cotton said. "That I'd get a little police protection but not enough to make the difference."

"Did he say that?"

"That's what he said."

Whan took a long drag off his cigarette and rocked back in his chair, staring at the ceiling. "If it works the way I want it to work, they won't know you've got any protection. You bought the ticket just to Kansas City, and under a phony name. There's no way for them to know you came here. When they find out you did, I'd like them not to know you're working with us." He rocked forward, leaned his elbows on the desk—looking at Cotton. "I think that's the best bet."

"Like bait," Cotton said. "You don't want them to see the trap. Somebody shoots me, you grab 'em red-handed, they talk to get a lighter rap, and you solve the McDaniels killing. Trouble is, I'm dead. But if I had a cop with me, I see Harge, and I point him out, and you arrest him, and I'm still alive."

"You said Harge was hurt. Besides, they wouldn't use him after you got a look at him." Whan opened the door, held it for Cotton. "Next time it will be somebody else."

> 16 <

Habit aroused John Cotton from a restless sleep at 6 A.M. He awoke tired, hazily aware at first only that he was in an unfamiliar bed and then abruptly and nervously alert. He showered slowly, examining the collection of scratches and abrasions accumulated in yesterday's desperate scramblings on the West Fork of the Brazos. Only one spot was painful—a bluish bruise on his left thigh which he could not remember inflicting. It was a long, narrow thigh ending at a bony knee. Cotton considered it as he soaped it. A good enough leg attached to a serviceable body. More elongated and thin than popular tastes required, perhaps, but generally satisfactory and usually trouble-free. It didn't tend to fat, which was fortunate because he enjoyed eating, and it would probably last about another forty years. Cotton toweled himself briskly, avoiding thought of the next forty years, dug his shaving gear out of the suitcase, and lathered. The face in the mirror was not the face he would have chosen for himself. The jaw was a little long, the nose bony and slightly bent, and the ears more prominent than necessary. He had once—long ago—made an idle shaving-time effort to capture the face in a paragraph, in a simile and in a single word. The word he had settled on was "nondescript" and the simile "like a plow horse on poor pasture." The face smiled slightly at him now, not resenting the insult.

At the door, he stopped for the automatic backward look at the room of the man who has long lived alone. And then, hand on the knob, he remembered that outside the door there was something to dread. He spent a second telling himself he was safe for a while. And then he went down to breakfast in the motel coffeeshop.

While he ate, he read with practiced speed through the *Capitol-Press,* the *Morning Journal* and yesterday's state edition of the *Tribune.* He read Hall's column in the *Journal* carefully. Nothing much had happened in politics in his absence.

By seven he was back in his room, on the telephone to Danilov, giving the managing editor his address and number and telling him of the arrangement with Captain Whan. Danilov didn't sound happy or friendly, but then he never did.

"I'm pulling Tom Rickner off that urban-renewal stuff and sending him to the capitol to sub for you," Danilov said. "He'll do any leg work he can for you. And we'll insert a box on the editorial page saying you're on vacation or something like that. What do you think it should say?"

"Why not say I'm on an indeterminate leave because of a sudden illness?"

"O.K. Now, as soon as you can I want you to write a long memo outlining all this and sign it and get it to me."

While he worked his way through McDaniels's notebook again, Cotton considered why Danilov wanted the memo. Danilov would want the written report to keep the story leads alive in case something happened to the reporter. But that wouldn't be the only reason. He would want it because Cotton had become more than a reporter in this affair—and thereby less than a reporter. He had become involved in his own story, which made him suspect. He had lost his official, sanitizing detachment. To Danilov he had become an ambiguous figure. On one hand he was still the reporter—the man the news desk must trust or the system would not operate. And on the other, he was part of the story, a news source from whom information must be automatically doubted. Danilov would decide—would have to decide someday if the story ever could be broken—just who John Cotton was. If he was the reporter, it would be:

> After the *Tribune's* capitol correspondent began investigating he received a call at his apartment. A man Cotton could not identify warned him that unless he left the city by the next morning he would be killed.

Or it would be:

> Cotton said, in a signed statement, that a man called his apartment and warned him he would be killed unless he left the capital the next morning. Cotton said . . .

Notice, reader, we tell you only what John Cotton said. He said this in a signed statement. We certify only that he said it. We do not certify that it happened. We had no disinterested fly on the wall in his apartment, overheard no call. You decide if Cotton lies.

The sound of rushing water. In the next motel unit someone had turned on the shower. Cotton called a rental service and arranged to have a typewriter delivered. Then he went back to his study of McDaniels's notes. Nothing suggested anything. He turned the page. Near the top in McDaniels's neat script was written *"Houghton??"* He had noticed it once before, and wondered who, and why the underline, and why the question marks. Now he knew who. Houghton was the Second Highway District Maintenance Engineer. Wingerd had mentioned that McDaniels had interviewed him. And he remembered Volney Bowles, at last week's poker game, gossiping about McDaniels's car parked often at the district highway office. But why the question marks? He flipped forward in the notebook, calculating. The name apparently had been written the day before McDaniels tricked Roark into confirming that tip. Had Mac mentally removed the question marks after the Governor's indiscreet confirmation that Houghton was an accurate and informed leak?

Cotton read the list he was compiling on a sheet of motel stationery.

It read:

Check ownership structure of Wit's End, Inc.
Background A. J. Linington.
Who reinsures for Midcentral Surety? Who owns it?
Why was Mac trying to get highway-project hauling slips? What slips?

Cotton added, "Check Houghton. What did Mac learn from him?"

He worked slowly through page after page. No ideas came. Hunger caused him to look at his watch.

While he ate a hurried hamburger in the motel coffeeshop, the state edition of the *Tribune* arrived. The box was there on the editorial page, set in boldface type.

> The political column by John Cotton, the *Tribune* State Capitol Correspondent, which normally appears on this page, will be discontinued for an indefinite time. Cotton has taken a leave because of illness. His duties have been assumed by Thomas J. Rickner, long-time *Tribune* city-government reporter.

He paused at the door of his room, hearing a voice inside. It was the television set—a network promotion for the Friday Night Movie. On the screen, a man with a pistol was climbing a fire-escape ladder toward an open window. Cotton sat on the bed and stared without seeing.

By now, long before now, Harge would have telephoned whomever had hired him and reported the failure. Or would he? Maybe Harge would gamble that Cotton would continue running, would disappear. Maybe he would report that Cotton was dead and that the body would never be found. Cotton considered this deceit, liking the idea. But it wasn't likely. He didn't think the man he had known as Adams would do it. Almost certainly he had reported accurately. Reported to X, to the unknown quantity in this equation, that Cotton was alive. A woman on the TV screen was examining a dirty shirt collar in a laundromat. Cotton closed his eyes—trying to imagine. Logic told him X would be disappointed, perhaps angry. He couldn't picture X. One man? Several men? A respectable corporation executive in a paneled office of Midcentral Surety, Inc.? Or a Mafioso type with sideburns and handmade shoes? Or someone in the Chicago Organization, as Captain Whan suggested? He visualized a florid, jowled, heavy-set man wearing a dark shirt and a white tie. A character actor in a low-budget, made-for-television movie. He pushed himself up from the bed. That was part of the trouble. It didn't really seem real to him. And yet somewhere, right now, at ten minutes before 2 P.M. there was a man—genuine flesh and blood—who must be extremely conscious of the existence of John Cotton. This man must be thinking of Cotton, deciding that maybe Cotton was still running and maybe Cotton wasn't running. He might be sitting behind a desk, or driving a car, or in conference with associates. Wherever he was, he would be adjusting himself to the unexpected knowledge that the threat posed by John Cotton had not been—as confidently expected—erased on a fishing stream in New Mexico.

Cotton walked to the window and stood behind the closed drapes, wanting a cigarette. What would this X decide to do? Watch Cotton's apartment and the capitol against his return? Logically, he would. And stake out whatever sources of information Cotton would have to tap to expose whatever X was doing? That, too, was logical. Cotton felt a sense of frustrated urgency. He should be moving fast today—making headway before this unknown person could adjust his plans.

Instead he was wasting the day in another fruitless hunt through McDaniels's notes.

He turned abruptly, picked up the telephone and called Danilov.

"I need two things," Cotton said. "Will you get the morgue to see if they've got anything filed on a guy named A. J. Linington, and if we don't have much, would you see what the city desk can find out. He's a lawyer. Represented the Amalgamated Haulers and Handlers Union a couple of years ago."

"Somebody will know him," Danilov said. "What else?"

"Who's on the business beat now? Could you see if he can find out who owns Midcentral Surety? It's incorporated, but it probably has some principal stockholders. And see if they can find out how it handles its reinsurance."

"Midcentral Surety? O.K."

"And one other thing. I may need to know whose money is behind an outfit called Wit's End, Inc. Operates a restaurant, I think, and has state-park concessions."

"What are you finding out? Sounds like you're getting somewhere."

"Nowhere," Cotton said. "I'm still guessing."

"Got the memo written yet?"

The question irritated. "No. Would you have somebody call me if they find out anything?"

He hung up and sat for a moment, thinking. Next he should call Tom Rickner at the pressroom. But there was a good chance that one of the other reporters would answer. If that happened, he could tell them he was calling from Santa Fe, or Los Angeles, or somewhere. Or maybe he could disguise his voice. He thought about it. His associates would have missed him since yesterday. They would have seen the box on today's editorial page, and they would be speculating at full steam. He wanted no risk of starting gossip that he was still in the city.

The knock at the door was no more than a tap—three quick, thudding sounds barely heard over the mindless background chatter of the television set. But it awoke in Cotton what he had kept sleeping all day—a wild, primeval, trapped-animal fright. He stared at the door, overcome by sudden enervating nausea, without the will to move. Behind him, the television speaker changed its voice to soprano: "Yooo've got a lot to live, aaand Pepsi's got a lot to give."

The tap came again, louder now. "Cotton. You at home? This is Whan."

The voice was Whan's—clipped, abruptly cutting off the sound of each word. Cotton drew in a deep breath.

"Just a minute." His voice sounded natural but his legs were weak.

Whan glanced at Cotton and then looked past him into the room. "Everything O.K.?" A small man, neat, trimmed, washed, in a neat, trim, pressed gray suit.

"Fine. You startled me."

"I've been to see Mrs. McDaniels—the widow. He'd left these copies of letters in a file case with his personal papers." Whan placed three sheets of paper beside the TV set on the motel-room table and looked at them, his expression pensive. "Maybe they'll mean something to you. The first one is dated twenty-two days before McDaniels died." He handed it to Cotton. "And the second one the following week, and the last one four days before it happened." The sheets were Xerox copies.

Mr. McDaniels:

Some facts, questions—and a suggested answer.

First the facts:

The chairmanship of the Highway

Commission pays no salary. Traditionally the job is sought as a launching platform for a statewide political candidacy. Since his unsuccessful race for reelection as Attorney General six years ago, Jason Flowers has shown no ambition to re-enter politics as a candidate. He has, in fact, no such ambitions. Flowers built the connections he made as Attorney General into a lucrative corporate law practice. Since he took the time-consuming commission chairmanship, his law firm has farmed out legal work for several clients—including General Utilities and Rowe, Beane and Pierce. This is expensive.

Now the question:

Why did Jason Flowers want this unpaid chairmanship?

And a suggested answer:

Rule out disinterested public service. Your paper knows Flowers.

But don't rule out the following peculiar chain of circumstances. There were rumors during the last year of Flowers's term as A.G. They were that

Gov. W. L. Newton and Flowers joined forces to hush up a scandal in the Highway Department. Reports current at that time were that Sixth Division Construction Engineer Herman Gay and two project engineers were taking payoffs from contractors. The records will show that Gay was transferred into the Right of Way Division, one of the project supervisors resigned and the other was shifted into the drafting office. However, reporters trying to work the story ran into denials from all sources and the story didn't break. But the rumors were true. Gay, for example, was "leasing" trucks to contractors under his jurisdiction.

Now, the personnel records will show that the same Herman Gay was promoted to State Construction Engineer a month after the appointment of Flowers to the commission chairmanship. They will show that the vacancy was created artificially when the new Executive Engineer, Delos Armstrong, moved Larry Houghton out of the job and made him Second District Maintenance Engineer. The records will also show that others whose names were linked to the affair of seven years ago have been promoted since Flowers and Armstrong took office.

Flowers is losing at least $18,000 in shared fees since he took the chairmanship. Why? Because he has found a way to make the job pay him substantially more than that.

There was no signature.

"Well," Cotton said. "Flowers has an enemy."

The letter was typed flawlessly with a modern electric typewriter face. There was something obscene about it. The right thing done for the wrong reason. Public service based on hate. The blow struck from the dark.

The second letter was shorter.

Mr. McDaniels:

The grapevine informs me you are checking the leads suggested last week. So here's another one. Within a month after Flowers's appointment to the Highway Commission a Harold L. Singer was hired in the Construction Division. Shortly thereafter, the department instituted what it calls the "Quality Experiment" on certain secondary highways. Mr. Singer seems to have been supervising project engineer on all such projects since the inception of this program. His background is interesting. Less than a year before he was hired by the Flowers administration, a Cook County grand jury in Chicago indicted four of Mr. Singer's associates for grand fraud and falsification of records in a case involving kickbacks in Chicago construction projects. Although the circumstances implicated Mr. Singer, he was no-billed by the jury.

It is also interesting that Reevis-Smith, Constructors, Inc., has been awarded all of these "Quality Experiments" projects. Who owns Reevis-Smith?

Again no signature.

The last one was a single paragraph.

Mr. McDaniels:

I was pleased to notice you talked to Houghton. I trust he cooperated. But I gather from other feedback that you have some doubts about the reliability of this correspondent. I am reliable. My sources are sound. To prove it, here's a tip to be held in confidence.

> Within four or five days Governor Roark will ask the legislature to authorize a highway bond issue in the range of 150 million. I don't want this printed because it could close off one of my leaks. If you use it in advance of the actions, I will have to discontinue this assistance.

Cotton frowned, letting these new bits and pieces find their places in the puzzle. When he had first found Mac's notebook, these letters would have been immensely useful. Now, at first thought, they only seemed to help a little—helping complete a pattern that was already taking shape. Reinforcing his educated guesses. He grinned suddenly, thinking of how McDaniels had handled the last letter. It was an interesting reaction. By confirming the tip of the bond plan in advance at the Governor's office—and then agreeing not to break the story—he had killed two birds. He earned a favor from the Governor while he made sure of his tipster's reliability.

"What do you think?" Whan asked. His eyes were on the television set, where a young man with horn-rimmed glasses was engaging two housewives in some sort of competition. It seemed to involve guessing what was behind a screen.

"I think whoever wrote these is mean as a snake," Cotton said. "And I think he's got some interesting leaks—like into Flowers's law business. And that he did a hell of a lot of legwork on this revenge job." Cotton stopped talking and thought. "And that makes me wonder why. Is hatred enough motive for that?"

"You know what I think?" Whan asked. He turned the audio on the TV all the way down. The lips of the master of ceremonies moved soundlessly in a charade of laughter. "I think we're no place. I don't have any idea who killed McDaniels. I don't know why it happened. I don't know where to start looking." Whan took out his handkerchief and carefully wiped a smudge from the TV screen. "You used to be a police reporter," he said. "You know how it works. Ninety percent of the homicides are busted when they happen. Guy strangles his wife and calls us to come and get the body. Guy knifes somebody in a bar with fifteen people watching. Or if it isn't that easy, it's just a matter of finding out who had reason to do it. Or talking to your informers about who was in town with a gun and a need for quick money. Here we got nothing. We got a guy who falls down the capitol rotunda while drunk. Officially an accident. We got a guy who gets his borrowed car run off the bridge in a hit-and-run case. And we've got the owner of the car who tells us he got a telephone death threat and then got shot at in another state. We've got nothing. Nothing solid."

"You've got a cigar box, and a toy booby trap and a Polaroid picture of my back," Cotton said. "If you think I'm lying, there are some things I didn't imagine." Cotton took out his apartment key and dangled it. "The box is on the coffee table."

"No box," Whan said. "We looked this morning. Where did you leave it?"

That wasn't hard to remember. "It was on the coffee table," Cotton said again. "And I locked the door behind me."

"The door was locked."

"So somebody got in, somehow, and took their cigar box back."

Whan put down the handkerchief and looked up. "Why?"

"Why? Why, goddamn it, so if I talked to the police there wouldn't be a shred of evidence that I wasn't lying."

"That's what I thought too," Whan said, ignoring Cotton's anger. He was standing now, half a head shorter than Cotton, looking up at him.

"To tell the truth," he said, "I can't imagine how we're ever going to have anything to take to a grand jury."

"What are you telling me?" Cotton asked. "That you don't have time for this?"

"If we had a couple or three men to watch you three shifts a day—which we don't have—maybe we'd put 'em on you. And they'd watch for maybe a month and nothing would happen, because then nothing can happen. So maybe after a month you get tired of having somebody at your elbow and we call it off." Whan looked up from the television directly at Cotton. "So then if somebody wants to kill you, they kill you. And what has anybody gained?"

"So how do you handle it?"

"Let's say we keep a man in the background when you're someplace risky. You let us know where you're going, and when. And we try to stay invisible. And then, if somebody tries anything overt, we have him and it's all wrapped up."

"Anything overt? You mean like shooting me? Like he shoots me, and you guys make a quick arrest, and everything is neat and tidy. You've got a suspect with a smoking gun and a body on the floor with a bullet in it."

"It wouldn't be like that," Whan said mildly. He picked up his hat. "Look. We've got maybe thirty people in this city right now under peace bond. They're under peace bond because they told the estranged wife, or the landlord, or somebody they were going to kill 'em. And there's a lot of other people—cranks, deviates, like that—that we try to keep an eye on. There's no way we can babysit everybody we need to babysit." Whan stopped at the door, glancing back. "So you're going someplace, call us thirty minutes ahead and let us know where you're going. And keep your door locked."

Cotton called the Second District Highway Maintenance office first and made an appointment to see Lawrence Houghton. And then he called the Legislative Finance Committee switchboard and asked for Jane Janoski. The telephone rang, and rang, and rang, and rang and clicked abruptly and said, "Janoski." The sound was so abrupt and short-tempered that Cotton laughed. He hadn't laughed for at least two days.

"Come on, Jane," he said. "I haven't even asked you to do me the favor yet. Cheer up."

"Is this John? Are you all right?"

The question surprised him, touched him. "Sure. Why not?"

"I saw in the *Tribune* you were on sick leave. What is it?"

"I'm not sick," Cotton said. "It will take a while to explain it." He paused, thinking how much he should tell her. Enough, he decided, so she would understand why he didn't want anyone to know he was in town—and enough so that she would be alert to danger, aware that the time she had spent with him in the Highway Department records room might have involved her in some risk. He told her of the telephoned death threat.

"They—whoever *they* is—think I've left town and I want to keep it that way," Cotton said. "Tom Rickner is replacing me at the pressroom and I need to get a message to him, but I don't want to call there because, if Rickner's out, somebody answers for him and then it's all over the capital that I'm still here."

"You should go to the police," Janey said. "You should . . ."

"I did," Cotton said. He kept the cynicism out of his voice. "I've got police protection. What I hope you'll do for me is call Rickner for me and ask him to check in the Highway Department personnel records on Herman

Gay and Harold L. Singer—when hired, promotions, transfers, anything interesting. And then I want him to check back during Governor Newton's administration—probably the last year of it—and see if he can find when Gay was transferred out of a job as Sixth Division Construction Engineer and get me the names of everybody else who was transferred, or demoted, or anything at about the same time."

"Slow down," Janey said. "I'm taking notes."

"The names are Herman Gay and Harold L. Singer," Cotton said. "Tell Rickner I'm interested in whether any of the same people transferred or demoted six or seven years ago have been promoted, or moved around, in the past two years."

"I've got it," Janey said. "Do you think it was serious? The death threat, I mean?"

"Probably not. Probably just trying to make me nervous." He laughed. "It worked. I'm nervous."

"Then I don't understand why you don't just drop it," she said. "It's not worth getting hurt for. It's just a newspaper story. And it's sure to hurt somebody else even if you don't get hurt."

"Like the administration," Cotton said.

"Like the Democrats. If they don't steal, they don't get hurt."

"I didn't mean Democrats," Janey said. "I meant people."

"People like your Mr. Peters," Cotton said. "Well, this time Mr. Peters isn't so damned innocent—or helpless for that matter."

She didn't answer that. There was silence for a moment.

"John, last week when you asked me to go to New Mexico with you, were you joking?"

"Well, now—down deep at rock bottom I *was* serious."

"All right, I'll go. We can leave this evening." Her voice was shaky. "I'll tell them I'm having a nervous breakdown. Maybe I am."

It took John Cotton a moment to digest the meaning of what Jane Janoski said. And then, in the befuddlement of amazement, he looked for the reason behind it, looked at the picture on the wall (a Swiss village) and at the draped window and the soundless television screen. A man with a mustache and a younger man in a sweater were standing in front of a sofa. The lips under the mustache moved. Why would Jane Janoski do this? The faces of both men convulsed in a pantomime of laughter. There were two possible answers. The temptation was there, born of want, and for a moment he toyed with it. The screen was filled now with the face of the man with the mustache, contorted with an idiot hysteria. Cotton released his breath, turned from the temptation to logic. Janey wanted to protect Paul Roark's record. An admirable thing.

"First I have to wrap this up and be done with it," he said. "Then I'll show you the Land of Enchantment, with real sunshine just like you read about."

"If you're able," she said. "If you're still alive." The seriousness left her voice. "Now or never," she said. "I'll find somebody else to take me."

"Anyway," Cotton said, "before you do, get my message to Rickner, will you?"

He called Whan's number then, and told the captain he was going to the Hertz office to rent a car and then he would drive out to the Second District Highway Maintenance office. He would be there by 3 P.M. and didn't know how long he would stay.

» 17 «

The first law of political reporting—as Leroy Hall sometimes expounded the code to new hands in the pressroom—was: "If his lips move, he's lying." And the second law was: "Find the one who got screwed." The one who got screwed, Cotton thought as he drove his Hertz Ford toward the Second Highway Division Maintenance office, was Lawrence Houghton. Under the logic on which Hall's laws were based, that meant that Houghton would be willing to talk with unaccustomed frankness about the affairs of those who had screwed him. It was logical, but it didn't always work. And it was less likely to work in the Highway Department than anywhere else because of the peculiar nature of that agency. Cotton turned it over in his mind—planning his tactics, wishing he'd had more time to research Houghton's background. He was—almost certainly—one of the agency's "good old boys," one of the long-timers hired as a political patronage appointment before the merit personnel system had been imposed. Thus he probably had been active in politics, perhaps still was. It would help to know where his loyalties lay. Probably indirectly with Senior Senator Eugene Clark. Not directly, because Eugene Clark's method of operation did not depend on a broad base of personal loyalties. His organization was a confederation of factional leaders, held together by the opportunity to serve their individual interests. Houghton's loyalty—if he owed one—would be to one of those Clark allies, perhaps a county chairman, or the Land Commissioner, or one of the city-hall machines. Cotton had been nervously aware of a dark blue Pontiac which had followed his Ford onto the freeway. He peered into the rearview mirror, trying to see the face of its driver.

The Pontiac flashed past him, driven by a blond boy in a leather jacket. Cotton glanced in the mirror. The car behind him was now a Cadillac, driven by a white-haired woman. He chewed on his lip—thinking. It was absolutely essential that he persuade Houghton that he would be protected as a source. The department was split into a kaleidoscope of factions, between the "good old boys" and the professionals, between advocates of asphalt and fans of Portland cement, by partisan politics and by office politics. But it had its traditions. And one of them—deeply ingrained by years of suffering as the state's most popular target for legislative investigations, campaign abuse and hard treatment by the press—was a repugnance for the tattle-tale. "No atheists in the Highway Department," Hall said. "When a road falls apart, or a bridge collapses, or an alignment is surveyed wrong, it always has to be an act of God so nobody has to blame anybody."

Cotton pulled into the Maintenance Division parking lot. He was sure Houghton would talk only if he was convinced no one ever could guess he had talked. And that meant Houghton must not guess that anyone knew McDaniels had gotten information from him. It would be tough, and Cotton didn't decide how to approach it until he met Lawrence Houghton in his office, and saw the sort of man he was.

He was an oversized man, six foot four, Cotton guessed, with an impressive shock of carefully combed hair, an impressive brigadier's mustache, a handsome pink face impressively scrubbed, and a clear, clipped loud voice with which he invited Cotton into a chair while he "finished signing some papers." Cotton felt an instant instinctive dislike, quickly tempered by relief. He had dealt with men like this before. They were easy.

"I don't have a lot of time this afternoon," Houghton said. "Perhaps this won't take long."

"I hope not," Cotton said. "Because I'm afraid I'm imposing on you. The fact is I need an authority on highway construction to talk to. Maybe there are others in the department as knowledgeable as you are." Cotton's tone indicated he doubted that. "But I also need someone I can trust." Cotton paused, looking into Houghton's eyes. Mustn't overdo this. "Trust absolutely, that what is said here will be held in absolute confidence."

"Of course," Houghton said.

"As you're already aware, a political reporter's reputation depends on protecting his sources. So I know you won't ask me the source of anything I'm going to talk to you about. I couldn't reveal that even to a grand jury." Cotton paused the proper moment for emphasis. "We go to jail first."

"I am aware of that," Houghton said.

"Things have been happening in your construction division since they moved you out of it," Cotton said. He ran quickly through the pattern of bidding and changing orders in the Reevis-Smith Quality Experiment projects. Houghton's face remained impassive—a study in blandness. "All that's clear enough. It's in the records. What isn't clear—at least to me—is what else is going on. There's not enough profit involved in these changed orders to make it worthwhile. There must be something else going on to make it pay and I don't know enough about highway construction to see it."

Houghton was rubbing his chin and the side of his mouth.

"This is in absolute confidence?"

"It is."

Houghton smiled, a patronizing smile. "It's really very simple."

Cotton waited a moment for him to continue, then realized the game the engineer wanted to play. Oh, well. Let him enjoy it.

"Simple? It's not simple for me."

"Cement," Houghton said.

Cotton thought about cement. "I don't understand," he said. His dislike for Houghton grew.

"The jobs you mentioned were all part of Delos Armstrong's Quality Experiment. His way of getting quality is spending more money on base stabilization and enriching the slab mix." Houghton laughed, an expression of scorn. "Eight sacks to the yard."

"Compared to what?"

"Usually about five. Five sacks gives you the strength you need. But the surface isn't completely waterproof, of course, and in this climate the water freezes and you get chipping." He laughed again. "Armstrong thinks you can make it rich enough to stop that. Or he pretends he does."

"But how is anyone making money out of this? You think the cement supplier is paying off?"

"I didn't say that."

"O.K.," Cotton said. He kept the impatience out of his voice. "I guess I'm dense, but I don't see how it works."

Houghton smiled again. "How much profit would you make, Mr. Cotton, if your work-in-progress sheets showed you were putting eight sacks per yard but you were only using five, or maybe six?"

"Um-m. Quite a lot, I'd guess. But wouldn't that be easy to catch?"

"No."

"Why not? Wouldn't a core drill show it? If

somebody got suspicious and had it analyzed in the lab?"

"The test is for lime content, Mr. Cotton. And there's a substantial variation of lime content in the aggregate—the sand and crushed rock you mix with the cement. And after a while the lime content of the base under the slab affects it. A lab test wouldn't prove a thing."

"I see. But how about the hauling slips?"

Houghton's expression shifted from amusement to mild irritation—the teacher losing patience with a student's slowness.

"You asked me to speculate, Mr. Cotton. That's what I'm doing. Those hauling slips are handled by the project engineer. If he's in this, as you believe he is, they would be easy for him to falsify. The supplier delivers bulk cement in hopper trucks. They're sealed with a tape and bonded. But if the project engineer and the contractor's weights man have an agreement, it would be easy enough to have the records show eight trucks were dumped at the batch plant, instead of five trucks."

It would, indeed. Cotton felt a growing excitement. He knew how he could pin this down, with a bit of luck. He guessed Houghton wasn't speculating at all. He was talking from sure, certain knowledge. Knowledge which McDaniels had confirmed before he died. And if this was happening with other smaller items, with roadbed watering, with tamping, with cubic yardage of excavations, with gravel tonnages, though much smaller in money, and harder to prove, they were probably enough, taken together, to double whatever the cement graft amounted to.

"So how much money would you guess would be involved?"

"Figure it up," Houghton said. "It's about $1.18 per sack, now. If you're stealing three sacks out of a yard that's $3.54. And five yards per running foot of standard with slab. That's $17.70. Times 5,280 feet per mile, and you get about $90,000 per mile. And you double that if it's a four-lane project."

Cotton whistled. "That's enough to make it worthwhile." More than enough. It would amount to maybe $2 million in the projects Reevis-Smith had handled so far, with no end in sight. And, since it was the kind of money that wouldn't show on the corporate-income-tax form, it was worth maybe $4 million in honest profits.

Cotton reached the Highway Department records room just after 4 P.M., pausing only long enough to call Whan's office and report his movement. He wrote his name and employer in the check-in register and then wondered, suddenly and belatedly, if he should have. But the risk seemed small and was now unavoidable. A quick check of the specifications confirmed what Houghton had said about the enriched cement mix. He jotted down the final bulk-cement delivery figures from the last worksheet on the first project and noted the name of the supplier—Alvis Materials. That was a big, old-line equipment and building-supplies dealer. A family corporation, Cotton remembered, and old man Alvis had once been something or other in state government. Adjutant General, he thought it was. And that might, or might not, be helpful. Cotton pulled out a thick stack of cement hauling receipts. If, by some slight chance, someone had been overconfident enough, or careless enough, not to falsify these receipts their total might not jibe with the worksheet total and that would save him a great deal of work. He noticed, first, that all the loads weighed a few hundred pounds more or less than nine tons. He would round it off at that figure and count the slips and multiply, which would be close enough to tell. When he reached the bottom slip he stopped, staring at it. Someone had done his arithmetic for him, done it in small, precise numbers in black ink. The total, Cotton noticed, was very close to the worksheet figure. And beside the total, also in the black ink of a fine-tipped ballpoint pen, an array of doodles desecrated Willie Horst's records. The doodles were small daggers, each with an ornate pommeled hilt. Familiar daggers. Daggers he had seen a hundred times, forming under Leroy Hall's pen on the margin of Leroy Hall's note pad at a hundred press conferences and committee hearings and dull legislative sessions. Hall was on the story too, and Hall had got here first.

Cotton put the haul slips back into the folder and the folder back into the filing case and walked slowly back to the entrance desk. If Roy was less than a day or two ahead of him there might be a chance to beat him—if Hall was unaware of the competition and working unhurriedly. Cotton ran his finger down the page of the check-in book, looking for the name. It wasn't on the first page, which went back to Monday. He felt a mounting sense of sick disappointment and defeat. With luck he could wrap this up in two or three days, but he wouldn't have two or three days. He checked the next page. No Leroy Hall there. And then, more rapidly and with growing surprise, back into the ledger. Finally, on pages dated September 7, he found Hall's signature—neat, tight, in black ink. Written almost six weeks ago. And written, he noticed as he continued checking, three times. Hall had been here on three consecutive days.

"Mr. Horst," Cotton said. "Do you know Leroy Hall?"

"Hall? No. I don't think so."

"He's about five-nine, sort of slender, gray hair, cut in a burr. He was in here early in September looking at the records."

"Oh," Horst said. "The reporter."

"With the *Journal*," Cotton said. "Has he been in here since then?"

"If he has been, it's in the book. Nobody gets in here without signing in and out. And I haven't seen him since then."

Cotton worked until almost five, recording the cement haul figures in his notebook, asking himself while he worked why Hall had sat on the story for more than a month. His first thought was that it hadn't checked out. But that didn't stick. This one would check out. His own notebooks already held enough for a solid story even without the cement angle. That left two alternatives. Hall might have missed the big rigging and the funny work with the change orders. Knowing how Hall worked, Cotton couldn't believe that. Something must have brought Leroy to this particular file among the thousands of files. He couldn't believe Hall would miss seeing what Cotton had seen. That left the last alternative. And knowing Hall, he didn't believe that either. Didn't like, even, to think of it. But two million dollars with more to come was a lot of money. Enough to corrupt a lot of people. As he signed out on Willie Horst's ledger, Cotton wondered if it was enough to corrupt Leroy Hall.

18

The telephone woke Cotton. He sat on the edge of his bed, groggy, and heard an efficient female voice establish his identity and tell him that Mr. Kenneth Alvis wished to speak to him. Mr. Kenneth Alvis wasted no words.

"Mr. Cotton? I've thought it over. You can come on down and look through the invoices."

"Good. When?"

"Right now," Alvis said. "You know where we are? Take the Industrial Avenue turnoff off the Interstate east."

"I can find it," Cotton said. He looked at his wristwatch, managing finally to focus. It was eight fifteen. "I'll be there about nine."

Cotton thought as he shaved that Mr. Alvis had almost certainly done more since their telephone talk last night than think it over.

He had probably talked to somebody in the Alvis Materials business office and in its bulk cement operation and assured himself that this subsidiary of his empire was innocent of collusion in any graft that Cotton might have found. Last night Alvis had been totally noncommittal.

Cotton had reached him at home and identified himself and Alvis had said that he followed Cotton's column in the *Tribune.* He sounded friendly. But he hadn't sounded friendly when Cotton finished his quick explanation of why he wanted to check the invoices on the cement deliveries to Reevis-Smith. He had sounded coldly businesslike.

"If it works the way I think it does, the Highway Department man and the contractor are falsifying your delivery records," Cotton had explained. "Your people wouldn't be implicated—wouldn't even know about it. All I need to do is to see the records at your end to confirm that's what's happening. It wouldn't be bad publicity for Alvis Materials—in fact, I might not even have to identify the supplier. No real reason to."

There had been a half-minute silence, and then: "What's your telephone number, Mr. Cotton? I'll think about this and I'll call you in the morning." No questions, no comments, just that. Cotton had sat beside the telephone for a moment, thinking—trying without success to decide whether to be optimistic. And then he had thought again of Leroy Hall's doodles on the hauling slip and he had walked out of the motel room and down the block through the dark autumn wind and turned into a place called Al's Backdoor and begun, methodically, to drink. He drank marguerítas—tequila cut with lime juice and served with the glass rimmed with salt. Drank and remembered. Frank's Lounge in Santa Fe, when he was young, and the Sunday edition had gone to press, with Mygatt, Peterman and Peterson, Hackler and Bailey and Alding, celebrating the end of another week, and the sweatshirt crowd jamming the bar, checking their parlay card point spreads against the sport-page results. And the bar on the top of the San Antonito in Ciudad Juárez, cool in the Mexican heat, when he'd been exhausted and exultant, with Rick Barzun, celebrating blanking AP on the finish of the Pan-American Road Race. How many was it? Eleven dead and eighteen hospitalized. A Porsche it had been. Not one of the Porsche team but an Argentine driver, skidding into the crowd on that fast final run from Chihuahua to the Juárez airport. And the luck of finding the Mexican colonel who had handled the army ambulances, and of having the radio-telephone link open to the Dallas UPI bureau. He remembered every detail. Perfect recall. But where was Barzun now? Where were they all? Scattered and lost. On the third marguerita he considered Janey, wondering if she *was* the Governor's much-rumored mistress. That led him to her offer to go to New Mexico with him and to her reasons for it. These he pondered gloomily and found, once again, to be admirable, but foolish. The story wouldn't hurt Governor Roark that much. Not beyond recovery. Not unless Roark's own hands were dirty.

The bar was dark and quiet. People came and went. Sometime about midnight, a newsie came in with the two-star edition of the *Gazette,* which Cotton bought, put in the booth beside him and forgot. He lost interest in numbering the margueritas. The tequila was cold in his mouth and warm in his stomach. Now, at last, he was ready to consider what had drawn him here. To think of Leroy Hall and the impossible alternatives. He preferred to believe that Hall had simply missed the story. But Hall wouldn't have checked that particular project file among those acres of files unless he had reason to be suspicious.

And, being suspicious, he would have been thorough. Hall wouldn't have missed the bid rigging, or the funny business with the changed orders. And, being Leroy Hall, he would have looked shrewdly beyond this minor thievery for the big money. And he would have seen what Cotton eventually saw. Hall must have the story. Probably had had it weeks ago, before McDaniels had been tipped to it. So why hadn't the *Journal* run it? Cotton tried to concentrate. It was important that he find an answer to substitute for another obvious but incredible answer. Janey Janoski probably wouldn't run it. Janey was smart like Hall. Maybe not quite as savvy in politics, but wise. And Janey wouldn't run it because she wasn't detached from it all. Janey would see H. L. Singer and Flowers and the rest of them as people with wives, and children, and lives to lead. (Or would she, above all, see Paul Roark?) She was not conditioned, as he and Hall were conditioned, to see beyond those who got hurt, the people with faces, to the three million faceless people whose money was stolen and who needed to know about it. But that was just part of it. Janey wasn't like Hall and him. Not like the metaphorical fly, seeing all, recording all, feeling nothing. No. Hall's reason for suppressing the story wouldn't be Janey's reason. Why did he try to deny that Hall, like any man, must have his price? Why did it hurt so much to admit that Leroy Hall, whose daily work was in the fields of compromise, where no value was absolute, had himself compromised? Why did he hate this thought? Hall was his friend. He thought about it, trying to concentrate. An answer came to him gradually. Maybe Hall suppressed it, not just for money they paid him, but as a gesture of contempt for all of it. Because the dry, brittle, witty surface cynicism Hall displayed ran right to his core. Because Hall, in his experience and his wisdom, had learned that the game they played in the pressroom—scoffed at and joked about and believed in—was indeed a game without sense or value. That was why he couldn't accept Hall's betrayal. Because it would mean Hall had concluded that what they did had no meaning. And Leroy Hall was—after all—smarter, and wiser, than John Cotton.

The glass before him seemed almost empty. He focused on it, and was suddenly aware of a man standing at his elbow. "Time to go," the man said. The voice was soft.

Cotton jerked his head up, looking at the man. He had forgotten that someone, somewhere, was hunting him, but he remembered it now.

"Two o'clock. Closing time," the man said. "Got to lock the place up."

"Oh." Cotton pushed himself to his feet, picked up his coat. He walked, unsteadily, toward the door.

"Wait," the man said. "You're forgetting your money." The man laughed. "Unless you meant to leave an eighteen-dollar tip."

Now, the morning after, Cotton felt the crumpled bills in his trousers pocket, and remembered all of this, although some of it was hazy and his head was aching. He pulled out the money. A ten, a five and two ones. The bartender had saved himself a one-dollar tip. Fair enough.

The shirt was his last clean one. He would try to find time today to buy some more, and some socks and underwear. He called Whan's office to report his destination. Whan was out and the officer he was referred to made no pretense of caring where John Cotton was going to be this morning.

In the office of Kenneth Alvis, the wall clock said four minutes after nine. The man Cotton thought would be Alvis proved to be a company auditor whose name sounded something like Crichton. Alvis was small and white-haired, with the weathered skin one attains either by working outdoors or playing a lot of golf. The third man Alvis introduced was named Harper and was, Alvis said, "in cement." Harper looked nervous and slightly belligerent.

"Here they are," Alvis said. He indicated a stack of papers on his desk. "Billing slips on what we've delivered to Reevis-Smith for the past thirty months. That's right, isn't it? The past two years, you said."

"I don't want to waste a lot of valuable time for you people," Cotton said. "I can do this. I just want to run a total on your bulk deliveries to Reevis-Smith on each of five highway jobs."

"We don't keep it like that," Harper said. "How could I figure it out?"

"I don't know. I guess we could check on the delivery point. We charge a haulage fee too, so we show on the billing slip where the batch plant was where we dumped the loads."

"That should do it," Cotton said.

The batch plant for project FAS 007-211-3788 proved to be at Ellis, a small town near the Lake Ladoga dam in the southeastern corner of the state. While Harper, Alvis and

Cotton sorted the Ellis deliveries out of the pile, Crichton brought in an adding machine.

Crichton was fast at it. Fast and sure. He tore the tape off the machine, glanced at it and handed it to Cotton.

"Thirteen thousand, seven hundred and eighty-six tons," he said. "Is that about what you were expecting?"

Cotton stared at the tape, incredulous. He had been a fool to think it would be this easy.

"Can you translate these tons into sacks?" But, even as he asked, he knew he was just wasting time. Twenty sacks per ton would be about 275,000 sacks—almost exactly the amount the state had paid Reevis-Smith for on that job.

"Sure," Crichton said. He tapped quickly at the adding machine. "It's 275,720 sacks." He was watching Cotton's face. "That's too much, I gather?" The question had a trace of satisfied malice in it.

"Mr. Alvis, I want to apologize for wasting your time," Cotton said. He felt sick. "I had some bad information, and I made a bad guess from it." He cursed Houghton, and then himself, for not being more wary of Houghton. The engineer had obviously been showing off. He should have guessed Houghton was himself guessing—trying to impress.

"Well," Harper said, "that is what we delivered to Reevis-Smith there. That's what they used for the jobs they had there. And if you want just what went into the highway, you'll have to get the breakdown from them."

"Jobs," Cotton said. "I don't follow you. Was there more than one job?"

"They worked them both out of the same batch plant," Harper said. "The structures and the slab on the highway and all that work at the resort. But you could get the breakdown from them. Both state jobs in a way, but they'd have to keep the books separate, I guess."

It was for Cotton one of those moments when time seems to slow down, when the words hang in the air. Another piece of the puzzle clicked neatly into place.

"Well," Cotton said. He was grinning now. "So that's how it works." Alvis was staring at him, waiting for an explanation. Let him wait. Cotton was thinking: Here's where Wit's End fits in. And maybe this explains Midcentral Surety—a bonding company which wouldn't make any nosy inspections. Cotton glanced back at Harper.

"Could Reevis-Smith be buying cement from someone else—using some other supplier for these Lake Ladoga resort improvements?"

"That would be pretty stupid," Harper said. "Anyway, they weren't. I get by there now and then and they're using the same batch plant for both jobs."

Alvis was smiling faintly now, understanding it, looking at Cotton with approval. He laughed. "The son-of-a-bitch is shorting enough cement out of the highway job to handle the resort construction. Getting paid for it twice."

"Just between us, I think it was even neater than that," Cotton said. "I think the same people who own Reevis-Smith own the park concession company. That would take the risk out of it. Reevis-Smith knows it's going to build the resort improvements—the roads and so forth. And, with some collusion in the Highway Department, it gets a lock on the highway jobs in the right places at the right time."

"How about that!" Alvis said. "Smart son-of-a-bitch. He gets paid twice for all his cement work."

"And for God knows what else," Cotton said. "But that will all have to come out in the wash. Now I just want to make sure that he didn't get cement from any other source."

"Joe," Alvis said, "who else could they get cement from? To that batch plant, I mean?"

"They didn't get it from nobody but us."

"But they could have gotten it from Perkins Brothers, or maybe Allied. Who else?"

"Them and maybe A & J, if they don't mind the extra shipping," Harper said. "But I'll bet my ass they didn't."

"You know the people. Get on the horn and find out for sure." Alvis turned to Cotton. "That's what you want, isn't it?" Alvis was enjoying this.

"That would save me a lot of time."

"O.K.," Alvis said. "Done. And you remember our deal. You keep us out of the paper."

"If you don't want in," Cotton said. "But you're doing a lot of public good here—cleaning up corruption. Why not get credit?"

Alvis was still grinning. "Get credit for screwing a customer? The smart son-of-a-bitch."

19

It was almost noon when Cotton left the office of Alvis Industries. It had taken less than thirty minutes for Harper to confirm what Cotton already knew—that no one else had hauled bulk cement to any of the Reevis-Smith Quality Experiment projects. And then Harper had another thought. He knew the foreman of the trucking outfit which subcontracted on Reevis-Smith jobs. This took a little longer, but when the last phone call had been made, Cotton had a tally of tons of mixed cement hauled from batch plants on all five of the contractor's highway jobs the past two years to state park improvement projects let to Reevis-Smith. Alvis ran the adding machine now, totaling tonnage and converting wet cement into money. The final amount on the tape was $318,427.

"That's more than we net out of this whole goddamn operation in a year," Alvis said.

On the way back to his motel Cotton noticed a police car behind him. A coincidence, or the first visible sign that Whan was providing any protection? If he needed it at all, he would need it now. Yesterday's activities would have alerted anyone who might be watching that Cotton was in the capital and working on the story. McDaniels had copied notes out of those contract files in the Highway Department records room and had been pushed over the balustrade down the capitol well. Leroy had visited the records and had been . . . He balked at the word, and then accepted it. Bribed. How much had they paid him? Cotton tried to imagine the scene and found it impossible. The Leroy Hall he knew—thought he knew—refused the role, refused to hold out his hand, refused to accept the imagined envelope thick with hundred-dollar bills. Then what was his price, if not money? Cotton turned away from the unanswerable question and sorted out his story. What he had. What he needed. He had nothing, beyond the circumstances of Highway Department policies and appointments, to tie Jason Flowers to the affair. He had nothing definite beyond peculiar coincidence to connect Wit's End, Inc., with this conspiracy. He had no doubt there was a direct connection, but with what he had now—and the way he would have to write it—Wit's End would appear a possibly innocent customer unaware that stolen cement was being poured into its park improvements. Nor had he anything to connect Midcentral Surety—not even a real clear idea of how it connected. Nothing more than the coincidence that it had interested McDaniels at the same time he was digging into Reevis-Smith—and perhaps that was simply because it was bonding Reevis-Smith contracts. Cotton had that, and a strong suspicion.

He glanced into his rearview mirror as he turned into the motel lot. The police car was no longer visible. Cotton pulled into the slot reserved for his room number, cut the ignition and sat, looking. Three men walked out of the coffeeshop toward him. They walked past his car, talking, seeming to ignore him. They got into a blue-and-white Chevy and drove away. A young woman in a tailored suit emerged from the walkway between the first and second blocks of motel units and stood a moment beside the ice machine, her eyes roving over the parking lot. She looked directly at Cotton, studied him, and then looked away. *Would they use a woman? Would they do anything in the cold light of noon?*

Cotton sighed and climbed out of the car. The woman had disappeared. He walked hurriedly to the stairway, trotted up the flight of steps and stopped behind the pillar at the head of the stairway. His room was six doors down this second-story walkway—at least thirty yards of wide-open exposure to anyone in the parking lot. He pulled his room key out of his pocket, took a deep breath and ran. And when he was inside the room, breathless, the door locked securely behind him—feeling simultaneously foolish and relieved—he hardened a resolution he had already made. Today would be the end of it. He would work until office closing time pulling together whatever loose ends he could. And then he would write what he had. The story would appear tomorrow and it would be over. No more hiding. No more panic. No more reason for anyone to kill him. Once the story broke, every reporter in the statehouse would swarm on to it—scrambling for whatever he had missed. But he'd give Danilov a head start on the rest of it.

He called Danilov first. Ernie had the rundown he had asked on A. J. Linington. Member of the bar. Owned little law firm with offices in the Exchange Building. Showed up in the file three times in the last eight years, twice as defense attorney in gambling cases and once representing a union business manager indicted for attempted extortion. The union was Haulers and Handlers, International, an independent.

"And," Danilov continued, "this Linington cat also turned up in that ownership check the business-page desk made for you. He's listed as agent-of-record for both corporations."

"Both?"

"Midcentral and Wit's End."

"But not Reevis-Smith?"

"No. That was owned by the estate of Frank Reevis until three years ago. A lot of labor troubles and it went into bankruptcy receivership. Then it was sold to Highlands Corporation. That's a Delaware corporation with a business address in Jersey City."

"Never heard of it," Cotton said. He was disappointed. Linington gave them some connection between Wit's End and Midcentral—but that connection was meaningless. What he needed was a link between the resort company and the construction firm.

"You'll hear more of it," Danilov said. "This

Highlands Corporation is also registered as owner of Midcentral Surety and Wit's End, Incorporated. They're subsidiaries."

"Wonderful," Cotton said. Another loose end pinned down. One less crumb left for the opposition papers. "I'll use that Wit's End–Reevis-Smith connection in the story. Check it with the business desk to make sure I say it right."

"Yeah," Danilov said. "How's it coming?"

"Count on it for tomorrow. First edition."

"How big is it?"

"Be a banner," Cotton said. He told Danilov briefly what he had. There was a short silence. Danilov preparing a compliment, Cotton thought. He had never heard a Danilov compliment. He would ignore it, he decided.

"I guess it'll take room on the jump page," Danilov said. "What'll it run? Galley and a half or so? You write too loose. Try to keep it tight."

A Danilov compliment.

"It won't run a word longer than it has to," Cotton said.

"I guess I won't need the memo," Danilov said. "Not if we have the yarn tomorrow morning." There was a click.

Cotton hung up the dead receiver, cutting off the dial tone. He thought: You'll get a memo, you son-of-a-bitch, because I'm quitting. You'll get all I can wrap up today in the story, and a memo with it. And the memo would tell Ernie Danilov what was left to be checked out and confirmed and it would tell Ernie and the *Tribune* to go to hell, effective on receipt.

And then it was time for the unpleasant part, the part he had always dreaded, the chore demanded by the conventions of objective reporting. He called Singer first, finding him finally downstate at the Seventh Division construction office. Singer's voice was pleasant.

"What can I do for you?"

"I'm looking into change orders on some jobs you handled," Cotton said. He identified the jobs. "It looks like just about all the change orders you signed increased the amounts on items Reevis-Smith bid high on, and cut back on items where they were low."

He realized he was trying to imagine what Singer looked like—trying to connect a man to the voice. Thinking as Janey Janoski would think. Cotton provided examples. "Is there an explanation for that?"

Singer's voice changed from pleasant to frightened and guarded. Conditions on the job required the changes, he said. It happened on every job with every project engineer. That was part of their duties, adjusting the project design to fit the site as construction developed.

"Just happened to be that way then?" Cotton said. "Coincidence?" Would Singer be married? Have children?

"You could call it that."

"Another thing," Cotton said. "The records show that you signed slips to pay Reevis-Smith for 13,786 tons of bulk cement on that FAS 007-211-3788 job. And that's the total amount delivered to the Reevis-Smith batch plant there at Ellis. But it looks like part of the mixed cement didn't go into the highway job. It went to the Reevis-Smith project over at the state park there—that Wit's End park improvement job." How much would he tell Singer now? Just enough to lead him into a lying explanation? And then just enough more to get a modification of the lie? And then enough more to demolish the lie? It was effective. Cotton felt slightly sick. To hell with it. If he handled it right, he was sure he could present the readers two or three contradictory lies. Singer's, contradicted by a separate lie from Herman Gay, and both contradicted by whatever spur-of-the-moment story the Reevis-Smith manager could come up with. Flowers would be smarter. He would refuse to comment. Three contradictory lies would make the story stronger. But to hell with it. He'd settle for a denial, spare Singer the role of public liar.

"We've got the records on it," Cotton said. "Exactly a grand total of 13,786 tons were delivered to the batch plant. You signed haul slips showing the same amount going into the highway. But we've got witnesses who can prove cement from that plant built the park improvements." Cotton paused, hesitating between the question leading to denial (wondering inanely if Singer had worked his way through college for the civil-engineering degree which would now be useless to him) and the question which would bring the "no comment," which would be smart for Singer but weak for the story.

"Do you have any comment on that? Do you have any comment on why you signed falsified hauling slips?"

"I didn't falsify any . . ." The voice was tight, frightened. "No comment," it said. "I don't want to say anything."

"You started to say you didn't falsify anything," Cotton said. "You don't want to say anything about that?"

"No. For God's sake. Is this going in the

paper? Look, I've got a daughter in high school."

"I'm sorry," Cotton said.

And he was sorry. It surprised him, reminded him of something. How long ago? Fifteen years. The Carter County sheriff (What was his name?) fat and frightened behind his desk. The sheriff (Lowden it was, or maybe Logan, a fat man with the waxy complexion of those who have weak hearts) trying to explain how he had happened to be collecting more money than he had coming for feeding county-jail prisoners. A clumsy, inept affair—the sheriff's name signed to affidavits swearing his wife's café had served 760 prisoner-meals for the month. The county-jail roster showed only 208 prisoner-days served that month; 208 times 3 meals a day equaled 624 meals. Could the sheriff explain why he had claimed and cashed vouchers for 136 more meals than had been served? The sheriff could not. It was some mistake. An error in paperwork. A slip-up somewhere. Then could he explain how the error happened to be in his favor every month of that year, and how each month of his term the error grew slightly larger? And the sheriff sitting slack behind his desk, saying he would not discuss it, his face ashen. Cotton remembered it. He had felt an immense pity then. Pity for the man who would be removed from office, indicted by a grand jury, destroyed.

That had been the first one, and the worst one. The next one had been much easier—an assistant city manager cheating on travel expenses, who had simply lost his job. And after a while you hardly thought about it.

But he thought about it now—about Singer and his ruin.

Herman Gay was easier. Older and tougher. He denied, first, that it could be happening. Then blustered. Then complained that, after all, the construction engineer couldn't keep an eye on everything at once. Gay didn't have his signature attached to any false records, therefore saw escape. But there would be no escape for Singer. And, since Singer would be easy prey for any district attorney, there would be no escape for Gay, either. Singer would certainly implicate him.

Cotton caught Flowers at his law office.

Flowers listened with no more than an occasional grunt.

"Where are you calling from, Mr. Cotton? I'm busy now. I'll call you back." The voice was icy.

"That won't be necessary," Cotton said.

"Why not just tell me what you have to say about this happening in your Quality Experiment highway program?"

"I think you're lying. Obviously I want to look into it before I say anything. But I'll check it out and call you back. Where can I reach you?"

"You can call our city desk at the *Tribune* and give them the statement," Cotton said. "They'll get it back to me."

"But I may need to reach you."

"You won't be able to," Cotton said. He would see to that. "I'll be out of pocket."

At Reevis-Smith, Cotton was referred to R. J. Putnam, the construction division manager. Putnam seemed genuinely puzzled and passed him on to the executive vice-president, a man named Gary Kelly. Mr. Kelly was not at all puzzled. He interrupted Cotton's preliminary account before Cotton could reach his concluding questions. The voice was slightly froggy.

"O.K., Cotton," it said. "This sort of stuff is going to cause us some public-relations problems. I think we could afford a nice fee for a public-relations consultant."

"I'm not in public relations."

"I think we could afford a lump sum. Like twenty-five thousand."

"I don't think you can afford me." Cotton's voice was tight with anger. How much had they offered Leroy? Did Hall place his value at $25,000?

"I think we better get together and talk about it then."

"All I want from you is some questions answered. Do you want to explain how you happened to charge the Highway Department for cement that didn't go into the highways?"

"Just a minute," Kelly said. "Be right with you in a minute."

No sound on the telephone. Mouthpiece covered with a hand, Cotton thought. He's seeing if he can get this call traced. Cotton hung up. Reevis-Smith would be reported as declining comment.

He sat a moment, thinking. The hunt for him would be in full cry now. No question of that. Could they find him? No way. Not unless there was a leak in the Police Department. Anyway, it didn't matter now if the pressroom knew he was back in town. He picked up the phone again.

"I've been trying to call you," Tom Rickner said, "but your line's been busy."

"Did you get anything out of the highway personnel files?"

"I've got some names and dates for whatever they're worth," Rickner said. "But fill me in on all this. What's this secrecy jazz that Ernie's giving me, this sick-leave business, and . . ."

"I'll explain it later. Give me what you've got."

What Rickner had added little. It confirmed what the writer of the anonymous letters had told McDaniels about a flurry of transfers and demotions eight years ago, with many of the same names involved in another flurry of job shifting two years ago. Most of it would be useful only with more checking in the contract records—to connect the same names with roles in Reevis-Smith projects for follow-up stories later. But it did provide better ground for tying Herman Gay into the story.

Memos in the H. L. Singer personnel file transferred him from district to district to handle the Reevis-Smith projects. Each bore Gay's signature as construction engineer. That pleased Cotton. It meant that Singer, with his pleasant voice and his daughter in high school, would not stand alone in the villain's role in this first story.

"One other thing," Rickner was saying. "There's a letter here for you. Guess it's a letter. Marked personal. Sealed envelope somebody left at the desk here for you."

20

In the car it was warm, even with the heater fan now silent. Outside in the pools of dim yellow light under the old-fashioned statehouse street lamps it would be at least ten degrees below freezing—the cutting damp cold of early winter. Cotton buttoned his overcoat and glanced at his watch. Twenty minutes until three. A little too early. He pulled the letter from his coat pocket and read it again—carefully. Something about it tickled his subconscious—suggested vaguely that there was some odd fact that he should consider. But nothing came. It was like all the letters, the same tidy electric typewriter face, the same insolent arrogance of tone.

Mr. Cotton:

I gather that you have learned from Mr. Houghton that all is not well in

Jason Flowers's so-called "Quality Experiment" highway projects. From what my sources tell me, you have been diligent and therefore deserving of a reward.

But first let me warn you to be careful. The late Mr. McDaniels of the *Capitol-Press* was working on this story in his inept fashion before his death. When one considers the personality of Jason Flowers and how much this story would embarrass him, one wonders if McDaniels's clumsiness was helped with a shove.

And now for the reward. I doubt if I can expect you to find enough to link the shrewd and careful Mr. Flowers directly to the thievery he has arranged. I have arranged for you to have some good luck.

The state income-tax return filed by Mr. Flowers and the corporate tax return filed by Reevis-Smith, Constructors, contain some interesting figures. As you know, these records are closed by law to all except tax officials. The law makes it a felony for tax officials to reveal information contained in returns to anyone. NOTE: The legal penalty is for revealing the records, and not for inspecting them.

Therefore, if you happen to be at the capitol at 3 A.M. Thursday morning, you will find entry of the east-wing basement utility tunnel unlocked. If you happened to be in the Bureau of Revenue wing on the third floor of the capitol building at 3:05 A.M. you will happen to find that the door connecting the B-of-R records stacks with the east hall happens to be unlocked. If you enter you will find the tax file of Jason Flowers in the fifth row of file cases from the door. The file is about a third of the way back in the drawer. It is in the top drawer of the seventeenth file cabinet. The drawer is labeled "Individual, Fla-Flo." The Reevis-Smith file is in the thirteenth row from the door, the eleventh cabinet east of the aisle, near the front of the top drawer. If you want copies, as I suspect you will, you'll find a Xerox machine at the file clerk's desk.

While 3 A.M. is admittedly an inconvenient hour, I felt it advisable for two reasons. The person who will unlock the door for you does not, as you will

> appreciate, wish to risk being seen doing so. Second, you will wish to minimize the chances of being seen during your research in the bureau files. If you are early, you may frighten away our friend with the key. So be punctual.

And here he was, being punctual. Following orders just as McDaniels must have done, serving as a tool of some anonymous hater. Cotton stared into the darkness. He had parked in the executive lot in the space marked RESERVED, ASST. SECY OF STATE—the space nearest the small side door which his own key would unlock. In four or five minutes he would climb out of this car, walk through that door, take the elevator to the third floor, do exactly what the-man-who-hated-Jason-Flowers had told him to do. Why? Was it simply because fifteen years as a newsman had hardened him against leaving a hole in a story? Because the artistry of the craft demanded maximum completeness? Was it because of some sense of righteousness—an urge to punish and destroy? Or was it because it seemed cruelly unfair that H. L. Singer (the pawn, cheerful voice, the teenaged daughter) should stand almost alone as thief in the first break of the story? He found the last explanation most comfortable. But he wasn't sure.

Cotton glanced at his watch again. Now it was time. He stepped out of the car, flinching against the cold air, walking slowly. He thought he knew what the income-tax records would show. It would be a legal fee. Flowers would report it as income from Reevis-Smith. Reevis-Smith would claim it as an expense deduction. The payoff bribe on the record under a polite name. Reported because state tax returns and bank deposits were cross-checked by the Federal Internal Revenue Service inspectors against federal returns. That's what he would find. (But why, then, had the letter writer sent him to look at both returns? He could confirm a legal fee in either one. Was that what bothered him about the letter?) The fee would be large. And if he could confirm it in the file, it would be all the link he needed. He could handle it in one additional paragraph.

"Records of Reevis-Smith show the construction firm paid a . . ." How much would it be? $50,000, probably more. ". . . a $50,000 fee last year to Jason Flowers, chairman of the State Highway Commission and author of the Quality Experiment program on which the contractor has been working."

Maybe the tax file would show a series of annual payments. But one year, one fee, would be enough to show the corruption came from the top, to tie in the top man, enough to modify for the reader the role of H. L. Singer. Singer would become a man who might—after all—be nothing worse than a fool and a weakling following orders from above.

The darkness at the side door was almost total and Cotton fumbled a moment at the lock. (Was this who teased him? That his anonymous hater—who knew everything—didn't know that statehouse newsmen carried building access keys and—not knowing this—had arranged to have another door unlocked?) Inside, he stood a moment, still thinking about the letter. The hallway here was lined with glass cases—a display of natural predators mounted by some forgotten Game and Fish Department employee for some bygone state fair and exiled now to gather dust in this basement corridor. Cotton, who had walked past this array of taxidermy for seven years without a glance, glanced now at the snarling bobcat beside him, and past it at an owl, its wings spread, rising from a bush with a woodmouse caught in its talons. The taxidermist had added a touch of macabre realism to the tableau by preserving the mouse's death throes, its teeth bared in an eternal silent squeak of death. Cotton's eyes rested on the mouse, thinking of mousetraps and cheese. But the letter wouldn't be bait. Couldn't be. Its anonymous author wanted his story broken, wanted Jason Flowers destroyed. The letter writer's interests were opposite to the interests of those who had hunted him—those who must be hunting him even more frantically now. But they would never think to hunt in this empty state capitol building at three o'clock in the morning.

Yet he stood motionless, listening. Somewhere far away in the hollowness of the corridors something produced a sound. Something made unidentifiable by the echoing distance. A thumping. Brief, replaced by the ringing silence. Cotton was conscious that while those who hunted couldn't know he was here, neither did the police. Calling Whan's office to report that he planned a 3 A.M. trespass on the state capitol building would have demanded explanations which he couldn't give. Cotton realized he was feeling something he hadn't felt since boyhood—

not exactly a fear of the dark, but of the hobgoblins which inhabit it. Another dim sound reached him from somewhere in the echoing building. Someone moving. A janitor, perhaps? Or a night guard? Was there a guard in the building at night? If there was, Cotton couldn't afford to be heard. He squatted, removed his shoes, and left them atop a glass case housing a weasel frozen in an eternal crouch behind an unwary quail.

Avoiding the clanking elevator meant trotting up five flights of stairs to third floor main. The architects of this massive old granite pile had given its interior a spurious spaciousness by making its main-floor corridors two stories high—each floor with a mezzanine corridor overlooking it. Cotton reached third floor main out of breath. He leaned against the wall beside the stairhead window, puffing. The letter in his inside coat pocket, the touch of stiff folded paper against his armpit, again tickled his subconscious. And this time his memory abruptly answered the question.

This letter was different because it was the original copy. Those Whan had brought him from McDaniels's files had been Xerox copies. But why should his subconscious be warning him that this mattered? The question almost instantly produced its response. Another question. Where were the originals? Cotton caught his breath. McDaniels obviously had made the copies for his file. Had the originals been in Mac's coat pocket before he made his long fall? They weren't among his belongings at police headquarters. Or had they been on his desk when the man in the blue topcoat came looking for the notebook? In the microsecond it took these questions to form, Cotton became conscious of the cold tile under his socks, of the coldness of the marble against the back of his head, of the coldness of his neck, of a chilling, dreadful fear. It took him a moment to control it. To think rationally. He found himself remembering the strange seven minutes or so which passed between the time Mac left the pressroom and his dying scream. If he was being held and searched this gap in time would be explained. But there could be other explanations of what happened to the original copies of the first three letters. And the letter addressed to him had the same tone, the same arrogance, as the ones written to McDaniels. Apparently the same typewriter—although any of a hundred thousand electrics could have done the job. Cotton felt his panic ebbing. This almost certainly wasn't a trap set by his hunters. But he would take a precaution. He would climb another flight of steps to the third mezzanine. He would work his way quietly along the balcony around the corner to the long wing. From the balcony, out of sight behind its ornate waist-high granite railing, he could see if there was any sign that anyone was waiting near the doorway to the Bureau of Revenue file room. He pushed himself away from the wall.

On the mezzanine balcony the floor seemed, somehow, even colder. He eased himself around the corner in a crouch and peered over the railing down the main-floor hallway below him. At the far end, almost a hundred yards away, the dim yellow light of a single bulb lit the west stairwell and cast the office doorways in sharp relief. And below him the dim light from the rotunda pushed weakly against the darkness. But much of the central section of the corridor was lit only by a vague illumination reflected from the polished floors and the grimy walls. The door Cotton would enter was in this area of almost total darkness. He stared, finally identifying the blacker rectangle that would be the doorway. Nothing moved. Nothing seemed to be there.

Cotton squatted, thinking, Owls see in the dark. Mice do not. Inane thoughts. He heard the faint sounds that old buildings make in their sleep. Somewhere in the dim distance the almost inaudible whirring of a heater fan was turned on by a sleepless thermostat in an office far below him. Somewhere a creak of stone or steel contracting. And beneath it, indistinguishable even in moments of utter stillness, a humming no louder than the blood moving in his own veins.

An abrupt sense of the silliness of what he was doing—crouching here above this empty hallway like a frightened child with his bruised thigh aching in a cramp—washed over him and overpowered fear. He would climb down the stairs, walk into the Bureau of Revenue file room, be done with his business, and get the hell out of this spooky building. He felt a sudden impulse to break the ringing silence, to waken the haunted sleep of these hallways with a shout. He looked at the luminous dial of his watch. Nine minutes after three. He was no longer punctual.

The sound reached his consciousness just as he started to rise. It said, "Whisk." Whisk, whisk, whisk, whisk. A regular cadence. Cotton froze. Puzzled. Then no longer puzzled, but afraid. The cadence was of footsteps. The sound of cloth on the tiled floor. Whoever walked had, like himself, removed his shoes. The sound came from Cotton's left, from across the rotunda, moving almost directly toward him. He sank lower behind the railing, staring out between the granite posts which supported it.

A man came into view, walking across the open rotunda floor toward the corridor. Cotton's view from above foreshortened the figure, but he appeared to be a tall man. Bareheaded, lank dark hair falling over his forehead, a blue topcoat. It was the man who had come into the newsroom looking for Mac's notebook. The coat pockets bulged (his shoes?). He walked almost directly under Cotton, the whispering sound of his socks on the floor plainly audible now in the silence. And then a voice, very low:

"He's in the building."

And a reply, too low for Cotton to understand. There were two of them. And one had been waiting in the corridor all this time—from the sound, not more than fifty feet from where Cotton now crouched. To his right and on the main corridor floor below.

"His car's in the parking lot north of this wing," the first voice said. "The door's unlocked and he left his shoes down there."

"So that's why . . ." Cotton couldn't make out the rest of it.

"Probably. I locked the other door so that's his only way out now. We screen him off from that end and it shouldn't be hard to find him. Just a matter of checking out these corridors."

There was a squeaking sound which Cotton couldn't identify. Perhaps a door hinge. Someone had been able to pick the lock on his apartment door. These old capitol locks, he guessed, would be easy. The voices were now too muffled to be understood.

Cotton stood up, looked frantically around him. He would run. Run down the mezzanine floor to the stairwell at the end of the hallway and down the stairs, and out of the building. And once out he would be safe. But, before he could take a step, the men were in the corridor again.

"Right, I've got it." The voice was that of the man in the blue coat.

And a second later the back of another man was in Cotton's view—a stocky man in a heavy red windbreaker walking rapidly and silently away, skirting the railing around the rotunda under the capitol dome, disappearing from Cotton's view in the direction of the west wing. There had been something white around the man's right hand and he carried his left arm stiffly. A cast, Cotton thought. Was it the man on the airplane? The man who called himself Adams. Whom Whan knew as Harge. The fall in the Brazos must have hurt his wrist. But Cotton's heart sank at the thought. Adams was a hunter. Adams would never let a quarry out of a trap as hopeless as this one. Cotton squatted back on his heels, feeling panic again and trying to concentrate. He had to think. To calculate what Adams would do.

Cotton rubbed his knuckles fiercely across his forehead, forcing thought. The other man, the blue topcoat, had walked in the other direction. Toward the east-wing stairwell. Would he go down to ground level? That seemed likely. One—probably the blue topcoat—would make sure he didn't reach the unlocked door by the Game Commission offices. And then when Adams had searched the basement and the ground floor they would both work upward—making sure he couldn't reach the stairwells unseen. It wouldn't take them long. A simple matter of trotting through the corridors on each floor. No place to hide anywhere. Was there? Cotton tried frantically to think. Searching the service tunnel into the basement post-office area would take a few minutes. Usually some crates and boxes were stacked there which would have to be checked. So would the old Game Department exhibits stored in the hallway he had entered. And in the floor lobby the hall of statuary would use up time. Someone would have to check behind each of the marble figures. It would take them, if they were methodically careful, perhaps thirty minutes to work their way from the basement to the top floor. And it would be almost three hours, maybe more than three, before the first shift of custodial personnel came to work. Where could he hide? Break into an office? The noise would reverberate through the silent building—bringing them on the run. What else, then? He tried to concentrate. There was nothing else. He could only work his way downward toward the ground level—hoping for luck. Hoping that Adams would make a mistake. But Adams wouldn't make a mistake.

Cotton considered his possibilities. The elevators were out of the question. They moved slowly, with great whining of motors and clanking of cables. Using one would be fatal. That left four stairwells. The broader, more used stairs at the ends of the shorter north-south wings or the narrower stairwells at the end of the east-west wings. He had come up the south stairs and they would take him very close to the door through which he had entered. But approaches to that door would be watched. Using the north or west stairs involved crossing the open rotunda. He had no intention of doing that. That left the east stairs, following the footsteps of the man in the blue topcoat. That was better than Adams, the hunter.

As he reached the third floor main corridor he thought suddenly of fire escapes. But where the devil were they? The building surely must have some. The fire code would demand it. He visualized the exterior of the massive old building, trying to see it in his mind's eye as he had seen it every day for years. He saw dirty granite, ornate cornices, arrays of high, old-fashioned windows, the equestrian statue of some early governor, who had been an undistinguished general in the Civil War, in front, the broad sweep of steps flanked by stone lions leading to the formal front entrance. But he couldn't remember where the fire escapes were located. Couldn't remember ever noticing them. He dismissed the fire-escape idea and thought of the pressroom. His key would unlock that. And he could telephone the police for help.

But if they watched any room it would be the pressroom—the natural place for him to go. Where else could he reach a telephone?

He stopped at the doorway where the two men had talked below him. The lettering, barely visible in the dim light, said AD VALOREM TAX DIVISION. The knob wouldn't turn. Down the dark hallway he stopped again at the door labeled INCOME TAX DIVISION: FILE ROOM. That, too, was locked.

He remembered then that on the second floor main below him was a janitor's room. If there was a nightwatchman (There *must* be a nightwatchman. Where could he be? Asleep somewhere? Or dead?), then this room might be his hangout. The door might be unlocked. And it surely had a telephone.

He ran down the stairs, carefully, soundlessly. At the bottom he paused to listen. Silence. Then a faint, faraway clattering sound. Perhaps a box toppling in the basement. Silence again. The janitor's room was across the rotunda in the west wing. He walked rapidly (too much risk of sound with running). Now that his logic assured him that death was likely, his mind made it seem unreal. He crossed the rotunda floor without the dread he had expected. And now the janitor's door was less than fifty feet away.

"Be open," Cotton prayed. "Be open."

The door was closed, but the knob turned easily in his hand. He closed it behind him. Inside there was almost total blackness. Cotton stood with his back to the door trying to recall the layout of the room. There was a desk, he thought, against the west wall, and shelves with bucket, soap and so forth. But what else? What to stumble into? He had only glanced into the room on walking past. He couldn't remember.

Cotton was aware of a strong chemical aroma—a mixture of something astringent (ammonia perhaps?) and something which smelled sweet and sick and reminded him somehow of accidents and hospitals.

He moved cautiously toward where the desk should be, his hands groping blindly in front of him. They found the edge of the desk, touched a wire basket, papers and finally the smooth, heavy plastic of the base of a telephone.

He wouldn't risk a light. He would dial 0 for the operator and ask her for the police. But his finger paused as it reached the proper hole. The receiver was cold. Cold and dead. No dial tone. He held it against his ear, thinking that this made no sense.

Then he heard, faintly in the dead silence, the sound of breathing.

The sound of air inhaled through nostrils, exhaled slowly, inhaled again. Regular, slow breathing. Just to his left. Only a few feet away. Cotton stepped backward. Opened his mouth. His vocal cords seemed numb. "Who is it?" he whispered. The whisper was loud, almost hysterical. "Who's there?"

Only the sound of breathing. Someone standing there? Staring at him in the darkness? "Who's there?" Cotton whispered again. The breathing didn't change. Asleep? The night watchman? Cotton fumbled in his pockets, found his matches, lit one.

The flare of the light blinded him for a moment. Then he saw behind the desk a fat man looking at him. The man wore the blue uniform of capitol custodial personnel. His gray hair was mussed. His eyes, half opened, looked at Cotton's coat front. He was asleep. Asleep with his eyes open. Then Cotton noticed the blood, a trickle down the side of his neck. And at the same instant he recognized the smell. It was chloroform.

Cotton shook out the dying match, struck another, and examined the man. The blood came from a bruised cut on his left ear. He had been apparently struck on the side of the head and then subdued with the anesthetic. Now he was sleeping it off—probably for hours. Cotton held the match high, inspecting the room. The telephone wire had been cut. The watchman's heavy belt hung from a coat rack, its holster empty. There was no window in this interior room. Two walls were lined with shelves, cans of cleaner, jugs of liquid soap, tool boxes, rolls of insulating tape, cleaning cloths, sponges, boxes of paper towels and toilet paper. And the back wall was partly occupied by the gray metal shape of a circuit-breaker box. Cotton stared at it, at the small lock which secured its metal door, seeing a way to even the odds against him.

He moved two jugs of liquid soap to the desk top out of the way and sorted through a tool box, selecting the heaviest screwdriver. It would be noisy, so he'd have to work fast. With a fourth match, he inspected the lock. Then, working in the dark he jammed the screwdriver under the edge of the door and wrenched it outward with all his strength. The metal screeched and bent. He jammed the screwdriver further in, and wrenched again. This time the lock snapped. Cotton fumbled inside the box, snapping the circuit-breaker toggles down. There seemed to be four rows of five—four circuits for each floor of the building. He flicked them all down.

As he opened the door to what was now utter blackness, there was the sound of running feet, and then a thump and a muffled curse. One of the men—at least one—was on the second floor with him. Across the rotunda, not seventy-five yards away. And the man would know where the circuit breakers were. Where he was. Cotton fumbled at the door knob, found the locking lever, pushed it up to keep the man from restoring the power. Then he grabbed wildly at the desk for something to use as a weapon and ran from the room, slamming the door behind him.

He ran down the corridor toward the stairwell, realizing as he ran that the weapon his hand had reached was one of the plastic jugs of soap. Almost useless. He slowed abruptly, panicked at the thought of crashing blindly down the stairway. As he slowed, he heard running footsteps behind him. At that moment it occurred to him that the soap might save him. He screwed frantically at the cap and ran down the stairs, leaving a splashing stream of the liquid behind him. He reached the bottom, the bottle still gurgling, and sprinted up the dark first-floor hallway. Behind him there was a yell, turned mid-breath into a scream. And then a clattering confusion of thumping, and the sharp crack of metal striking the marble on the stair landing. Then a man moaning.

The Attorney General's office was about here. Cotton felt along the wall, found a doorway, felt the glass pane which bore the gilt lettering. He smashed at it with the soap jug, reached through the shattered glass to unsnap the lock. In the reception room he crashed into the corner of the secretary's desk, lost his balance and fell. Outside, somewhere, a voice was shouting: "Harge, Harge. Where are you?" Cotton was up again. Finding the door to the office of Second Assistant Joey Walters. Finding his way through it, past the desk and the chairs to the window where Joey had removed the heavy screen to keep his bird-feeding box on the sill. Sliding the window up. Jumping six feet into the shrubbery below. Cursing the tearing, breaking branches. Blessing the finches which came to this window to feed, and Joey for feeding them. And then running wildly, sock-footed, across the dead dark grass under the starlight, gulping icy air, and freedom, and safety, and life.

21

When he finally looked at his watch in Janey Janoski's apartment it was eighteen minutes before 4 A.M. Either the nightmare occurrence in the capitol had been incredibly brief or he had set something like a cross-country speed record in traversing the six blocks to Janey's address. He had arrived here without really planning to do so. In his panicky race from the capitol building, his instinct for preservation had led him first down the blackness of the alley behind the Health-Welfare Building and from there down an equally dark residential alley. And then his bursting lungs and a bruised foot forced a halt which allowed his first coherent thought. The only hope of flagging a cab would be on Capitol Avenue. But at this hour there would be no cab—nor any other traffic. The first car which came along might well be his hunters, cruising the streets, knowing that anything that moved would be he. His second thought was to arouse some householder and ask to use the telephone. But when that thought arrived, he was halfway down a third alley and only three blocks away from Janey's place. He had stood in the darkness a long time—watching and listening, making sure he wasn't followed—before he rang her bell.

"I'm warning you right now," Janey Janoski said. "When you finish that cup of coffee you're going to have to answer two questions. If you don't I'm going to make you go home."

"Which two?" He could think of a dozen.

"What did you do with your shoes, for starters? And why are you out jogging at four in the morning? And why not tell the police to come and talk to you? And what in the world happened at the capitol tonight? And . . ."

"That's more than two. I don't want the police to know where I am because I don't want anybody to know where I am," Cotton said. "And that's because I just had the living hell scared out of me, and I'm still scared, and if you give me a minute or two to recover my normal lion-hearted courage, then maybe I'll decide I don't mind if the police know where I am."

"I think maybe the man at the police station thought I was drunk," Janey said. "He wanted to know how I knew the nightwatchman had been chloroformed, and how I knew somebody broke into the Attorney General's office, and how I knew they should be looking for a man in a blue overcoat and a man in a red windbreaker with a cast on his arm, and . . ." Janey paused, and took a breath, "who I was."

"They'll send somebody." It didn't seem important at the moment whether they did or not. With the panic and adrenaline gone, Cotton felt exhaustion, release and comfort. He liked looking at Jane Janoski early in the morning; her hair tousled, eyes still sleepy, no makeup, and her slender shape wrapped in a housecoat or something with rosebuds all over it.

"I like looking at you," he said. To his immense embarrassment, Janey blushed—a genuine, thorough blush—and looked away. Cotton could think of nothing to say, so he said, "I left my shoes in the capitol."

"You don't really have to tell me anything," Janey said. She spoke to the coffeepot—refilling his cup. "I was just kidding about that."

"But we had a deal," Cotton said. "Remember?" He was glad he remembered. It was an opportunity to restore the old bantering relationship. "I was going to tell you how that highway-contract story came out and you were going to tell me what to do with the rabbit—if we caught one." That seemed ironic now. He was the rabbit, nosing into a den of foxes.

"I gathered from what you said on the telephone you'd caught something or other." Her face was grave. "And it sounded dangerous. It still is, isn't it?"

Cotton laughed, wondering, as he listened to it, what he had to laugh about. It was just that he needed sleep. "It was for a while. But it's all right now. Now the only problem is I left the story in my motel room and I don't want to go back there. So, if you have a typewriter here, and paper, and carbon paper, and so forth, I'll try to borrow it from you."

"All I have is an old portable."

"That'll be fine. Why don't you go back to bed?"

"I don't get much excitement," Janey said. "I don't want to miss it when the posse starts pounding on the door. Will *they* be barefoot too?"

"If they're wearing black hats," Cotton said, "tell them to go away."

The rewriting was easy. It's axiomatic in the business that the big ones practically write themselves. This one, when he first tried it, had presented some organizational problems. But, once solved, they were easily remembered. Only the typewriter was balky. Cotton jammed the keys and paused to unjam them, muttering under his breath.

"Come on now," Janey said. "It's a gift horse."

"Here's the lead," Cotton said. "Here's what your looking up 'borrow' in the dictionary led to." He read: "More than a third of a million dollars' worth of cement—paid for with public road funds—has been siphoned away from five highway projects in the past two years and used for privately financed construction."

Jane Janoski's reaction was all that Cotton could have hoped for.

"My God," she said. "Really!? But if that's happening . . ."

Cotton interrupted her, reading on: "The affair was hidden by erroneous Highway Department construction records. They indicate all of the cement was used in the roadbed and bridges of highway projects. Actually, thousands of tons of it were diverted for construction of lodges and recreation roads at nearby state parks.

"Contractor on all five jobs was Reevis-Smith, Constructors, Inc. The same firm was also contractor for Wit's End, Inc., the company picked by the State Park Commission to build and operate state-park concessions under a $30 million recreational bond plan approved by the Legislature three years ago."

"Poor Paul," Janey said. "His recreation thing is in this, too." She got up, put her hand on the coffeepot, and then sat down again. "Poor Paul."

Cotton became aware that the bottom of his left foot was hurting—bruised by something he had stepped on in the alley, that a toe he stubbed was probably bleeding. That his hip was bruised. That he was tired to the point of exhaustion, and that someone was trying to kill him.

"Yeah," he said. "I'm sorry about that." He wasn't. Neither sorry nor pleased. Simply tired. A moment ago he hadn't been aware of it.

He wrote rapidly, pausing no more to read, aware of Janey sitting opposite him, elbows on table, chin on hands, watching him write.

"All five of the road projects involved were

in the Quality Experiment program instituted by Highway Commission Chairman Jason Flowers—projects in which cement content of concrete slab was to be enriched 37 percent.

"On all five projects, Reevis-Smith obtained the contract by offering bids far lower than other contractors on certain items—such as roadbed material. But, after the contract was awarded, the amount of these low-bid items used was reduced by 'change orders,' and the amount used of items, such as aluminum culverts, on which Reevis-Smith had bid high, were increased.

"In each of the five projects, another contractor would have been the low bidder had the original specifications included the change orders. All the change orders were signed by H. L. Singer as project engineer.

"In a procedure unusual for the Highway Department, Singer was transferred from district to district to serve as project engineer on all five jobs. His signature also appears on the concrete weight slips, which erroneously indicate that all of the cement delivered to Reevis-Smith mixing plants was used on the highways.

"The records of hauling companies which also work on the jobs show that $342,000 worth of the mixed cement was actually hauled away from the mixing plants on the highway jobs and delivered to nearby Reevis-Smith projects on the parks."

Cotton paused, thinking. Was it here he stuck in the lying-out-of-it paragraphs? He thought it was.

"Singer declined comment when asked for an explanation. Flowers said he wished to 'look into it' before commenting. And Herman Gay, promoted to Construction Engineer under the Flowers administration, also withheld comment."

He pulled out the page, shook out the carbon paper and dropped the two copies on the table. She picked one up without a word. Cotton put together a second carbon-paper sandwich and put the three sheets in the machine. (Who was it? Some famous writer. Asked if he had any advice for someone who wanted to be a writer, he said, "Always remember the shiny side of the carbon paper has to face away from you." This morning it wasn't amusing.)

Cotton typed, reporting the ownership link between Wit's End and Reevis-Smith through the Highlands Corporation, wishing again that he knew how Midcentral Surety fit into this picture, and wishing fervently that he had something more than circumstance to pin Jason Flowers into this complex corruption. Given a couple of days of digging, and he could nail Flowers.

"This time it's somebody named Singer," Janey said. "Who is he?"

"He's identified there. The project engineer. On all five jobs." The typewriter keys jammed again.

"I mean *who* is he? Is he like Leroy Hall's Mr. Peters? Is he a little skinny man with a mustache? Is he shy, like Arthur Peters?" Janey was staring at him. "You talked to him. It says here he said 'No comment.' Don't you know anything about him? Weren't you curious?"

"Oh," Cotton said. (Janey's eyes were dark, dark, dark. Who are you, Janey Janoski? You're not what they say about you.) "Yes," Cotton said. "But it was on the telephone." He looked down at the typewriter, unclogging the keys. And then back at her. She might as well know it. "But he had a nice voice. And he has a daughter in high school."

"Then why don't you . . ." Her voice trailed off. She just looked at him.

"Why don't I what? Use the child's name? Singer is the father of Alice Singer, a junior at Washington High School, the fat, homely girl who already has social problems and pimples. Point your finger at her, classmates. Her daddy is a thief."

Cotton typed. Changed pages. Typed again. Details now of how the bid rigging worked. Background on the Quality Experiment program. Background on the way the park-concession contracts were granted—with private firms like Wit's End submitting the development plans, using allocations from the state bond fund for construction, paying it back with concession fees.

And finally he was finishing it, with the final paragraphs based on the information Rickner had given him about the pattern of transfers within the Highway Department. And Janey broke the heavy silence between them, talking over the sound of the typewriter keys.

"I can't understand it," she said.

Cotton's anger surprised him. "Goddamn it. It's easy enough to understand. Some bastard steals the public's money. The public has a right to know about it."

"And if you don't do it somebody else has to," Janey said. Her voice was very low. "That's what my husband said. In the Navy. Flying a fighter-bomber. He said somebody had to do it. But it wasn't really that. When he had the hundred missions he volunteered for another tour."

Cotton looked at her. (She wasn't explaining it to him. She was explaining it to herself. Now I see a little more of you, Janey Janoski. Now I know you a little better.)

"He didn't hate anybody. The bombs didn't really hurt anybody. It was Dick against the antiaircraft guns. It was a game you played."

The room was silent again. Cotton could think of nothing to say.

"But people do get hurt," Janey said. "Mr. Peters and Mr. Singer—and somebody threatened to kill you." She looked at him. "Somebody tried to kill you tonight, I think. That's what was happening at the capitol, wasn't it? Somebody trying to kill you because of this article?"

"Somebody doesn't want it printed. I guess that's obvious."

"So why do you do it?" It was an honest question. Not part of an argument. "Everybody gets hurt. Mr. Singer and Mr. Singer's daughter and Paul's reputation as Governor, and his chance at the Senate. And maybe you get killed."

Cotton was tempted to tell her. To explain that printing it was his way of not getting hurt, of ending the hunt for him. But why?

Why not let her think he too was playing some Don Quixote game of ethics and morality? Anyway, that was part of it. And her interest really wasn't with him, or with Singer, or Singer's daughter-in-high-school. It was with Paul Roark. (Know yourself, Janey Janoski. Examine your own motives.) His anger returned, hardened, the decision quickly made, the product of fatigue and emotion.

He pushed the chair back, got up, handed her the last pages of the story, jammed the carbon copy in his coat pocket.

"I'm going to let you try it for yourself, Janey. I told you I would. I said I'd give you a chance to rescue the rabbit. So you decide."

He walked to the telephone table, flipped through the yellow pages, looking for "Taxicab." "You'll have to play by the rules. That means you can't put it off. You have a deadline. If you take it to work with you and get it to Rickner in the pressroom by 9 A.M. that makes the first edition. He teletypes it to the city desk and they have it in time."

Cotton found the Checker Cab number and started dialing. "There's another rule. Between thinking about Singer and Paul Roark, you have to think a little bit about this cab driver I'm calling. He pays his taxes out of money he could use for his own daughter in high school. He has a right . . ."

Somebody at the cab company answered the telephone.

Cotton gave him Janey's address and ordered a cab. The dispatcher, sounding sleepy, promised it in ten minutes.

"Keep this cabbie in mind," Cotton continued. "If he doesn't know somebody's stealing his money, the mess doesn't get cleaned up."

"This isn't fair," Janey said. "It's your story. What if I . . ."

"The best you can do is give Singer a reprieve," Cotton said. "My managing editor knows a lot about this now. They'll dig it out." He thought about telling her that if she didn't give Rickner the story for today, he would have to deliver it tomorrow. Would have to because he owed that much to the *Tribune.* He was their man. At least he was while he was working the yarn, and until he could get his resignation to Danilov. And the yarn belonged to the *Tribune* just as much as its printing presses did. But why make it easy for her?

"There's another way to do this," Janey said. "You could tell Paul about it. He could clean it up. The cab driver doesn't have to know."

"What if Paul already knows about it?"

"You don't believe that."

As a matter of fact, he didn't believe it. But the outrage in Janey's voice hurt and he wasn't going to admit it.

"If he doesn't know, he's supposed to. It's his administration. His Highway Commission and his Park Commission."

Janey picked up the coffeepot, took it into the kitchen.

"One other thing," Cotton said. "Discount what you said about me getting hurt. There's no reason left for anything like that now. It's all over with."

Janey's answer came from the kitchen. "Not quite," she said. "It won't be over with for Mr. Singer."

> 22 <

At the truck-stop café where the cab left him, Cotton realized there was just one thing left to do. Then it would be as complete and tidy as he could make it. He would call in his IOU from Joe Korolenko. He would tell the National Committeeman everything he knew and ask Korolenko to examine these facts and tell him what was behind them. He had no doubt that Korolenko's generation-spanning knowledge of the state's politics, politicians and power structure would make it easy for the old man to put it all into perspective. Korolenko would be able to guess who was behind Flowers, how the deal was set up, how the fixes were arranged. And he had little doubt that Korolenko would tell him. It would have to be off the record, but that wouldn't matter. Korolenko would tell, unless the facts caused the old man to suspect that Paul Roark was the fixer. If that was the case, he would be evasive, because Roark was one of his own. Otherwise Korolenko would talk freely, because he owed Cotton a favor.

The IOU dated back more than four years to another session of political maneuvering. It involved persuading a man not to file as a candidate for Congress in the Democratic primary. Korolenko hadn't asked the favor. He had simply approached Cotton in the Senate lounge and explained the problem, letting his eyes make the request.

And Cotton had done it. He had called the would-be candidate, and had obliquely let the man know the press hadn't forgotten a grand-jury investigation involving him. Two days later the man had announced he wasn't running. It seemed a small favor.

Later Korolenko had stopped him in a statehouse hall and said simply: "Thank you very much." And a dozen times since then, Korolenko had suggested he would like to return the favor, wipe out the debt. It was one of the oldest and most necessary rules of the game. No successful politican could afford to forget either a favor or an offense. Both had to be repaid or the system wouldn't work.

Now he would make an appointment, call

in the IOU, pass the information on to Danilov to exhaust any debt he owed the *Tribune.* And that would tie a string around it. He would be finally finished, done.

On the fourth ring, someone picked up the phone. It was Korolenko's soft voice.

"This is a hell of a time to be calling, Governor," Cotton said. "I hope I didn't interrupt your breakfast. But I need to talk to you."

"Old men rise early," Korolenko said. "What do you need?"

"Probably about forty-five minutes of your time. Just as soon as possible if you feel up to it."

"I'm fine. Come on out to the house."

The sleet started as the taxi pulled onto the freeway, an icy flurry which rattled off the windshield and inspired a curse from the cab driver. The driver fiddled with the dial of the transistor radio on the front seat beside him and finally found a newscast. An oil slick from a leaking tanker was fouling Virginia beaches. Governor Roark had signed seven bills into law, including a measure authorizing the transfer of the criminally insane from the state prison to a new maximum-security facility at the state mental hospital. Senator Eugene Clark was addressing the annual convention of the State Dental Association at noon today—at the Senate Downtowner Hotel. He was expected to officially announce his candidacy for reelection. The Secretary of Defense warned—in a speech before the U.S. Chamber of Commerce—that the growth of the Soviet missile submarine fleet was a critical threat to national security. The first serious storm of winter was invading the state. Highways in the northern counties were icing and sleet and snow was expected in most counties during the day. The weather bureau forecasts . . .

Cotton hardly heard the forecast. He was hearing Janey's voice. "Who gets hurt this time?" Those were the words. But what was the tone? Not angry. Not until he lost his temper, and not even then. He shook his head. He shouldn't have left her with the decision. It wasn't fair. A senseless act of anger.

The cab took the interchange ramp leading to Hillsdale Avenue. The sleet was steady now—tiny granules of white tapping the glass, whipping across the concrete in grainy flurries. Without the newsman's conditioning to deadlines, Janey would probably decide by not deciding—by putting it off until time made its own automatic, negative decision. Or perhaps she would call Paul Roark. That would be the second inviting compromise. But he wasn't sure, because he wasn't sure he knew Janey Janoski. He would know when the *Tribune* mail edition hit the newsstands. Either it would carry the story or it wouldn't. This would mean simply that he would send his carbon copy to Danilov and that he would have one more day of hiding to survive. And it would confirm that he had failed in his effort to make Janey understand him.

Korolenko's curving driveway, protected from the wind by a high wall and a double row of poplars, had collected enough sleet to cause the taxi to slide as it braked to a stop. Cotton stood for a second, hunched in his coat, admiring the house. It was a graceful place, warm and dignified, fitting its occupant.

Korolenko met him at the door, hung his coat in the entryway closet and ushered him through the dark living room. In the light from the door to the den, the bigger room looked formal and unused and somehow lonely. No logs in the fireplace, no magazines on the coffee table, every chair exactly in place. Cotton remembered that Mrs. Korolenko had died five or six years ago. Did the old man live all alone in this big house?

"If you haven't eaten," Korolenko said, "I

can get you something like a sandwich. But Mrs. Ellis is always off on Tuesdays. Goes to visit her sister."

"Thanks," Cotton said. "I've eaten."

"A drink then? You still take a sip of bourbon and no water?" He waved Cotton toward a deep leather-covered chair.

"You've got quite a memory, Governor. It's been three years since I've been here."

Korolenko poured, his back to Cotton. "Too long. Much too long. But I even remember you don't have that uncivil prejudice against whiskey in the morning."

The den was a startling contrast to the living room. Here, obviously, the old man lived. A fire burned in the grate. Sections of the *Morning Journal,* yesterday's *Tribune* and the *Capitol-Press* were scattered on the worn sofa and the table beside it. A coffee cup sat on a *Newsweek* atop the television set. A chair beside Cotton's was stacked with bound editions of county-by-county voting tabulations from past elections. The walls were lined with framed photographs of bird dogs and paintings of ducks; the parts of a disassembled shotgun, oily rags and a cleaning kit littered Korolenko's big desk.

Korolenko delivered the drink and waited in easy silence while Cotton sipped.

The whiskey was good, warming the mouth and the throat and, finally, the stomach. Cotton hadn't realized how badly he had needed it. It had been a hell of a long night.

"Drink up and I'll fix you another. You look shot."

"Thanks. Maybe later." Cotton paused, looking for a way to start. What he had to say would be bad news for the old man. It could only reflect on the Roark administration, on Korolenko's wing of the Democratic party.

Behind his desk, Korolenko polished a part of the dismantled trigger assembly, put on his bifocals, and inspected his work. Cotton took another slow sip of the bourbon, savoring the warmth and the comfortable silence.

"I saw in the *Trib* that you're on sick leave," Korolenko said. "I hope it's nothing serious." He smiled at Cotton. "If Catherine was still here, she'd be having us both saying prayers for your recovery."

"It's nothing serious. In fact I'm not really on leave at all. That's part of what I want to talk to you about." He put down his glass. "What I want to do is tell you about some bad business in the Highway Department, and in the Park Commission, and maybe in the Insurance Commission. Then I'm going to remind you that I once ran an errand for you.

And then I'm going to ask you to return the favor by backgrounding me on what you guess is behind this bad business."

"You don't have to remind me I owe you something. I don't forget." Korolenko's smile was gone now. "But I hope this business isn't too bad. There's an election coming up."

"Here's what you've got. You've got bid rigging in the Quality Experiment highway projects. You've got one contractor getting these special jobs. Then you've got change orders increasing his high-bid items and reducing the parts of the job where he bid low. Then you've got . . ."

"Who's the contractor?"

"Reevis-Smith."

The old man's frail hands were still at work on the shotgun parts—polishing cloth on metal. But his eyes were on Cotton, his face totally intent. "Yes," he said. "It would be Reevis-Smith."

"That doesn't amount to a lot of money. Not the change orders. Where it gets big is in cement." Cotton explained how the cement shipments were diverted into the park improvement, into the Wit's End projects. And then he outlined his suspicions that another dimension of the affair involved Midcentral Surety, which bonded all of the companies.

"I don't have that pinned down yet," Cotton said. "But I'm sure it's there."

"So that part's speculative," Korolenko said. "How much of the rest of it is guesswork?"

"None of it. Except for Midcentral I've got a lock on everything I told you about. It's solid."

"So you plan to print it." It wasn't a question. It had a toneless quality, a sort of despair that touched Cotton and then touched off a conditioned alertness coupled instantly with a sense of self-disgust. He looked down at his coffee cup, away from Korolenko's still face.

"Yes," Cotton said. "The people have a right to . . ."

"Let's save that," Korolenko said. It was a tone Cotton had never heard him use before. "Have you thought about the implications if you print it now? The timing? The effect on the election?"

"Sure, I've thought about it. It won't do Paul Roark any good. I can see that. But maybe it won't hurt much." He wanted Korolenko to understand. "That's why I'm here. I want you to tell me what's behind it. What the implications are."

"Don't you see them?"

"I see it with the Roark campaign," Cotton said. He was leaning forward, his voice earnest. "We nail corruption in the Highway Department and probably in the Park Commission. Roark reacts immediately by firing his commission chairman, rooting some people out of the department, cleaning house over in parks. He calls a series of press conferences. He gets the Attorney General to investigate. On one hand, he's hurt by it at first. But in a week or so, he's the man on the white horse. He's Mr. Clean again, brushing out the stables."

"Is that what you think?"

"It makes sense," Cotton said. "What I need to know from you is another sort of implication. Flowers isn't the brains behind this business. Who is? And where did the money come from to take over Reevis-Smith? Where did the money come from to set this up? That's the important question."

Korolenko ignored it. "You see Paul being Mr. Clean again," he said. He got up, stiffly, unlocked the glass door on the gun case behind the desk and replaced the reassembled shotgun in the rack between an automatic with a choke on its barrel, and an old-fashioned-looking pump-action duck gun.

"What do you think of Paul?" he asked. "How well do you know him?"

They were not casual questions. Cotton thought before he answered. "Not as well as I know you, I guess. And I like him. I respect him. He's a good man."

"Better than Eugene Clark?"

Cotton laughed. "I'd say that."

The weight of the glass gun-case door was swinging it slowly open. It reflected now Joe Korolenko's profile, a fragile skull covered with taut translucent skin. In the reflection, Cotton noticed that part of the lobe of Korolenko's left ear was missing. He had never noticed that before.

"So we'll start with that, then," the old man said. "Roark's better." He walked around the desk and stood looking out at the rattling sleet. "It would be tolerable if Clark believed in anything. I can respect a man who is conservative. Who believes it. You need the Tafts and the Dirksens, and even the Goldwaters." Korolenko was talking to the window, his hands clasped behind him. "But Clark believes in nothing but opportunism. Did you notice his vote on the forestry conservation bill last week? He voted with the Republicans. A lot of honorable men voted that way because they think it will bring the price of lumber down. But Eugene Clark voted because the Hefrons and the Federal Citybank are up to their ears in papermill investments."

"Hefrons?"

"Richard Hefron, Randolph Hefron," Korolenko said. "And their kinfolks. They own that new shopping center here, and Commercial Credit, and a lot of small loan interests, and real estate, and now big interests with Citybank in paper and lumber." Korolenko turned away from the window, hands still behind him. "Or take his vote on that second phase of the disarmament treaty. Clark tells the Democratic grassroots bunch that he'll probably be for it and three days later he has lunch with some people in Washington and they remind Clark that Citybank had underwritten all those defense-industry bond issues. Anyway, Clark votes no." Korolenko turned now, away from the window, looking at Cotton. "That's always been the story with Clark since he was the youngest man in the state Legislature. When it counts, Clark's vote has always been where Clark benefits and to hell with philosophy." Korolenko paused. "He's talking to the dentists at lunch today. He'll be conservative. Next week he speaks at the AFL-CIO meeting. He'll be liberal."

Cotton was uncomfortable under Korolenko's eyes. "No argument," he said. "Roark's better."

"Look at Roark then. City Commission chairman at twenty-nine. Broke the hold of the real-estate people on zoning and planning. Straightened out the Police Department and got rid of the shakedown artists. And on the State Board of Finance he's the one who forced the holding banks to pay interest on state general-fund deposits. And he's . . ." Korolenko shook his head. "I don't have to recite what you already know. Roark's a dedicated Jeffersonian. He's . . ."

"O.K.," Cotton said. "I buy it. I like him. I like his politics. But I don't let whom I like show in how I do my job."

"Goddamn it. Listen to me. Only a fool can be neutral. You're not a fool. I don't think you're a fool."

"Look," Cotton said. "You listen." He was tired, exhausted, and feeling the bourbon and his rising anger. "You fault Gene Clark for having no political philosophy. Well, I've got one. I believe if you give them the facts the majority of the people are going to pull down the right lever on the voting machine. A lot of them are stupid. And a lot of them don't give a damn. And some of them have closed minds and won't believe anything they don't want to believe. But enough of them care so if you tell them what's going on they make the right decisions." Cotton paused, thinking how to say it. "So I don't believe in playing God," he said. "I don't buy this elitism crap. I don't go for suppressing news because the so-called common man won't know how to handle it. I don't . . ."

"Sure," Korolenko said. "Sure. But in this case that leaves a question. You just print part of the facts. Sometimes there's a difference between facts and truth. Here you show them the dirt you've uncovered in the Roark administration. But you're not going to say: 'On the other hand . . .' You're not going to say, 'But this mess is relatively minor. Because Eugene Clark has sold out to Citybank. Because the Senior Senator doesn't represent you people, he represents only the financial interests which benefit him.' You won't say that because that's another level of truth. It's not the 'verifiable truth' you people talk about in the pressroom."

"That's part of not playing God," Cotton said. "It's not enough to just think it's true."

Korolenko turned from the window, walking slowly back behind his desk. He stood there, leaning on his knuckles, staring at Cotton.

"How can you say you don't play God? Is destroying a good young man not playing God? Let me tell you what happens when you print that story. You say Roark cleans his own nest and survives. But here's what happens. George W. Bryce is District Attorney in this judicial district. George is part of what Clark is building in this state. He's Clark's boy. While Roark is asking the Attorney General to investigate, George Bryce is summoning a grand jury. Some of this stuff you have is criminal and a lot must be at least on the border. And I don't have to tell you how a D.A. can manipulate a jury. He can string it out from now until primary day. And Roger Boyden will be right at Bryce's elbow, looking for the dirt and telling George where the damage needs to be done, doing Clark's hatchet work as he always does." Korolenko stopped, took a deep, sighing breath, looked down at his hands and then back at Cotton. "Boyden's already at it, you know. Ever since he flew in from Washington he's been collecting the mud for the primary campaign. You know how it will work with Boyden and Bryce. There'll be a dozen indictments released the day before the election. And what difference does it make if the court throws half of them out six months later? And what difference does it make if the trial jury finds them innocent? He builds the impression that Roark's administration is a mare's nest of corruption." Korolenko paused, with the orator's instinct for impact. "And you've ruined the best hope this state has had."

Cotton said nothing. He was thinking of Boyden. Boyden—who had been AP's second man at the statehouse for ten years before becoming Clark's press secretary. Boyden—who would know exactly how to start a political reporter hunting where Boyden wanted a hunt made. Boyden—who would have access to the sort of information given to McDaniels. He saw with sudden certainty that Boyden must be the author of those three unsigned and arrogant letters. On the other end of the string which had pulled McDaniels and now pulled him was Gene Clark's hatchet man. The fourth letter, the one addressed to him, was another matter. Flowers wrote it, probably. Or someone working with Flowers.

Korolenko was talking again. No anger in his voice now. Just a flatness. "So what do you decide?" Korolenko was asking. "Do you print it?"

But the decision was made. Or maybe Janey had made it. If she believed in him, the copy had already been handed to Rickner, had already been teletyped to the city desk, already converted into part of the day's merchandise of news, capped with a headline. And what would it say? GRAFT FOUND IN STATEHOUSE, STATE CORRUPTION AIRED. He thought of Paul Roark. Roark behind his desk, with his wry smile, discussing his future. He saw Roark the man, with a razor cut on his chin and wrinkles around his eyes, and he turned away from the thought. The headline wouldn't shout, PAUL ROARK'S HOPES SLAIN, GOV. ROARK'S CAREER ENDS.

"Look, Governor," Cotton said. "It's not as black as you make it. Roark has his own access to the press and you know it. And we'll be watching Bryce. He can't get away with much and the Governor can make it clear that he wasn't personally . . ."

Korolenko held up his hand. "Then you intend to print it."

"I haven't told you all of it," Cotton said. He was talking fast, desperately wanting the old man to understand. "Not quite. When Mac died last week. That wasn't an accident. He was working on the same story and somebody pushed him over the railing and then tried to get his notes. And Robbins. That wasn't a hit-and-run case. He was driving my car, and the next night I got a death threat. And three days ago they tried to kill me. It was . . ."

Cotton's voice trailed off, stopped by the pain in Korolenko's expression. The old man's face was bloodless, slack. What was it? Shock? Or grief?

Cotton half rose from the chair. "Governor, are you all right?"

Korolenko turned away, one bony hand on the gun-case door. "I'm all right," he said.

Cotton looked away, out the window, out at the sleet blowing through the barren trees, out at the gray, cold, bitter world. "How could I suppress it? I could run away again. I did it once and I could do it again. Run away and leave it. But damn it, Governor, the people need to know about it. You've got to believe in them. You've got to believe in something. Can you understand how I feel about it?"

Korolenko's voice was dim, barely audible in the silent room. "I can understand," he was saying. "And you can understand what I'm doing, and why I have to do it."

Korolenko was holding the pump shotgun, its barrel pointed approximately at Cotton's chest. He could see the blackness of the muzzle and above it the bright bead sight. "But knowing you're the kind who understands won't make it any easier," Korolenko continued. "It makes it harder."

"Put it down, Governor, put down the shotgun."

"I can't possibly let that story be printed."

"You're not going to shoot me," Cotton said. And he laughed, a laugh touched with hysteria. This was beyond reason, beyond belief. He sat back in the chair, dizzied by this, trying through the alcohol and fatigue to digest it. "You wouldn't do it."

"I would," Korolenko said. "But you need to know why that story can't be printed. Not ever. If it is, if it gives Bryce the leads for a grand jury there's no hope for Paul or the party. No hope." Korolenko raised his left hand slowly from the desk top and rubbed it downward across his face—wiping away something invisible. "Because the grand jury will find that Midcentral Surety is the principal—almost the only—contributor of funds to the Effective Senate Committee. And it will find that the Effective Senate Committee bank account has been used to pay for Paul's precampaign expenses. Underwriting the organizing costs."

Cotton stared at the shotgun. None of this was real.

"You're telling me Roark sold out," Cotton said.

"The Governor doesn't know about it. Not unless he's guessed. But you can see that doesn't make a damned bit of difference. The voters would never believe it. The point is Bryce's grand jury would have subpoena power. It would tie everything in your story right to the Governor's campaign."

The shotgun wasn't loaded. Korolenko, the bird hunter, wouldn't keep anything loaded in his gun case. It probably wasn't loaded. This was just a desperate bluff. "But for God's sake," Cotton said, "how could Roark possibly not . . ."

"Come on," Korolenko said. His voice was impatient. "You know how it works. There are always approaches. Every day. Every campaign. A trucking company would like to contribute ten thousand dollars to a campaign fund and it would appreciate a little sympathetic understanding by axle weighers at the ports-of-entry scales. Or a real-estate developer would like to kick in to the kitty and he could afford to do it if he was fairly sure where interchanges would be located on one of the interstate highways. Or the State

Manufacturers Association is looking for a place to spend its political-action funds and it wonders if the Governor would veto any bill increasing workmen's compensation rates. Or Citybank and First National and Financial Trust would like to help finance a campaign, but they're worried about a proposed branch banking law and they want a little reassurance. You've seen it."

"Sure," Cotton said. The shotgun had dipped. It pointed now about at Cotton's lap. "But there's a little difference, Governor. In cases like that you can argue that all the contributor is buying is someone who sees things his way. What Roark sold was a license to steal. And . . ." Cotton paused, choked suddenly by his anger. "And a license to murder. How much did Paul charge for the lives of McDaniels and Robbins?"

"You're very moral, aren't you?" Korolenko's voice was shaking. "Let's talk about morality then. What happened to those two men shouldn't have happened. You can't forget it, and you can't forgive it, and you go to your grave thinking about it. But let's talk about murder. You were covering the Legislature when the Taxpayers Association had the votes in the Appropriations Committee to gut the Health Department budget. This state damn near had tuberculosis under control then. But the testing program went down the drain and the outpatient medication project was cut, and the rate slipped back up again. And the home nursing program was chopped back. And the sanitation inspections. And how many died because of all that? And six years ago, when Governor Hill vetoed that income-tax bill and cut back on the Welfare Department budget. I remember reading in your *Tribune* about a suicide that year. You remember that? Turned on the gas in the hovel she was living in and killed herself and her three kids. And you remember the note? She said her relief check had been cut from $160 a month to $118 and she just couldn't feed 'em. If you want to talk about morality, there's all kinds of morality. And there's all kinds of murder." Korolenko paused, staring at Cotton. "And, as I told you, Roark didn't know about it."

"He had to."

"He didn't have to, and he didn't. All Paul knew was what we told him. If Jason Flowers was named chairman of the Highway Commission and a couple of changes were made in the State Park Commission, we could assure ourselves of adequate financing for a statewide senatorial primary. That's all he knew. It's been done by every administration."

"We? We would be you, and Congressman Gavin, and who else? And how much money is 'adequate financing'? And where did it come from?" As he asked the questions, Cotton realized Korolenko couldn't answer them—not with an empty shotgun. What he was really asking was, "Governor, is the shotgun loaded? Would you really kill a man?"

"It was $200,000," Korolenko said.

The shotgun was loaded. Cotton felt his stomach tighten.

"About half of what it will take," the old man was saying. "But in cash. On deposit." Korolenko put the telephone receiver on the desk top and dialed while he talked, still cradling the shotgun on his right arm. "It's there for the early organizing, where it attracts the bandwagon boys, the bet hedgers. With that much to start we can run a $500,000 campaign. Clark can't raise much more than that and it's all we'll need. It means we can tie up television time in advance. And we pay an agency for the effective spots and the slick TV telethons and have a committee working in every county. And it means . . ."

The receiver Korolenko held against his ear made a squawking noise. "This is Joseph

Korolenko," the old man said. "Get Jason Flowers on the phone. Right now. It's important."

The receiver squawked again.

"Call him out of the meeting, then. Tell him he'll talk to me now or he'll go to jail." He looked back at Cotton. "And it means organized labor knows we can win and the unions will go all out. And it means all those who would help if they weren't afraid of Clark will help because they see a chance to be rid of him. With early money, we'll have our share of the uncommitted professionals. There won't be any more of this trying to campaign by borrowing cars, and using borrowed credit cards, and signing notes, and hiding from the bill collectors, and finding the prime TV time all contracted by the other side before you get the cash to—

"Flowers. I'm standing here holding a gun on a reporter. He's got you cold. I gather you turned out to be pretty greedy. Anyway, he has all your dirt dug up. I want you to . . ."

Squawk, squawk-squawk. Squawk-squawk-squaaawk-squawk.

"Shut up," Korolenko said. "It's John Cotton. Your connections seem practiced at taking care of problems like this. I gather they took care of McDaniels and Whitey Robbins."

The telephone made fast unintelligible sounds.

"Wait a minute," Cotton said.

"That or go to prison," Korolenko said. "I don't care about you, you son-of-a-bitch, but I care about Roark. Don't talk to me. Just do whatever dirty thing you have to do. I'll keep him here."

"Wait," Cotton said. "Governor, it's too late."

Korolenko was listening to the sound from the telephone, looking at Cotton. "Yes," he said, and hung up.

"It's too late. The story's already filed," Cotton said. "I teletyped it to the *Tribune* this morning—just before I came out here."

Korolenko held the shotgun in both hands now, pointing approximately at Cotton's throat. His eyes were fixed on Cotton's. Somewhere in the old house a timber creaked. A flurry of sleet rattled against the window.

"I don't believe you."

"It's true."

"If it's true, it's all over with. Roark won't have . . ." Korolenko stopped. "When will it be printed?"

Cotton thought about it. But there was no use thinking. Either Janey had believed in him or she hadn't. "It should have made the mail edition." He glanced at the clock above the fireplace. "That's on the street in less than a hour."

"We'll wait," Korolenko said. He lowered himself wearily into the chair behind the desk and sat, looking at the shotgun. Almost, Cotton thought, as if he couldn't believe it was in his hands.

"I believe you're lying," Korolenko said slowly. "Because why would you come here if the story was already at the paper?"

"Because I wanted to be done with it. Done with it once and for all. I wanted to tie up the loose ends, clean it all up, put it in a package so I wouldn't owe the *Trib* a thing. And then I was going to quit."

"Quit? Isn't it a little late to quit?" Korolenko laughed, but the sound was bitter. "Why not stick around and watch? The man who dynamites the dam should enjoy the flood."

Cotton ignored it.

"What's Flowers going to do?"

Korolenko laughed again. "He is going to wring his hands, and feel sorry for himself. And then he will call whoever it is . . . probably a man I can think of in Chicago . . . who-ever it is who arranged for McDaniels to be pushed and for you to be shot at. And he will tell this man what I told him. And then he will walk into his private bath and wash his hands thoroughly."

"And somebody will be coming here after me. The people who tried to kill me . . ."

"That's how I understand it. But now we'll all wait. If the story is in today's *Tribune,* all of this is done and over with. There's no more damage left for you to do."

Cotton pushed himself to his feet. "I'm not waiting for anything. I'm walking out of here."

"Not yet. Not alive."

"Governor. Don't be silly. You wouldn't shoot me. I never thought for a moment you would. You wouldn't shoot anyone."

Cotton turned, took one step, and the blast of the shotgun was deafening thunder in the room. By the door to the living room the wallpaper blossomed into an explosion of dust where the pattern of pellets smashed through paste, lathe and plaster. And then there was the clack-clack sound of the pump action putting a second shell into the chamber.

"Sit down, John. Please. Do me that favor.

If you try to leave, I'll kill you. And maybe it will be for nothing. If the story's in the *Tribune* it would be for nothing at all. You'll have destroyed Roark, and destroyed everything I've worked for. But you can spare me having blood on my hands for nothing."

Cotton sat down. "This doesn't make sense," he said.

"Yes, it does," Korolenko said. "It does if you understand." The shotgun still pointed at Cotton, blue smoke trickling thinly from its muzzle now, the room filled with the acrid blueness of burned gunpowder. "It does when you know the kind of man Eugene Clark is."

"What don't I know?"

"You weren't here when I made my run for the United States Senate. I was fifty-four then. In Congress. Too old to wait. And the time was right. Old Senator Johnson died and the central committee gave me the nomination for the special election to finish the two years left in his term. The Republicans put up old Judge Ainsley and there was no doubt how it would come out. And then about three weeks before the election the word started going around that I had cousins who were officials of the Communist party in Yugoslavia. It was during the Joe McCarthy days, the red-scare days with the right-wingers in full cry and the liberals on the run and the public frightened."

"I heard about that campaign," Cotton said. "That it was dirty."

"You heard about part of it. Ainsley was too good a man to use that stuff, but it was used. Used everywhere, by something called Save America . . . Mostly direct mail and handout pamphlets . . . It was all documented, names, party titles, the whole thing. And it was killing us." Korolenko smiled—a painful thing. "I remember talking to Eugene Clark about it. He was on the ticket too, running for his second term from the Sixth Congressional District against a nobody. I remember apologizing to him because it was hurting the party." Korolenko was in the past now, talking not to Cotton but to the room—reliving it.

The voice droned on, slow words without expression, as if the old man were listening to them himself.

". . . we got the last poll the Saturday before the election and it showed I was marginal, trailing the slate. And then election night it was obvious early, almost from the first precincts. The people were afraid of Communism and they were afraid of me. We were watching the returns right here. Gavin was here, and some of the younger people who had been working with me, and Catherine was in and out serving coffee and seeing about things and being the hostess. Catherine always stayed away from politics. She didn't understand it. She just understood being a wife, and my ambitions. And she was here that night because she knew that this was really all I had wanted all of my life. She didn't know why I wanted it, but she wanted it for me. So she was here that night—mixing with the politicians—because she sensed it might be going wrong and she wanted to be close in case she could help."

Korolenko drew a long, shaking breath and sat for a moment looking past Cotton through the doorway into the cold, dark living room. "So she heard the talk about the Communist cousins in Yugoslavia, and my people wondering where the radical right had found out about it, and, after a while, I noticed she was gone. And I found her up in our bedroom." He stopped again, looking at Cotton. "Crying. I'd never seen her cry before," he said, hoping this stranger before him could understand. "She asked me if I was losing, and I said I was, and she asked me why, and I told her. God help me. I told her it was because somehow they had found out about my family in the old country. And, and . . ." The old man's voice shook. "God help me, Catherine got down on her knees there, and begged me to forgive her, and told me that she had been the one who had ruined me. That she had talked about it to Eugene Clark's wife, chatted about the family coming from Pula, down the coast from Trieste, and how our grandfathers had known each other, and how my own family was split between Royalists and Social Democrats, and how some of my uncles had sided with Mikhailovitch Royalists and some with Tito's partisans, and how I now had a cousin who was the Mayor of Pula and another who was an official in the Bosnian People's party, and another was in Tito's Foreign Office."

Korolenko's voice stopped again. The electric clock behind him clicked. The pale light from the window reflected from a film of moisture in Korolenko's eyes, on his cheek. And then the voice began again, still flat and emotionless, the voice of a man reciting to himself a story he has repeated a thousand times. "And she begged me to forgive her, and I told her there was nothing to forgive. But she never forgave herself. She had always been a happy woman, a joyful woman, but it was never the same after that. She did *penance* for years and then she got pneumonia. That was her chance. She died of it because she didn't want to live."

The room was silent now. The sound of sleet on the windows. The sound of time ticking by.

"Have you ever loved a woman, John? Most men haven't. But, if you have, I think you know I'm willing to kill you if it would help retire Eugene Clark from the Senate."

"But Clark was a Democrat," Cotton said. "Part of your slate. Do you think . . ."

"I know. I took the trouble to find out, and to find exactly how he got the word out, and who he got it to. It's easy to see why he did it. Ainsley beat me and two years later, when he ran for the full six-year term, Clark got the nomination and beat him in the general election. If I had won, Clark could never have beaten me. Not in the Democratic primary. He did it to keep the job open for himself."

Korolenko made another call then, long distance. Asking someone to go down to the Tribune office, pick up a street edition as soon as it was out, and call him back.

And then they waited. The old man sat slumped in his chair, the shotgun on the desk in front of him, his eyes looking past Cotton at nothing. Cotton tried to think. His problem now had been reduced to a single dimension. If Janey had given Rickner the story he need only wait. In less than an hour the telephone would bring that news to Korolenko and it would be over. But, if she hadn't, he should be doing something. He should be trying to get out of here, to get the shotgun away from Korolenko before the call to Jason Flowers bore its fruit, before whoever had hunted him arrived here and found him helpless. Right now, at this moment, a car must be moving through the sleet toward this house—its driver knowing the quarry had been finally cornered. A sudden sense of desperate urgency overcame the buzzing fatigue in Cotton's brain. Korolenko's face was still, blank, intent on some remembered landscape of the mind. The ashtray on the table beside his chair was thick, heavy glass. Cotton reached his right hand toward it, hoping the motion would seem casual.

"No," Korolenko said. "Don't do that."

Cotton left his hand where it lay, feeling the polished varnish of the table under his palm, looking into Korolenko's eyes. He saw the dark brown pupils behind the film of old age. Opaque eyes which looked back at him now as upon an object. Cotton was aware of the lingering smell of burned powder, aware that the shot Korolenko had fired past him had not really convinced him that the old man would, indeed, be willing to kill him. Now the blankness in Korolenko's eyes convinced him. He withdrew the hand, dropped it in his lap, looking at Korolenko and considering this new insight into the human species. The thought led him to Leroy Hall. It explained what had baffled him for two days. Hall had suppressed the story—done the unthinkable—for the same reason old Governor Joe Korolenko was prepared to kill. Like Korolenko, Hall saw himself as part of it all. Involved. Hall hadn't been bribed. He had known more than Cotton. Known a lot more and felt a lot more.

Cotton stopped thinking of the peculiar nature of Hall's betrayal. He thought of Janey Janoski. Then he noticed the change in Korolenko's face. The tension had left it.

The old man sat behind the shotgun looking somehow content—as if some inner doubt had been resolved. The question shaped itself in Cotton's mind—normally not a question that he could ask, but the shotgun between Korolenko and him formed a sort of link, creating an odd intimacy.

"Governor," Cotton said, "I want to ask you

something about Mrs. Korolenko. Were there times when she thought what you were doing was wrong? And if that happened, how was it then? How was it between you?"

Korolenko looked surprised. "Weren't you married once?"

"No," Cotton said.

Korolenko was thinking about it. "Yes," he said, "there were times. But it was all right with us. Because she knew I did what I did because I had to do it." He stopped, trying to frame the words to explain—giving up. "Catherine understood me."

"If you were the reporter," Cotton persisted, "would she have understood why you had to write it? Even if she thought it was a terrible, damaging thing?"

"Yes. She would have." There was no hesitation in the answer. "And now I have a question for you. Entirely aside from the personal situation we have here now, would you publish that story knowing what I've told you?"

"I don't know," Cotton said. "Not for sure. I'd have to think about it. But I guess I would. Who am I to be judge and jury? I don't think I'd have the right not to print it."

"But you have to judge. You're a human being. You're in this, too. We're all in it together. You and I and all of us. We have to judge where the good lies, and where the evil. No man can hold himself . . ."

A car turned into the driveway. Korolenko moved to the window, cradling the shotgun, looking out. "Come to the door with me," he said.

The doorbell rang as they got there, a loud descending scale on the chimes in the entry hall.

"Who is it?"

Whoever was outside didn't answer for a moment.

"I'm supposed to pick up a man here," the voice said. "Pick up a man named Cotton."

Korolenko opened the door.

It was Adams. Or Harge. He glanced at Korolenko's shotgun and then at Cotton, smiling slightly. His right hand, Cotton noticed, was gripped on something in the coat pocket. Undoubtedly a pistol. The sleet whipped in the opened door, around the man.

"Come in," Korolenko said.

"No. We'll go now. Come on, Mr. Cotton."

"No," Korolenko said. "We're waiting a few minutes. We'll know then whether this has to be done. Maybe this is past the point where Cotton can cause any harm. Come on in and we'll wait a little."

The man stood, indecisive, gradually

aware that Korolenko's shotgun now pointed approximately at his lower abdomen.

"Take your hand out of your pocket," Korolenko said. The man stared at Korolenko, then slowly removed the hand. "Now, come in, and hand me your coat. I'll keep your gun until you're ready to leave." Adams came in, muttering something which Cotton couldn't quite hear. In the study, he stood beside the bookcase, watching them both.

"I don't know about this," Adams said. "The deal was I pick up this guy and be done with him. They didn't say anything about waiting around."

"The orders have changed," Korolenko said. "In a few minutes I'll get a call and that will tell us if this is necessary. If it's not, you can go away and collect your money without any more trouble or risk. If it's still necessary . . ." Korolenko paused, "then you'll leave with Mr. Cotton."

Adams was a tall man, taller than Cotton remembered, with heavy shoulders and an intelligent face. Maybe thirty-five, Cotton thought. And he looks like what? A young college professor? Maybe a minister? A lawyer? Certainly just like an office-machine salesman.

"I don't like the way this is working out," Adams said. "He can identify me."

"That won't trouble you," Korolenko said. "Will it, John? What could he accuse you of? Of coming here and frightening him? What could he tell the police?"

"Yeah? Well, maybe. O.K.," Adams said. "If we have to wait, we wait."

They waited. Korolenko behind the desk. Adams almost motionless against the wall. Cotton tense in the chair, his head buzzing with fatigue and aching alternatives. Either Janey went along with him or she didn't. She probably—almost certainly—hadn't given the story to Rickner. But maybe she had. The maybe, he knew, was mostly the product of his overpowering, urgent need for her to believe in him. Not in the story, or in the abstractions of philosophy, but in him as a man. If she hadn't believed in him, the story wouldn't be in the *Tribune.* And then he would have to decide something. He tried to think about it, but the thought receded. How many hours had it been since he had slept?

"Matter of curiosity," Adams said. "But what was that you poured on those steps? And where'd you get it?"

"Liquid soap," Cotton said. "Out of the janitor's closet."

"My friend damn near killed himself," Adams said. There was no rancor in the voice, only a slight ironic amusement. "And you were rough with me too." He held up his right wrist encased in plaster. "Pulled all the tendons."

And then the telephone rang and Korolenko picked it up. Cotton took a deep, involuntary breath.

"This is Korolenko. Yes. O.K. What's the top headline?"

He listened, his face bleak. "Yes," he said. "Yes, that sounds bad. But read me the first few paragraphs."

Elation flooded through Cotton. Delight. Joy. He wanted to shout. To sing.

"O.K., O.K. No. I'll get a copy here," Korolenko said. "And thank you. Thank you for the trouble." He hung up, looking at Cotton. "It's done." No emotion. Almost as if he no longer cared.

"So what happens now?" Adams said. "Do I take him, or do I go?"

"Neither," Korolenko said. "I have an errand to run. I want you to keep Mr. Cotton here for . . ." he glanced at the clock, "exactly thirty minutes. That phone call told us that Cotton can't hurt us any more than he already has. And there's no reason to harm him. If he's harmed, I'll give the police your description." Korolenko handed Adams the shotgun. "Don't let him make any calls," he said. "And ten minutes after twelve, you can leave and let him leave if he wants to go."

And with that Korolenko was gone. Cotton heard the clatter of a coat hanger in the entryway closet, the front door closing. A minute later Korolenko's old Lincoln was purring out of the driveway.

Adams was looking at the shotgun, examining its safety catch and the pump action. "Any objection to waiting thirty minutes?"

"None," Cotton said. "You don't even need the gun."

"Might as well keep it, if you don't mind. If you got away and screwed something up, maybe I wouldn't get my money."

"That's reasonable," Cotton said. He wondered what sort of mission Korolenko was on, but it didn't matter. He felt only euphoria, elation. Janey Janoski. Janey Janoski, whose dark eyes lit like candles when she laughed, had done it for him. She had read through the story, and she had hated it for what it would do to people, and then—still hating it—she had folded it neatly and walked down to the pressroom, and handed it to Tom Rickner.

The man was behind Korolenko's desk now, dialing the telephone, watching Cotton with noncommittal, incurious eyes while he listened to it ring, then talking in a low voice. "This is me. Yeah." He grinned. "Me. I'm at the old man's house. Cotton's here with me. The old man said I was just to keep him here thirty minutes and then leave." He paused, listening, looking at Cotton. "That's what he said. Got a call from somewhere that Cotton's story has already been printed. Yeah. Today. Just a few minutes ago, I guess. O.K. I'll hold on." He put his hand over the receiver, smiled at Cotton. "Just checking. I don't work for the old man here. Wouldn't want to turn you loose if I'm not supposed to."

"Or you wouldn't get paid," Cotton said. A thought struck him. "By the way, how much do you get paid for this?"

"I don't get rich." The man glanced away from Cotton, inspecting the photographs of hunting dogs on the walls, utterly unembarrassed. A gust of wind eddied around the eaves, rattling sleet against the window. Two or three minutes ticked away. He's like me, Cotton thought. Just doing an impersonal job.

"Hell of a day," Adams said. And then the telephone receiver squawked. "Yeah, I'm still here. O.K. I'm all done then? Is that right? O.K." He hung up. Looked at Cotton, grinning. "All done."

"All done," Cotton said. He intended to say more but his voice was shaky. He felt watery, weak. There was still almost fifteen minutes left of Korolenko's thirty-minute wait, but the man seemed to be ignoring Korolenko's instructions.

He put the shotgun back in the gun case and picked up his coat from the chair where Korolenko had draped it. He weighed it on his hand, surprised. "The old son-of-a-bitch stole my gun." He plunged his hand into the pocket, looking at Cotton. "How about that? That old bastard took it."

"Buy another one," Cotton said. In a moment he was going to get up and walk out of here and never come back. But now he felt dizzy and his legs were weak. He was thinking about why Korolenko had taken the pistol.

"Well," Adams said. "Goodbye now." He walked out.

"Goodbye," Cotton said. He knew why Korolenko had taken the pistol. There was the sound of the front door closing. He knew why Korolenko wanted thirty minutes. He glanced at the clock. Ten minutes now. Cotton pushed himself stiffly out of the chair, picked up his coat, walked through the cold, silent living room. In the entry hall, he paused. He hadn't heard a car start and he would rather not see the man again, not ever. He would rather wait until the man drove away. He hesitated a moment in the entry hall. And then he opened the front door.

Captain Whan was walking up the front steps. Behind him Adams was leaning with his good hand against a police car, being searched by a man in a tweed overcoat while another officer watched. Whan stopped, looking at Cotton, his face surprised. How long had he been waiting out here? Waiting for what?

"Too bad," Cotton said. "I'm still alive. You don't have a corpus delicti."

Whan ignored the words. "What's been going on in there?"

"Do you mean how come the man there didn't shoot me so you'd have a case? I don't know. It was damn sure no thanks to you."

Whan flushed. What he was saying, Cotton realized, might not be entirely fair.

"We figured he'd bring you out with him," Whan said. "That would have been the safest time to take him."

And, Cotton thought, the time when there

would be evidence that a felony was being committed. Something concrete to take before a grand jury. But Whan was just doing his job. Nothing personal.

"No gun," the man in the tweed coat said. "Nothing."

Whan turned and walked back to the car. Cotton followed, interested in this.

"Mr. Harge," Captain Whan said, "what brings you to our town? And where's your gun?"

"Just visiting," the man said.

"Mr. Cotton, anything happen in there?"

"Nothing that would interest you," Cotton said.

"Take him downtown and book him on something," Whan told the tweed overcoat. "I'll be down to talk to him later." He turned to Cotton. "You'll ride downtown with me."

"I guess not," Cotton said. "Thanks, but I've got things to do. I'll call a cab."

Whan's mouth tightened. "This man you're consorting with here is a known felon. There's no reason I can't take you in for an hour or two just on general circumstance."

"O.K.," Cotton said. "It'll give me a chance to thank you for all this close guarding you've been doing for me." He waited in the police car while Whan and a policeman checked the house.

Whan drove carefully on the icy street, flicking on his warning blinker as he pulled onto the freeway.

"You said Korolenko fired the shotgun into the wall. But you didn't say why."

"I said you should ask him why," Cotton said. "I had my back turned. Maybe he was seeing if it would work, or maybe it was an accident."

The sleet was snow now, small dry flakes which the wiper blades dusted off the windshield. Whan was looking straight ahead, driving very slowly. "You're not very talkative today," he said. "I can remember when you talked a lot. What happened?"

"That was way back when I thought I might get some police protection. Before I knew you'd just use me as a decoy."

"I'm not going to argue about it," Whan said. "What did he do with his gun?"

"To tell the truth, I never saw his gun."

The radio speaker emitted clipped, precise female radio-dispatcher words. A three-vehicle collision at the intersection of Seventh and Marberry.

"Look, Cotton," Whan said. "I can see why you're sore. But I told you we couldn't have somebody sleeping with you. We haven't got the people. And you know yourself the only way to end this business is to catch them at it. Now, what can we charge Harge with? If he threatened you, we might make an assault stick with the kind of record he has."

"Nothing," Cotton said. The radio interrupted him. Unit 17 was instructed to pick up Officer Matthiessen at the east entrance of the federal building. "If he had a gun, he didn't take it out of his pocket." Where was the gun now? Cotton glanced at his watch. Korolenko's thirty minutes were up. Expired six minutes ago.

Whan slowed, flicked the turn indicator, and angled gradually into the exit lane for Central Avenue. "Goddamn it," he said. "You can't expect . . ."

"Things have changed, captain. The story that wasn't supposed to get printed got printed in today's *Tribune*. Nobody's gunning for John Cotton right now. I wish you luck on . . ."

The radio interrupted again. "All units in vicinity of the Senate Downtowner at Capitol and Second . . ." This would be it. Korolenko had estimated the time he needed almost exactly right. Cotton closed his eyes as he listened. The female voice unflustered, unhurried, detached, reporting a homicide in the lobby of the Senate Downtowner. Homicide. Then Korolenko's bullets had hit where he wanted them to hit. That was exactly what you would expect of Joe Korolenko. The voice droned on, flat, no trace of emotion, reporting a statistic. Against his eyelids, Cotton tried to project the scene. The lobby aswarm with dentists. Korolenko among them. Greeting an old friend here and there, waiting. Eugene Clark arriving, as the Senator always arrived, exactly on time for the ceremonial entry into the dining room. And then the shots. Two or three. As many as were necessary. Nothing said because there would be nothing to say. And then Korolenko would shoot himself.

"Subject surrendered and is disarmed and in custody of officers," the voice said. "No additional units are needed." It paused. "Unit 17. Matthiessen is waiting at the east entrance of the Federal Building. Please confirm you're en route to pick him up."

"Hell of a place for a shooting," Whan said. "Some nut knocking off his wife, probably." He paused. "But who knows?"

Cotton kept his eyes closed. Why would Korolenko turn himself in? The answer was obvious. The death of Senator Clark would crowd the corruption story out of the banner headline spot today and tomorrow. But, by staying alive himself, Korolenko could keep the assassination story alive. Keep it alive through his arraignment, the preliminary hearing, all the way through the trial. And control it, timing his statements and even timing the trial, using it all as a forum to discredit whatever would be left of Eugene Clark's organization.

"I've got to use the telephone when we get to your office," Cotton said. Korolenko would need help.

The Armchair Detective Library was created in affiliation with *The Armchair Detective* and The Mysterious Press with the aim of making available classic mystery and suspense fiction by the most respected authors in the field. Difficult to obtain in hardcover in the United States and often the first hardcover edition, the books in The Armchair Detective Library have been selected for their enduring significance.

For the production of these collector and limited editions, materials of the highest quality are used to provide a select audience with books that will prove as timeless as the stories themselves. The paper is 60–lb. acid free Glatfelter for longevity, bound in heavy duty Red Label Davey Boards, encased in Holliston Roxite "C" grade cloth and Smyth sewn for durability.

Printed and bound by Braun–Brumfield, Inc. of Ann Arbor, Michigan, U.S.A.